SUPERIOR STORM

a lake superior mystery

by

TOM HILPERT

Copyright © Tom Hilpert 2012

All rights reserved. Without limiting the rights under copyrights reserved above, no part of this publication may be reproduced, stored in or introduced into a retrieval system, or transmitted, in any form or by any means (electronic, mechanical, photocopying, recording or otherwise), without the prior written permission of the copyright owner.

Cover by Lisa Anderson. www.opinedesign.com

ISBN-13: 978-1480224339

ISBN-10: 1480224332

For Kari

Because of Fish Lake

ONE

Three people were shot when the First National Bank of Grand Lake was robbed.

The first was a security guard, who appeared to be going for his gun. The bullet hit him low and on the side.

The third was one of the criminals. He left a trail of blood out to the sidewalk.

The second was a darn fool who grabbed the guard's weapon and started a gun battle in a bank lobby full of innocent people. He was the one who shot the robber. He was a lucky fool, because no one else was shot, and the bullet that hit him went clean through his calf without any major damage.

It still hurt like blazes, though. I know, because I was the lucky fool.

Besides the bullet, the robbery began a sequence of events that shook up my life, disturbed the quiet town of Grand Lake, and didn't end until I was half-drowned in Lake Superior.

Up until then, the day had been going just swell.

That morning, before the robbery, I was in my office, listening to The Eagles. I felt slightly uneasy, because I thought the lyrics might be dirty.

Julie, my part time secretary, walked into my office. I reflexively stopped my iPod and slipped off the headphones.

"Hey Julie," I said. "What does 'brutally handsome' mean? Does it mean he is so handsome that it is brutal, or that he is handsome in a brute-like way?"

She looked at me levelly for a moment. "How you find room in your head to remember your sermons is beyond me."

I grinned happily. That was as good as a point for me.

"Mail," said Julie, "and don't try to think up some stupid pun like fee-mail."

"Furthest thing from my mind," I said. "We all know that you are the funny one around here." Pastor two, secretary zero. It was going to be a good day.

Julie rolled her eyes and threw a small bundle on my desk. There was a book catalog, pleas for money from all four of my alma maters, and some other junk. She hesitated, and then tossed a thick eight-by-ten envelope on top of it. My name and the church address were hand-written. The envelope had a return receipt and insurance.

"Package too," said Julie. She sort of hung around for a minute.

"You can ask, you know," I said. "It isn't rude."

"I'm a Minnesotan. *Any* sort of communication is always considered slightly rude."

"It's from my mother," I said, looking at the return address. "I think it's some old papers of my dad's. We're working through some details left over about my dad's estate."

"Why did she send them to the church?"

"I don't know. Maybe she wanted to test your rudeness level." Actually, I had my mother send them to the church so that I would remember to take them to Alex Chan, my lawyer. However, Julie never needs an excuse to remember my absent-mindedness.

Julie snorted and turned to leave.

"Don't you want to know what I was listening to, when you came in?" I asked.

She didn't turn around. "No. It was probably just a song you were afraid was dirty, but almost certainly was not."

I stared at her. Score one for the secretary.

She turned, winked, and then left my office.

~

Our treasurer was out of town that week, and so I had to make the bank deposit later that afternoon. But, first, I went to visit the widow Ethel Ostrand. Ethel had been a member of Harbor Lutheran Church for forty years. Her house was a small white clapboard, decorated in original 1950s wallpaper and furniture. I was pretty sure she had bought it all when it was new. The shades were drawn and the living room lamps were on.

"I want you to do my funeral," she said.

"I'm so sorry, Ethel," I said. "I didn't know you were sick."

"I'm not sick, I'm old," she snapped.

"Oh."

"You aren't supposed to say 'oh,' you are supposed to say, 'Ethel you don't look that old.'"

"Well, how old are you?" I asked. I realized my mistake immediately, but it was too late to take it back.

"It isn't polite to ask a lady's age," she said.

I took a breath. "So why this talk about funerals?"

"Well, when you're old like me, what else do you have to sit around and think about?"

I let that one sit there without touching it. Even stunningly slow pastors can learn.

She grinned at me. "Actually, I'm enjoying the idea of planning my funeral. I want you to preach."

"I can do that," I said.

"And I'm picking out some hymns."

"We can do that too."

We discussed her funeral for a bit. She did actually seem to be enjoying herself. Everyone needs a hobby.

After about half an hour, we had nailed down the important parts. I got up to leave.

"Oh pastor, I'm sorry to bother you," she said, "but could you help me with something before you go? I have to get some things from the store, and I need some money."

I reached for my wallet. "How much do you need?"

"Oh no!" she said. "I don't need *your* money. I need your help to get *my* money."

"I'm not sure I understand," I said.

"Come with me."

She rose slowly from her chair. Leaning heavily on her walker, she led me into her bedroom. This was done in pink and gilt wallpaper with some obscure but flowery pattern. I squinted.

Ethel walked over to the bed. "Could you lift the mattress, please?"

"I beg your pardon?"

"Could you lift up the mattress for me? I need to get some money."

Curiosity struggled with propriety and won a first-round knockout. I walked over to the bed and heaved. The mattress was old – also probably 1950s vintage – and quite heavy. Under the mattress, and on top of the box-spring was money.

A lot of money.

Ethel hobbled over to the bed and began to paw through the piles of green. I started to sweat.

"OK, you can put it down now," she said at last.

I managed not to drop it too hard.

"Ethel," I said, "why do you have all that money under your mattress?"

"That's where I keep it," she said.

"What, *all* of your money?"

"Yes, of course."

We processed slowly back to the living room. I sat back down heavily in the green wingback chair.

"Ethel, we need to talk about this."

"Pastor, I'm not sure this is an appropriate conversation for us to have."

"This is important," I said. "What if you were robbed?"

"Who would rob an old lady like me?" she asked.

"Lots of people, if they knew you had money under your mattress," I said. "Does anyone else know?"

"I don't think so," she said. "And I don't see how they could find out unless somebody told them." She looked meaningfully at me.

"But what if you need to get more money from there and there's no one to help you? Whoever you ask to help you will see."

She thought for a moment. "It's only been the past month or so that I couldn't get at it. I just don't seem to have the strength anymore. I've been pulling out the bills that are on the edge, but before you came, I'd gotten almost everything I could reach. Maybe we should go back in there, and you can hold the mattress again, while I move more money to the edges."

"Maybe you should put it all in a bank."

She was quiet.

"Ethel, what if there was a fire? It would all burn, and you'd be left with nothing at all."

She was still quiet.

"How much do you have under there?" I asked.

"Oh, I don't know. A couple hundred thousand, I should think."

This time I was quiet.

"You really think I should put it all in a bank?"

"I really do. This is very dangerous for you."

"But what if the bank loses it?"

"Banks are insured. It's called FDIC. If the bank loses your money, the insurance will pay it back to you."

She was silent again. Finally, she sighed. "I guess if I can trust you with my funeral, I can trust you with my money."

"Trust the bank with it," I said.

"But you can put it in there for me?"

"You have to open an account."

"Can't you just have them keep it in the vault?"

"Well, you could put it in a safety deposit box, but the normal thing is to give it to them and they hold it in an account."

"But I don't need an account if they keep it in the vault?"

"Well, no, but that's a bit unusual, and you won't earn interest."

"Put it in the vault."

"I think you should come with me and open an account."

"Pastor, I'm an old lady. You just told me it isn't safe to keep it here. Couldn't you just put it in the vault for me?"

I kept at her, but after twenty minutes, I had gotten nowhere. I finally figured cash in a large safety deposit box in the bank vault was still better than under the mattress.

So that was how, when the First National Bank of Grand Lake was robbed, I lost the money given to the church that month, plus all $237,556 of Ethel Ostrand's uninsured cash.

TWO

The bank lobby was crowded. It was Friday afternoon on a payday, and a lot of folks in Grand Lake were coming in to cash their paychecks. Several owners of tourist shops and restaurants were there, like me, to deposit a fair amount of cash. I nodded at Drew Carlson, the owner of Dylan's, my favorite lunch café. He was holding a thick money bag, the kind businesses often use for deposits. He raised his eyebrows at me. I glanced back at the duffel bag slung over my shoulder. Ethel Ostrand had packed it, and given it to me a few minutes before. You don't fit a quarter-million dollars in twenties and fifties into a business deposit bag.

I was near the back of the line as it snaked over to one side of the room, and I found myself next to Arne Engstrom, retired cop and now the security guard for First National. Arne was sixty-ish, with thin gray hair and a solid Scandinavian face and build. He looked as sturdy as the bank building.

"Hey, Arne," I said.

"Pastor," he nodded. Arne went to the other Lutheran church in town, but he was a proper Norwegian, so he called me pastor anyway.

Arne's gaze lifted up over my shoulder, and I heard some kind of commotion behind me. I turned and saw that three people, dressed all in black, were in the lobby. They had ski masks on, the old knit kind that fit over your head and then pull down over your face, with holes for your eyes and mouth. I felt a sudden rush of adrenaline, and everything seemed to go into slow motion. There were several loud booms, and people screamed. One of the masked figures leaped onto the teller's counter of the bank. He waved a pistol at the tellers and shouted,

"Be still! This doesn't concern you, but if you move, I will shoot."

The other two had pistols too, big, black automatics.

"Everyone on the floor!" shouted the largest masked man. "Get down on the floor! Face down!" People were complying, but I felt like I was locked in molasses. One of the masked robbers, a short, slight guy, waved his pistol at me.

Slowly, still looking around me, I got down on my knees, and then lay on the floor. I was the last one down, and Arne was lying next to me.

I heard talking and rustling. I looked up and saw that two of the three robbers were crouched over someone. They appeared to be searching the person. But almost immediately, the man standing on the counter shouted "get down!" and a gun fired. I put my head back down. A short minute later, I felt a hard cold object pressed into the back of my head. Hands were grasping me, searching my coat, pulling my wallet out of my back pocket.

"Get the duffel too," said a strangely high, light voice.

"Shut up!" said another, deeper one. "Don't talk."

They pulled at my duffel bag. Without thinking, I tried to hold on, but the pressure on the back of my head increased. "It isn't worth your life," said the second, deeper voice. I let it go.

They moved on, and now that they were near me, I could see from the corners of my eyes that they were quickly and methodically robbing each customer.

I heard more rustling and looked up again. Arne stirred next to me and started to get to his knees. A gun roared again, and Arne fell back as though he'd been kicked by an invisible mule. I scrambled over to him and found a red stain spreading along his lower right side, just above his belt. Just above his hostler.

I reached down to search the wound, or put pressure on it, or do something. I didn't really know what to do, but I couldn't just leave him lying there. Something slammed into my leg just as another gun boomed.

I looked up, and the three robbers were moving back toward the doors, two of them holding a big black garbage bag each, and one with my duffel. The small one fired his gun again, and I saw the chips fly off the floor near Arne's head.

I slid my hand down to Arne's holster. It was already unbuttoned. I pulled out his gun, which, lucky for me, was a revolver. I didn't know how to work an automatic. I lifted and fired in the same motion. The small robber fired back again. I pulled the trigger manically, trying for the small guy, but behind him, the robber holding my duffel bag stumbled, yelled, and then they were all out the door.

My ears were ringing from the gunfire. I dropped Arne's gun, and shouted, "Someone call 911." Turning back to the solid Norwegian guard, I said, "Hang in there, Arne, you're going to be OK." Arne Engstrom was the proud grandpa of six. I had no idea if he was going to be OK or not. I didn't really know what to do for a gunshot wound, or how serious it was. There was a lot of blood. I put my hands down over the area, one on top the other, and pressed. Arne groaned.

Around me, nobody much moved. I could hear a man saying, "Oh my God," over and over again. A woman was crying, but quietly.

After what seemed like too long, I could hear sirens. The doors burst open with a blast of cool air, and there was a small stampede of uniformed people into the lobby.

"Over here!" I shouted, "He's been shot."

Two paramedics knelt down beside me. One of them gently removed my hands, and said, "OK, we've got it from here."

I leaned back against the wall of the lobby next to a potted plant. When I looked up, I saw Dan Jensen, Police chief of Grand Lake, walking towards me. Jensen was a big man, a little overweight, but still athletic. He was in his late thirties or early forties, with white-blond hair and piercing blue eyes.

"Shoulda known you'd be in the middle of this somehow," he said. Then looked at me closely. "Oh jeez, you've been shot."

About then, my leg started to hurt.

THREE

The wound was superficial, they said. That made me think I was a superficial kind of person, because it hurt like heck. One of the EMTs, a young guy, was bandaging me up. He was facing the door when suddenly he looked up very alertly. It reminded me of a hunting dog when it was pointing. He jerked on my bandage a bit roughly, and I grunted in pain.

"Sorry," he mumbled, looking back down at my leg.

I shifted my gaze to where he had been looking and saw Leyla Bennett coming through the lobby. Her long, dark hair was caught up behind her ears, framing her high cheekbones and dark, almond-shaped eyes. She was wearing khaki pants that were flattering to her shapely legs, which generally needed no extra flattery anyway. The navy top and stylish brown coat showed her figure without showing it off. She was a well put together woman.

"It's all right," I said to the EMT. "I still react that way myself every time I see her."

He shook his head. Possibly ruefully.

I saw Leyla say something to Chief Jensen. They both looked over at me, and then Leyla came running over, with Jensen following more sedately.

"Jonah!" said Leyla. She knelt next to me and hugged me tight. She smelled nice. For a moment, I didn't notice the pain in my leg. Then suddenly, she released me and looked over at the EMT.

"Is he OK? Can I hug him?"

"It's his leg," said the paramedic. "He'll be fine."

"You can even talk directly to him, as if he were actually here," I said.

She looked at me, and her eyes were watery. Her expression seemed to be crumpling. Without a word, she held me again, tight and long. Her hand stroked the back of my head. My cheek started to feel wet where her face was pressed against it.

The EMT made no objection. Neither did I.

At last, she let me go again, sitting back on her heels and wiping at her face with her hands.

"I heard on the police scanner," she said. "They said two people were shot, and one was pretty serious. Then the officer outside said you were one of the two." She took a shuddering breath. "And then they let me come in, and I see you leaning against the wall here, covered with blood."

I looked down at my jacket. It was dark with blood.

"Arne Engstrom was the other one," I said. "This is mostly his blood. It looked bad." I looked at my EMT.

He shrugged. "I haven't heard anything yet. He was alive when they took him out a few minutes ago."

Dan Jensen came over. "How is he?" he asked the EMT, nodding at me.

"What is with you people?" I said. "I wasn't shot in the throat. I can talk, you know."

Jensen shook his head sadly. "No better than usual, I see."

"I'm about done here," said the EMT. "I'm sure you'll be fine, but you really ought to see a doctor. You'll be hurting, and I think a doctor would get you some pain meds and antibiotics."

Chief Jensen thanked him, and he started to pack up his stuff. "Jonah,

I'd like to hear your version of what happened here. When we're done, you two love birds can go on."

He looked at Leyla and me. We didn't look at each other or him.

"Oh, no," he said. "What's the matter? What's going on with you two?"

I glanced at Leyla, and found her looking at me. "It's complicated," we both said at the same moment.

Jensen groaned. "You have got to be kidding." He looked from Leyla to me like a stern elementary school principal. "When I was your age, you liked somebody, you dated. You didn't like 'em, you broke up. If you kept liking 'em, you kept dating, and eventually got married and had kids and everything. We didn't have any of this 'it's complicated' crap. What is *wrong* with you two?"

"Dan," I said, "you're only like four years older than me."

"Exactly my point," he said.

The EMT was staring at Leyla in open admiration. Without turning to me, he said, "Seriously, dude, how complicated could it be?"

"Well," I said "that's a good point."

Leyla had the grace to blush very prettily.

The EMT finished packing up and then left.

"Why don't you give me your story?" Jensen said to me. He looked at Leyla. "Sorry, but this isn't for the press yet. I let you in because of him –" he nodded in my direction " – but could you just give us a minute, please?"

Jensen had me tell him everything I knew, which wasn't much, while Leyla moved away and made a few phone calls. He took notes with a little notebook and pencil. His face tightened when I told him about the shootout.

"I suppose it's too much to ask for identifying features?" he asked when I was done.

"Other than the fact that they all called each other by their full names – including middle initials – and the leader had red hair, only one hand, and a big scar on his face, there is no way I could ever identify them."

Jensen chewed on his pencil for a moment. "You're going to need those pain meds in a minute," he said.

"Sorry, maybe my problem is that I need them right now. No, they all wore black, all wore masks. One of them was a lot shorter and smaller than the others. One was medium sized. One was a pretty big guy. And one had a kind of high, light voice – I don't know which one. Not really anything to go on."

"We think you hit one of them with Arne's revolver," he said. "There was a bit of a blood trail going out to the curb."

"One of them flinched and yelled when I was shooting," I said. Honesty got the better of pride. "It wasn't the one I was shooting at."

Jensen nodded. "Handguns aren't like rifles. Pretty hard to be accurate in those circumstances, especially without training. Normally, I'd chew you out for doing it, but with them shooting at you in the first place, it seems like maybe you did the right thing. Plus, if you did hit one, and he goes to a doctor, we'll hear about it."

My leg had started to throb. In fact, I realized I could count my heart-rate by the pulsing pain in my calf. I thought about Ethel Ostrand's money, and noticed that my head hurt too. Jensen was looking at my face. Leyla had returned and was standing near.

"Probably about time you got to your pain meds. Why don't you two get your complicated selves out of here?"

He and Leyla helped me to my feet. With my arms around their shoulders like an injured football player, I hobbled into the brisk autumn air and over to Leyla's car.

"What about my car?" I asked.

"We'll figure it out," she said.

I slid into the passenger seat, while Leyla stayed outside the car, talking to Jensen for a moment. I pulled out my cell phone and called the church. Julie answered.

"I don't think I'll be in the rest of the day," I said. "I just got shot in the leg."

"What, *again*?" she said.

There was a brief silence.

"I was expecting a bit more sympathy," I said.

"Leyla already called and told me about it," said Julie. "She said it wasn't serious, but that pretty soon you'd call me, and be whining and complaining like a little girl, and expect a lot of sympathy."

"She said that?" I was slightly shocked.

"Well, not exactly. She said you'd been shot, but that it wasn't serious. I figured the rest out myself."

"It's good to know you are so perceptive."

"I knew you'd appreciate it," she said. There was another pause. "Seriously, are you really OK?"

"My life isn't in jeopardy, if that's what you mean. I'll be fine. It *does* hurt a little, though."

"See, I *knew* it."

"I give up," I said. "Anyway, I won't be in today. Hopefully I'll be OK for tomorrow."

"Do you need anything?"

"Just some sympathy," I said, and hung up on her laughter.

FOUR

Leyla took me to my doctor, who, as expected, prescribed both a painkiller and antibiotic.

"You never know where a bullet has been," was his comforting explanation for the antibiotic. We then went to the drugstore and got the medicine.

"It's getting close to supper time," said Leyla. "If you want, I'll take you home and make you supper."

"Thank you," I said. "That would be wonderful."

My home is a newer Northwoods-style cabin, up on the ridge, a mile or two above Lake Superior and maybe two or three miles south of Grand Lake. My living room and deck boast an ever-changing view of the largest freshwater lake in the world; a deep, clear, cold romancer of men and killer of ships, the lifeblood and livelihood of Northeastern Minnesota.

Most of Minnesota is not known for spectacular scenery. While there are plenty of quiet lakes and tall forests, it is also pretty flat, and most of the state is just good, fertile Midwestern farm land. But the coast of Lake Superior is the stunning exception. Granite cliffs plunge into clear, deadly cold water. Ridges rise mountain-like off the lake and waterfalls of tannin-stained streams hide in the folds of the hills. And always, lying to the southeast, is the giant freshwater behemoth, changeable as a diva, but twice as beautiful.

It was almost dark when we got to my cabin, but on clear days the water has a way of holding light, and we could see the glimmer far out to the empty southeast. My leg seemed to have stiffened up, and I was feeling the pain pretty severely.

Leyla got me on to the couch and came back with water and my pills.

"Thanks," I said. "I think there's some leftover spinach pie in the fridge. I don't mind if you just want to heat that up."

"You can make a pie from spinach?"

"Don't knock it 'til you've tried it," I said. "Spinach, Italian sausage, eggs, and cheese – all inside a pie crust – how can that be bad?"

"Well, I guess I could try it." She sounded doubtful.

"Make whatever you want," I said. "I hope to be in la-la land soon."

She found the pie and put it in the oven to warm up. Then she brought a glass of white wine over, and sat on the end of the couch opposite me, facing my direction. It was an ordinary couch, but with her on it, it looked like it belonged in a millionaire's mansion.

"Are you in la-la land yet?"

"No, but I'm starting to feel better."

"Jonah, why is it complicated?"

"What?" Maybe I was in la-la land after all.

"Why are we – us – complicated? That's what we said to Dan today. Because, I mean, I know we've talked, and I said it to Dan too, but the truth is, it isn't complicated for me."

I looked at her steadily. "What do you mean?"

"I know how I feel. I know what I want. It isn't complicated for me. I want to be with you."

I tried to look out over the lake, but with lights on in the cabin, the glass doors out to my deck were just black.

"You could say something anytime now."

I looked back at Leyla. "You're right," I said. "I am the one making it complicated. I hope someday it won't be."

"You still haven't forgiven me." Her voice was thick with emotion.

"No, Leyla, that's not it. I have forgiven you. But it takes some time to rebuild trust. When the chips were down, you trusted a multiple murderer before you believed me. It takes something to recover what was lost there."

"I was here for you today."

"Yes, you were. You are."

"But that's not all of it, is it? It's not just about trust."

I thought for a while. "No, I guess not."

Leyla had a trick of looking beautiful, even when she cried.

I reached out and grabbed her hand. "Leyla," I said. "I want it to be uncomplicated. I want to be with you freely, with no reservations. Like the EMT said, I often think I must be crazy to even let this be 'complicated.' But I will never give you less than total honesty."

She sniffed and nodded.

"I'm working on it. I'm trying to figure out what my problem is – because it *is* my problem, not yours. The trust thing is part of it. I don't know what the other part is yet. But I will figure it out."

"What does that mean? Do you want to date other women? Do you want me to be looking for other men?"

"No," I said. I may have said it a little bit firmly, because Leyla actually smiled. "I'm not interested in anyone else. That wouldn't help me."

Her smile broadened. "You sound pretty sure about that part."

"I can't ask you to," I said, "but I was hoping that you could wait for me while I work on this. You know, not date anyone else."

"So you want to date me exclusively – except you don't want to date me."

"Couldn't we be kind of, I don't know, friends with a future?"

"*Friends with a future?* Sounds like a slogan for the Army or something."

Maybe it was the drugs. I couldn't help myself. I began to laugh, knowing it was inappropriate. The more I tried to suppress it, the funnier it got. Soon, my whole body was shaking, and I felt tears coming to my eyes.

"Join the Army; find *friends with a future?*" I was gasping for breath.

To my relief, she began to smile, too. She shook her head.

"I'm letting you off easy, because you've been shot, and you're on painkillers."

"Thank you," I said wiping my eyes. I felt slightly more serious. "For everything."

She looked at me, and her open vulnerability was like a powerful drug. "Still, I like the sound of it. Especially the part about the future."

"So you'll wait?"

She looked me in the eye. "I will wait Jonah. But not forever."

She cleaned up the dishes and then came and sat back on the couch. I was starting to feel pretty good from the painkillers.

"We always seem to have this tension," said Leyla, "but I was wondering if I could ask you about the robbery, as a journalist." Leyla was the managing editor for the *Grand Lake Gazette*. Circulation was around 12,000, but I knew the Associated Press, and possibly even Reuters, would be likely to pick up Leyla's story from the wires.

"I'm not sure how much I'm allowed to tell," I said.

"That's what I was talking to Chief Jensen about while you were waiting in the car," she said. "I'll abide by his wishes. Whatever he said is off limits, is off the record."

"Freedom of the press?" I asked.

"Maintaining good relationships with my sources," she countered.

I told her what I had experienced.

"Ethel Ostrand's money is killing me," I said. "How many people are ever present at a bank robbery in their whole lifetime? And yet I'm there with a widow's life-savings in cash right when it happens."

"Bank robberies are usually investigated by the FBI. The resources of the federal government will be all over this one. They'll get it back."

I was starting to get sleepy. The support of the FBI seemed like a good reason to relax and not worry about it, at least until I slept a little.

I didn't wake up until morning. Leyla was gone, but my own pillow was under my head on the couch, and I was tucked warmly under a wool blanket.

FIVE

"What do you mean the FBI won't be investigating this? Don't they investigate all bank robberies?" I was holding the phone a little too tight.

"This wasn't a bank robbery, Jonah," said Dan Jensen. He sounded tired, but I was too unsettled to care much.

"Dan," I said, "I was there. I was in a bank. It was robbed."

"No, Jonah," he said with excessive patience. "The *people* in the bank were robbed. They didn't take any money from the bank itself."

"You mean they didn't rob the *bank*?"

"That's what I'm trying to tell you. They only robbed the customers. No money was taken from the bank itself."

"So it's not a federal crime?"

He sighed through the phone. "No federal crime. No FBI."

I was quiet.

"They aren't exactly the saviors the movies paint them as anyway," said Jensen.

"Sorry Dan," I said, finally paying attention to how he might be feeling. "I didn't mean to insult you. You guys do a great job around town. It's just that I lost a quarter million dollars of someone else's money. I want all the help I can get."

"The state police will be in on this to help us," said Dan.

"OK," I said. "What can I do?"

He was quiet for minute. "Nothing right now, Jonah. If you think of anything new you might have forgotten, call me right away."

"Dan," I said, "you think you'll get any of the money back?"

"I really don't know Jonah," he said. "But we'll get the suckers who did this. I promise you that."

We hung up, and I limped out of my home-office into the kitchen for a cup of coffee. I had slept late, so I wasn't quite done with my first pot. I was experimenting with a chicory blend that was popular in New Orleans, in the theory that coffee from the South might help keep me warm in the North.

I fed a few more logs into my fireplace, and then limped around my living room. It was a cold day in early autumn. The ridge fell away from the house like some gaudy ocean wave, decked out in gold, red, yellow and green. The lake lay at the bottom of the hill like a silent blue monster, biding its time until it could roar with the force of November storms.

I thought about the robbery. There was an athletic man of medium height who could jump onto the bank counter from the floor. There was a bigger man. There was a short slim guy. Possibly, they had a getaway driver. They had a quarter million dollars just from me; possibly as much as a hundred thousand more, considering the business owners making deposits and the people cashing paychecks.

Now all I had to do was take these facts and solve the case, because surely I could do it better than any of the professionals who were working on it. After all, they had only devoted careers to this sort of thing, whereas I was a highly trained pastor.

One thing was inescapable. Ethel Ostrand deserved to hear from me personally. Reluctantly, I shaved and dressed in my pastor uniform of Dockers and a mostly clean, blue button-up shirt. Clerical collars make me feel like I'm choking. Because it was fall, I added a sweater and my brown leather jacket. Grand Lake was a small town. Very few people there needed a white collar to know who I was and what I did.

With a certain amount of pain, I drove to Ethel's house and limped to her door.

"Have you heard the news?" I asked when we were both seated in her museum-of-the-1950s living room.

She did not look happy. "I heard the bank was robbed."

"They took all of your money, Ethel," I said. "I'm so sorry."

She looked confused. "Wasn't it in the vault?"

"It never got that far," I said. "They took it before I could deposit it."

"But it was insured?"

My head began to hurt. "Remember, Ethel, you didn't want it in an account, so it would not have been insured anyway. But they took it before the bank could lock it up. I'm afraid it's all gone."

Ethel had big glasses, and it was hard to read her expressions, but she looked angry. "You were the one who told me it wasn't safe here," she said. "You said it was dangerous. It might burn up, or someone might rob me. But it got lost in the nice safe bank."

Sometimes, abject humility is entirely appropriate. "You are absolutely right, Ethel," I said. "I am so sorry."

"I needed that money," she said. Her voice had a quaver to it.

"I know," I said. "I hope the police will recover it soon. But until they do, I want you to know that I will make sure you are taken care of. I won't let you suffer as a result of my mistake."

She did not seem particularly mollified. I didn't blame her. I let her vent some more anger on me. I may have even encouraged it. I didn't even mention the fact that I got shot. Both the fact that I had been shot, and that

I didn't bring it up, made me feel slightly more righteous. Even so, it wouldn't pay Ethel's bills.

We eventually made a list of some of her upcoming needs and expenses. It was going to be one of those months for me.

Afterwards I drove down to see Alex Chan. Chan was my lawyer, and maybe my friend too. His office was in a newer building that looked like a fancy house, but was actually designed to hold several upscale office suites. The other suites were taken by a real estate company, an architect, and some kind of small engineering firm. The reception area had stone pillars and stone tile and a common area with carafes of coffee and couches and a flat screen TV playing CNN to an empty room. I sampled the coffee, and finding it old and stale, took a cup with me into the Law Offices of Alex Chan.

Alex had a part-time secretary, a pleasantly plump, attractive blond woman in her late twenties. She smiled at me as I entered the little reception area at the front of the suite. "Hello, and how may I help you?"

"Julie," I said, "it's me. I'm here to see Alex."

"Do you have an appointment, sir?"

"Julie, seriously," I said.

She grimaced. "Alex wants me to bring sense of professionalism to this office," she said. "I'm supposed to be kind of formal and sort of give people the impression that he is a serious lawyer, or something."

"He is a good lawyer," I said. "But this is a bit silly."

"I know." She sighed.

"I know I gave him your name when he was looking for help, but I also told you I wasn't sure you'd like it."

"Do you have any more hours for me at Harbor Lutheran?"

"No. We're small, with a small budget. You know that."

"Well then, this is my solution. Besides," she grinned "I don't have to remind him about his appointments all the time. He's very organized."

"Thanks for the uplifting conversation," I said, and limped into Chan's office.

Alex Chan was a little under medium size, with the kind of ivory skin that some Asians get when they never go out in the sun. There wasn't a lot of time to get a good tan, this far north. He had eyes that he liked to think were inscrutable, but to me they always looked mischievous, and maybe a little insecure. He nodded at me as I walked in, and then leaned over to look around me through the door to the reception area.

"Julie," he called. "You're supposed to buzz me and announce clients before you send them back."

"I know," she called back. "But it's *him*."

Alex sighed and turned back to me. "It's hard to find good help these days."

"I think she's great help," I said loudly enough so Julie could hear.

"That's 'cause you need me more than he does," called Julie. "But compliments don't pay the bills."

"Would you like to join us for our private attorney-client meeting?" said Chan, his voice dripping with acid.

"Oh, can I?" said Julie girlishly.

Alex sighed. "Shut the door, will you?" he said to me.

I closed it and said, "I told you what you were getting with her."

"I know." He lowered his voice and looked at the door as if Julie had her ear on the other side of it. "But she is very good, actually. Plus, she's kind of cute."

I just grinned widely.

"Shut up," said Chan. "What do you want?"

I threw the envelope from my mother onto his desk in front of him. "My mom sent some more papers of my dad's."

He pulled the envelope toward him and extracted the contents. "Have you looked at these?"

"No, that's what I pay you for."

"How do you know she didn't send you a letter?"

"She told me on the phone she was sending more of this stuff."

He started glancing through the thick stack of paper my mother had sent. "Why did he make you executor of his will anyway? Why not her?"

"I don't know, maybe he figured she would die first. She's not very good with this kind of thing anyway, so she didn't mind."

"You're not so great with paperwork and details yourself."

"Yes, but I have you."

Chan sighed and shook his head. The window behind him looked out onto a well-kept green lawn dotted with trees that were bright with autumn. Two squirrels were playing at the base of a white-trunked birch that was gaudy with golden leaves.

After a minute, Alex shuffled the papers and tapped their edges on the desk. "I don't see anything here that is relevant to your dad's estate. These look like old case files from his days as a Washington state police detective." He slid the papers back into the envelope and handed it to me.

"Yeah," I said. "Mom is just sending me anything and everything that looks kind of official or important."

"That's OK," said Chan, grinning at me with startlingly white teeth. "It all works out into billable hours for me."

Now it was my turn to sigh.

SIX

Much as I wanted to solve the crime and recover Ethel Ostrand's money, I still had a job as pastor of Harbor Lutheran Church in Grand Lake. So on Sunday, as usual, I preached a heck of a sermon. I could tell that at certain points, some folks would have said "amen" if they hadn't been Scandinavian Lutherans. As it was, they showed their rabid enthusiasm by not overtly falling asleep.

Leyla was there, as she had been every week for several months now. She had joined the ladies Bible study group as well, but she never talked to me about it. Despite my complicated ambivalence, I was happy to see her.

After church, I pulled her aside. "Wanna watch the game at my place?" I said. "I'll make lunch." She gave me a long look that I guess I was supposed to understand.

"I don't think so, Jonah," she said.

"OK," I said. I had a vague sense that it had to do with our conversation on Friday night.

I liked Leyla. Her attitude unsettled me slightly. Even so, I was rarely unhappy at the prospect of an afternoon alone. After a nap, I made a simple dough from flour, salt, oil, water and yeast. While it was rising, I fried up some ground beef with garlic, onions, pepper, basil and oregano. I also chopped up some tomatoes, fresh mushrooms and black olives. I opened a can of tomato paste and mixed it with water, black pepper, more basil and garlic, some salt and a lot of black pepper.

When the dough was ready, I pressed it onto my pizza stone. I spread the tomato sauce onto it, and then the other ingredients, and topped it with mozzarella cheese, and put it in the oven for twenty minutes. Voila! Pizza.

Belatedly, I remembered the football game. It wasn't the Seahawks or the Forty-niners, but I was doing my best to stay current with the Vikings this year. When in Rome, one ought to cheer for the Roman team. Or something like that.

I watched most of the second half, munching on my pizza and drinking a bottle of Woodchuck's hard apple cider. It was a game the Vikings were expected to lose, so, naturally, they won. It was fun to watch a team do that. On the other hand, the Vikings also had a tendency to lose games they were supposed to win. I thought it might have something to do with the Scandinavian temperament of their fans. Too much success was morally questionable.

The late game came on, still not the Seahawks. I had read somewhere that someone had done a bunch of blood tests on pastors, which seemed like a good idea for so many different reasons. They found that most pastors, over the course of a week, gradually built up to a massive adrenaline spike on Sunday mornings. Once the church services were all done with, there was a corresponding physical low, and most of them crashed, waking up with big headaches on Monday mornings.

I had so far escaped the headaches, but I believed in the adrenaline and the following crash. The crash began to hit me as I watched the Bears battle the Packers, and even the drama of a battle for first place in the division failed to keep my eyes from growing heavy. I scooched down on the couch, set my plate on the floor, and fell into the blessed embrace of my Sunday afternoon nap.

~

About a year ago, a bunch of thugs had broken into my cabin and trashed it, as a warning to me. I was too obtuse for the warning to be effective, but many staunch, worldly wise friends and church members had insisted afterward that I get an alarm system. I finally caved in when I came home one day to find it was already installed, and Julie was programming it for me.

Generally, I only turned it on out of guilt, because I hadn't paid for installation. I left it off when I was personally at home. But I had never figured out how to turn off the brief, loud, series of beeps that happened whenever anyone opened a door or window.

That loud beeping sound is what startled me out of my nap.

I looked up, and there was a man dressed in black standing in the sliding door that opened onto my deck. He wore a black ski mask, covering his face except for holes where his eyes and mouth were.

Talk about adrenaline spike. It was like no sermon I'd ever preached before.

I've heard about an instinct that some natural fighters have to attack relentlessly without pausing. My Tae Kwon Do coach used to tell me I had it. I do know this: it's usually a good thing if your reactions surprise your opponent and he doesn't have time to think. I leaped from the couch, and stooping at the fireplace, I grabbed a chunk of wood with my right hand and the poker in my left. I heaved the wood directly at his face. He ducked, and it hit him on the head because my aim had been too low. He cursed and staggered back while I switched the poker to my right hand and ran at him. Perhaps if I had paused he might have drawn a weapon, or suddenly remembered he was a champion street fighter or something, but as it is, he did what was natural for almost anyone who is attacked by a crazed, poker-bearing pastor who has just been wakened from his post-adrenaline nap: he ran.

The triple beep of the alarm system went off again, suggesting another intruder. I shouted as loud as could, whirled, ran to the alarm keypad, and hit the panic button.

Wild sirens went off while I spun back around looking for the second invader. No one was in sight. Within ten seconds, my phone rang. It was the alarm company.

"We show that your alarm is going off," said a calm female voice at the other end. "Is everything OK?"

I felt like I was on a TV commercial. "No," I said. "Someone – maybe two people – just tried to break in while I was napping."

"The police are on their way," she said. "Please stay on the line with me until they get there."

In the TV commercials I'd seen, the burglars always ran away when the sirens went off. I could understand why – it was so loud, I wanted to run too, but I left the sirens on, and I stayed put by the front door, with the poker in hand, just in case anybody had been wearing earplugs.

While I waited, I noticed that my leg had begun to hurt again. Looking down, I could see that the bandage was soaked with fresh blood.

When the police arrived, I shut off the alarm. They were from the county, since I lived well outside the town limits. One was a young, short, blond woman named Sam. Her partner was a tall, lean, middle-aged guy with a shaved head. His name plate said Nelson.

Officer Sam noticed my leg immediately. "Are you hurt?" she asked.

I shook my head. "I got this a few days ago at the bank. Probably just busted it open chasing that guy out of here."

"I heard about that," said Nelson.

"I know you," said Sam. "You were involved in that courthouse business last year. Didn't you get shot in the same place then?"

"Other leg," I said. "But thanks for remembering. I'm Jonah Borden."

"Sam," she said. "And this is Officer Nelson."

"Rick," he said, sticking out his hand.

"Are you kidding me?" I said. "Ricky Nelson? What happened to the hair?"

"Careful," he said. "I'm a lot bigger than you." But then he grinned.

"So what's up here?" asked Sam.

I told them about the intruders. They poked around a little bit and found the window to my office was open. We couldn't see that anything was missing or disturbed.

"Not much more we can do," said Nelson. "No description of the suspect. According to you, nothing taken or damaged."

Sam finished writing in her notebook. "Call us if you realize later that something is missing," she said. "In the meantime, keep your doors locked and your alarm on."

I'm not normally nervous or jumpy when I'm alone in my cabin in the woods overlooking Superior, a mile from my nearest neighbor. But for some reason that evening, every time I glanced up at the night outside the glass of my patio door, I could swear a man in black clothes and a ski mask had just stepped away from the light into the darkness beyond.

At around eight, I heard a subtle noise coming from my office. It sounded like someone was moving around, but trying to be very quiet about it. I remembered that the window had been opened there this afternoon. My heart began to pound. I stepped over to my stereo, plugged in my iPod, and turned on some tunes. I glanced over my shoulder but no one was coming out of my office door yet. Covered, I hoped, by the sound of the music, I walked over to the fireplace and picked up the poker again. Then I stepped softly in my stocking-feet toward my office. I could have hit the panic button on the alarm, but I would have felt pretty stupid if it was nothing.

I waited outside the office door for a long time. Now I regretted putting on the music, because I couldn't hear as well. At last I heard it again, a soft rubbing, maybe someone's pant-leg against a chair. Then there was a quiet thump, and then a louder sound of papers being pushed off my desk.

I leaped through the door, poker raised, yelling, and then I stopped.

Flattened in fear on my desk was a scrawny orange kitten, its fur puffed up to twice its size. I lowered the poker weakly. Then I collapsed in the chair, laughing.

The kitten watched me with wide eyes, like I was a Martian just descended from my space-ship.

"Well," I said to it, "I'm glad I didn't hit the panic button. You must have come in when the window was open before."

Slowly, the animal relaxed, its fur settling back down into place. Its orange coat was long and fluffy, like a Persian cat. The kitten looked small and helpless and very hungry. It continued to stare at me out of large round eyes.

"I had a vet friend who told me once that orange cats are almost always male," I said to it. "That true?"

The kitten slowly sat up, and then yawned and started to clean itself.

"Well, I'm going to take that a yes. You new in the neighborhood?" He had to be a stray. He looked ill-kept and hungry, and there were no houses for a mile around my place.

The cat stopped licking himself and stared at me again.

"What?" I said. "You got something to say, say it."

"Mew," he said, and then started purring.

"I guess I can see that," I said. I leaned forward slowly. "You OK if I pick you up?" As I reached out my hand, the kitten arched his back and rubbed against my computer monitor. I stroked him and the purring got louder. I gently reached under him and picked him up, pulling him back to my chest. He immediately thrust his head decisively under my chin, the purring going like a chainsaw.

After a minute I carried him out into the living room, where I replaced the poker and stepped into my kitchen. I put him on the floor and got him a little bowl of milk. He sniffed at it curiously, and then tasted it. After a second or two he began lapping furiously. When he was finished, he came to me where I sat on the couch. He climbed up my leg, and then wormed his way up my chest to shove his face under my chin again. I petted him and blew fur away from my face. Eventually he fell asleep and I moved him up against some pillows on the couch.

Before bed I checked the doors and windows. I leaned the poker next to my bed. Even so, I laid there for a long time staring into the dark. I heard a little sound and then the kitten padded softly into my room. "Mew?" he said, and the scrambled up my comforter. He wormed his way under the covers until he was tucked under my chin, purring loudly.

"Goodnight," I said, and slept peacefully the rest of the night.

SEVEN

It was fall, and the counseling appointments were starting to line up. Minnesotans didn't waste time with relational or psychological problems during the short, beautiful summers. They tried to eke every last second of enjoyment out of each precious degree above sixty. So every fall, after school started up, I had a rash of appointments. This year, the favored topic seemed to be marriage problems.

On the Tuesday after the bank robbery, I had an appointment with someone new, a woman named Angela. She had called the church out of the blue, and Julie had set up the meeting. At eleven, she came into the church office.

She was probably five foot seven, with a mass of frizzy, dark-blond hair. I thought it was a natural frizz. I couldn't imagine anyone paying to get that done to her hair. All the same, she had it pinned and barretted so that it cascaded attractively down one shoulder.

I stood up and walked around my desk. "Come on in," I said. "Do you want some coffee?" To my approval, she accepted. I decided to have a cup with her. Just to be sociable.

I ushered her to the sitting area and went to get the elixir of the gods. When I came back, she was sitting on the love seat, both legs crossed under her, her sandals lying on the floor. She looked comfortable. On both wrists, she wore a bunch of thin metal bracelets, the kind I used to call bangles. I never did know if I had that right, but that's what I called them. They clinked in a sort of enticing way when she moved her hands. She wore loose fitting, thin trousers that looked vaguely Indian. Her top was long and orange-ish and definitely East Indian. The overall style of her look, I figured, was classy hippie. I thought she might be in her mid-thirties, and well kept.

After we exchanged the normal banalities, I said, "What I can do for you, Angie?"

"Angela, please." She said. "I never go by Angie. That is what my father used to call me."

"OK, Angela," I said. "How can I help you?"

She turned her hand palm up and twisted her wrist around aimlessly. The bangles made little clinking sounds.

"I have had an affair," she said.

I waited. Sometimes I think one of my biggest jobs in counseling is simply not to appear shocked. That was easy this time, because I had heard this sort of thing before.

She twisted her hand in the air and clinked some more. "The problem is," she said, "I feel guilty."

I waited some more, mostly because this time I didn't really know what to say. Finally, I said, "It's pretty normal to feel guilty after you have an affair."

"Guilt is an artificial construct, created by a patriarchal society to enforce its arbitrary mores." She said it with a straight face, unblinking. She pronounced mores properly too, like 'mor-ays.' I wanted to compliment her enunciation, but I restrained myself.

"I know better than to fall for all that patriarchal social oppression," she added, "but somehow I still feel guilty."

"I'm not sure I understand," I said. "What do you want from me?"

"I want you to help me to not feel guilty," she said.

"Angela," I said, "do you understand what it is I do here?"

She laughed, a short laugh, but genuine. Then she cocked her head at me. "You don't seriously still believe in sin and all that nonsense, do you? You seem so educated."

"I am, in fact, ridiculously over-educated," I said. "Even so, I'm wondering why you chose to come to me, rather than a therapist who might share your same views."

"I've been taking a few classes in Feminism and Counseling at the University of Minnesota Duluth," she said.

That explained a lot about her misconceptions concerning guilt

"One of my professors is also a certified therapist. I've been seeing him. Unfortunately, he can't really help me in this matter."

"You had an affair with your *professor?*" I blurted.

"How could you possibly have known that? Did Ethan call you?" She looked shaken.

"No, I don't even know who he is," I said. "Sometimes I get these – insights. I think it's a God thing."

"Well, anyway, there is nothing wrong with our affair."

"Actually," I said, "there are all kinds of things wrong with it. Not least of which is malpractice. As a therapist, he is liable in a civil court for that, and possibly a criminal one too. I imagine UMD still frowns on that sort of thing also."

There was an awkward silence. She didn't meet my eyes. "Anyway," she said very quietly, but firmly, "I still feel guilty, and I don't think I should have to."

"All right. Why do you think you should have no guilt?"

"It was a beautiful thing," she said. "Nobody else even knows it happened, so it doesn't hurt my husband. And besides, like I said, guilt is an artificial construct created by a patriarchal society to enforce arbitrary mores."

"Nice diction," I said. She didn't seem to think it was as amusing as I did.

There was a slight pause. "If guilt is artificially created, then why has every single human society in every time period and every place come up with that same idea?"

She shrugged, "It *is* effective."

"Angela, that's not really an answer, and you know it. And it isn't just guilt. Marriage is a universal idea too. Throughout history, every single culture has – most of them independently, mind you – arrived at some sort of idea of 'marriage.' Some cultures disagree about who can marry whom. Others disagree about how many people a person can marry. But all cultures have always agreed there is something called marriage, and that adultery is wrong. Most cultures came to that conclusion independent of the influence of any other culture. That can't be an accident."

She seemed to shrink inside herself. "That doesn't really help me to feel not guilty."

"In my profession, I deal with guilt quite a bit," I said.

"That's why I came here," she said. "I thought you would know more about how to get rid of it."

"I guarantee I know more about it than your therapist, or professor, or whatever he is," I said. I sipped some coffee, and felt no guilt myself. "In all my experiences and studies, I know of only one thing that can deal effectively with guilt."

There was silence. "What is it?" she asked finally.

"Forgiveness."

"*Forgiveness?* But that would mean that I had done something wrong, something that needs to be forgiven."

"Precisely."

"But there was nothing wrong with it. It was a beautiful thing. My husband doesn't even know about it, so it doesn't hurt him. It doesn't hurt anybody."

"And yet, you feel guilty."

She was quiet.

"Angela," I said, "I have seen people try to deal with guilt in all sorts of ways. They try to work it off, fight it off, pay it off, or suffer it off. They try to drown it in drugs or alcohol or pleasure. They try – like you – to pretend it doesn't really exist. But the only thing that really takes care of it is forgiveness. And to receive forgiveness, you have to admit that you need it. That means you have to admit you were wrong. Your therapist was even more wrong than you – he took advantage of you – but you were wrong too."

She started to cry, softly. "But it didn't *hurt* anybody," she said.

"Who made that the only basis for deciding right and wrong?" I said. "Surgery to remove a tumor can be very painful. So can setting a broken leg. The right thing is, at times, desperately painful. And sometimes the wrong thing is easy and pleasurable, at least in the short term." I watched her for a moment longer. "Besides, if it didn't hurt anyone, why are you crying?"

"So you want me to go tell my husband, and beg for his forgiveness? *He's* the reason I had to have an affair!"

"Now we're getting somewhere," I said. "But, no, I don't necessarily recommend telling your spouse, and certainly not until we understand the situation a little more clearly."

"Well, then, if I need forgiveness, but I don't tell my husband, where can I find it?"

I told her.

EIGHT

After Angela left, I saw another couple who were struggling in their marriage. By the time they left, it was all starting to bug me a bit. I did enough study to have some material to think over, and by early afternoon, I was sitting in a canoe on Fish Lake, not catching any fish. Every fall for three years, I had been trying to catch crappie. For some reason, I was never very successful. Maybe they knew that secretly, I would rather be wading in a stream, catching trout.

"It was too late in the day to go all the way to Wisconsin for trout," I said to my motionless float. "So why not give me a break here?"

The crappie had no pity on me.

I did, however, have a thermos of hot fresh coffee and a couple of flaky croissants, and so I drank and munched and ruminated on my study material.

Like all good voyageurs, I had my cell phone with me. Normally, I would have shut it off, but I was feeling slightly guilty for leaving the office so quickly. About five minutes into my second croissant, the phone rang. I didn't recognize the number.

"Borden," I said, answering it, and tucking it between my ear and shoulder.

"Hello, Pastor Borden?" asked a man's voice. My bobber slid smoothly, but without haste, under the water.

"Shoot," I said, jerking up on my rod and reeling in. The phone slipped. "Dang," I added, as the fish came off, still well underwater and away from the canoe.

"I heard you weren't much for swearing," said the man at the other end. "Is this a bad time?"

"Sorry," I said. "It's fine now. How can I help you?" I set my rod down, leaving the bait in the water.

"My name is Red Hollis," said the man. "I got your number from Mike Schwartz." Schwartz was a counselor I knew down in Minneapolis.

"What can I do for you?" I asked.

"Well, I own a sailboat up on the North Shore. When I'm not using it, I have it chartered out. Sometimes Mike charters it for a marriage counseling weekend. You know, he takes two or three couples on the boat; they sail around, experience the beauty of Superior, and talk about their problems and so on. Mike says the atmosphere of the sailing charter really makes it a unique experience. Really helps the folks, you know."

"Sounds interesting," I said.

"Well, this year, I'm keeping the boat in the water a few weeks later than normal, and so I have some time still free for a late-season charter. Trying to fill it up, pay the bills you know," he chuckled. A genial, friendly guy. "Mike thought you might be interested in doing one of those 'marriage cruises' with some of your people."

"Could be," I said. My float began to dance back and forth across the surface of the water. As I watched, it slid under again. "What dates are we talking about here, and how much per person?"

My bobber stayed under. I gave in, picked up my rod, and began to crank. The float popped back up and I could tell there was no fish on. I put the rod back down.

"I'm sorry, could you repeat that?" I asked Red Hollis. "Bad reception or something."

He told me again. "And you'd be free," he added. "And I'll captain the boat, so you don't pay any extra for that either. Desperate times call for desperate measures, you know."

The bobber disappeared again, this time with violent little sploosh. I turned and looked the other way. Red and I talked for a few more minutes. We arranged to meet for lunch for the next day.

I hung up, turned around, and found my bobber floating placidly next to the boat. When I reeled in the line, my bait was gone, of course.

Those were the only bites I got all afternoon.

NINE

I met Red Hollis at an Applebee's in Duluth. All Applebee's restaurants are the same. No matter where in the country you find them, the bar is laid out the same way, the tables are arranged the same way, and the menu is also the same. That can be either very comforting or quite boring, depending on your outlook. Just for the heck of it, today I decided it was boring. Even so, they do know how to cook, especially appetizers.

"I'm buying," said Red. He was a big guy, several inches taller than me. Whatever had given him the name nickname "Red" was no longer in evidence, since he had, like many balding men, shaved his head completely. He was probably in his mid or early thirties. I wondered what a man so young did to get enough money to buy a yacht. On the other hand, in my experience, doing almost anything was likely to make more money than being a pastor. Hollis was wearing casually expensive slacks and a lightweight black sweater under a nicely tailored blue blazer. He looked pretty much like what he was: a successful, wealthy businessman who owned his own big-water sailing yacht.

Maybe if he had looked poor, or even sad or something, I would have argued with his offer to buy lunch. As it was, I just said thanks. And after all, it was Applebee's, not the Saint Paul Grill.

"Sometime when you're down in the Cities, look me up, and I'll take you to a real lunch," said Hollis after we were seated. "I don't know Duluth that well, so I just picked Applebee's. You can always count on them being the same everywhere. It's almost kind of comforting."

"Yeah," I said. "That's what it is."

He gave me a funny look. People are always giving me funny looks.

"How do you know Mike Schwartz?" I asked after we ordered drinks and appetizers. Hollis was having a beer, and I had a Coke. On the rocks.

"Don't really know him well," said Hollis. Our drinks came, and he took a sip. "I met him over in Bayfield one time when I was sailing. We got to talking, and I ended up taking him and his little group on a cruise."

"So, you are kind of wining and dining me here," I said. "I'm wondering what you get out of it."

He looked at me thoughtfully. "I thought pastors weren't supposed to be so blunt."

"I'm a lot of things pastors aren't supposed to be," I said.

He shrugged. "I'm a businessman. If you fill the boat for me for a weekend, that's a month's payment I don't have to make." He took a sip of beer. "If you have a good experience, maybe you'll do it again next year. Maybe you'll do it more than once a year. It's worth my investing a little time and a meal or two in you."

"So tell me again how it works for Mike."

"Your buddy Mike Schwartz is not the only I guy I do this for, but here's generally what happens."

He was interrupted by the arrival of our appetizers. Mine was a Tuscan-style cheese dip with ciabatti bread. I remained calm.

"Anyway," said Red as our server left, "Mike, or you, or whoever, has people he counsels. Sometimes, you know, it helps to have a change of venue if you really want a change of perspective. So you get these people out of town, out of their ordinary life, and put in them in a situation where everything is new and different and stimulating."

I was trying not to look like a pig as I ate my cheese dip. I'm not sure if I was successful.

"First off, they are going to have a good time. If it's married couples you're counseling, maybe this is the first time they've enjoyed themselves together for a long time."

I had to admit, Hollis was making good sense. He'd obviously thought it through. I also had to admit, the cheese dip was as good as I remembered.

"And then," Hollis went on, "not only are they actually enjoying themselves together, but also, being in that new and different environment makes them more open to changing, to actually dealing with their same old patterns of behavior."

"So, you been counseling long, Red?"

He grinned. "I got most of this from Mike Schwartz, but I pay attention."

I guess you don't earn enough money to buy a yacht without being pretty bright and observant.

"Actually," said Hollis, "that's what got me to buy this boat in the first place. Another counselor-friend of your buddy Schwartz wanted to do this thing, but he didn't know how to sail. He knew I was into sailing and had some experience, so we chartered the boat, and I took care of the sailing and stuff, and he did the counseling. Then Schwartz started doing it too."

He finally paused to take a bite of his quesadilla. It was probably cold by now. "Anyway, I saw pretty quick that these folks were shelling out some coin, you know, for the boat. I did the math, and figured I could buy one if I just did so many counseling trips a year. I already had two counselors on board – so to speak, a little pun, you know – and so I went for it."

"When was that?" I asked, just to be polite. I'm not a huge fan of puns.

"A few years ago now," he said, waving his hand vaguely. We paused as our entrees were served. An old Elton John tune was playing in the background.

"So, what's the name of your boat?" I asked. Hollis took a bite of his burger. He washed it down with a sip of beer.

"*Tiny Dancer*," he said finally.

"Hey, just like this song," I said, gesturing in the air to indicate the music.

"Yeah," he said, sheepishly. "I love this song. I figure I spend this much money on a boat, I can name it whatever I want." He took another sip of beer. "Do you have any more questions?"

Now I was chewing. "I thought Mike still chartered his trips," I said.

Red Hollis was chewing now. He spoke with his mouth full, gesturing. "I don't know what all Schwartz does without me." He swallowed and took another drink. "Truth is, he isn't real regular with me, which is why I was hoping you'd be interested."

"Where is your boat?" I asked.

He looked uncomfortable. "I've been having slip troubles," he said. "I'm over by Bayfield, but that's tough over there, to find a permanent slip. I'm hoping to get her up to Silver Bay before winter."

"That's closer to Grand Lake, but that one's hard to get into, I hear," I said.

"I know, but I know a guy,"

"That's the plan," said Hollis.

"Isn't that a little late in the year to be going?"

"Naw," he said. "Like I told you, I'm just trying to make the most of things, times being what they are."

"But what about storms and bad weather?" I asked.

"Well, obviously, we won't go if the weather's bad, but there's no reason to assume it will be."

"What if you can't get into Silver Bay?"

"Then we'll go from Bayfield," he said. "Listen, if you schedule this with your folks, I'll make sure it happens, one way or the other."

"Fair enough," I said.

TEN

I was beginning to think that Red Hollis might have a pretty good idea. There are no magic bullets when you are dealing with real live people, but it couldn't hurt to get some couples on a yacht in the middle of Lake Superior and threaten to throw them off the boat unless they started behaving like adults.

Another couple had called, again out of the blue. They were new to the North Coast. Apparently, the wild beauty of the cliffs, the impossibly clear water, and the golden autumn on the ridges had not yet solved their marriage problems. Aside from my occasional fits of frustration, I did enjoy counseling couples, and it was often a good way to connect new folks with our church community.

She was small, with dark hair and olive skin, bursting with suppressed energy. She stalked into the main church office like a cat, looking all around her, touching books and running her hand along the reception desk.

She turned, quick and smooth, when she saw me. "I'm Jasmine," she said, holding out her hand. Her grip was firm and cool.

He was medium height, badly cut brown hair, with broad shoulders and a powerful handshake. His face was coarse, his features blunt, and quite frankly, he was ugly to look at.

"Tony Stone," he said.

Where she seemed to be full of energy and curiosity and passion, he seemed reserved and distant.

"Come on in to my office," I said. I offered them coffee, but they both declined. The pot was half-full however, so I figured I had better drink some without them. The pot was always half-full, with me.

Jasmine Stone walked around my office, looking at pictures, and always touching something – my books, my desk or stroking chairs as she moved past them. Tony stood impassively.

"Please sit down," I said to them. They sat next to each other on the little love seat in the sitting area in front of my desk. I sat in one of the armchairs in front of them.

"So how long have you been in Grand Lake?" I asked.

"Actually we live north a little ways," said Jasmine.

"Well, how long have you lived there?" I asked.

"Not long," said Tony Stone.

There was a pause.

"So what brought you up here?" I asked.

"Business," said Stone. It was quiet again. Usually when I wait, people will start talking.

"Oh, let's cut the crap," said Jasmine, tossing her hair. "We're miserable." She looked at Tony with shining eyes and stroked his arm. "We need your help." She turned back to me. Tony sat impassively in the love seat. His legs weren't crossed, and he looked completely comfortable.

"What seems to the problem?" I asked.

"We fight all time," she said. "Don't we, honey?" she added in a little-girl voice, squeezing Stone's arm.

He stirred, as if coming out of a daydream. "Yeah," he said. "We fight a lot."

"What do you fight about?"

"Money," said Jasmine quickly, her eyes flashing.

Stone seemed almost to smile slightly. He looked straight ahead, not at me, not at her. "Yeah," he said. "We fight about money."

We all sat there for a moment and contemplated this.

"Anything else?" I said at last.

"Oh, we're just all messed up," said Jasmine. "We fight all the time, and we're unhappy. We need some serious help. Like, if you could lock us up in a cabin somewhere or something, off away from it all and help us work it out."

Stone looked at her speculatively and nodded slightly.

"Well, I'd want to know more about you before I had you locked up," I said. Jasmine locked eyes with me and gave me a stunning smile that, for some reason, made me want to blush. Stone's lips twitched slightly.

I asked some more questions, and we talked further, but when they left an hour later, I still had no clear handle on what their problem was. We scheduled another appointment for the next week.

ELEVEN

A lot of North Coast towns don't really understand what they have in terms of tourist potential. Granted, the season is short, but even so, many of the little towns along Highway sixty-one between Duluth and Canada almost ignore the fact that they have a drop-dead gorgeous freshwater ocean right in front of them. You have to look hard even to find a restaurant with a water view. Grand Lake is an exception. Some far-sighted town planners purchased a nice strip of waterfront downtown, a little north and east of the old ore docks. They turned the lake-front into a nice park. The street running behind the park is filled with restaurants, bookstores, little touristy craft shops and a small indoor mall set in a renovated lumber mill. Several of the restaurants look out to the park and lake.

Dylan's is one of these. It's a small café and coffee house, named in honor of the North Coast's most famous son, Duluth native Robert Zimmer – better known to the world as Bob Dylan. Dylan's is the perfect combination of a Starbuck's, a French café and a log cabin. Leyla and I were having lunch there.

"You know," I said, "the chicken salad itself is as I good as I can make –"

"High praise," murmured Leyla. I ignored her.

"But the brilliant thing is to put a slice of aged Swiss on it. I don't know why nobody else puts Swiss cheese on chicken salad."

"You sound like you are eighty years old," said Leyla. "Are you going start talking about your intestinal health soon?"

"Aren't we crabby," I said. "The fact is, I love food. I love to create it, to smell it, to taste it, and yes, talk about it."

"Sorry," she said briefly. She closed her eyes and took a deep breath. I took the moment to enjoy watching her. She opened her eyes.

"Why do you look at me that way?" she asked.

"I can't help it," I confessed.

She shook her head and looked away like she was a bit angry. "I don't get you, Jonah Borden."

"I'm sorry," I said. I had no idea what for, but it seemed like a good thing to say.

I chewed some more chicken salad. "A couple came in the other day," I said. I told her a little bit about Jasmine and Tony Stone, without naming them.

"I don't know what to make of it. I mean, she seemed almost excited. If it didn't sound so weird, I'd even say, 'turned on.' He sat there like a pile of bricks, but at the same time, he didn't seem uncomfortable or anything."

"Is that unusual?" asked Leyla.

"Well, yeah. I mean, normally, there's quite a bit of tension between couples who come in. But I didn't get that. It was almost like they were coming to marriage counseling just because they felt like they should, or something, but not because they really need it."

"Maybe we need counseling, Jonah," said Leyla suddenly.

"What?"

"Maybe we should get counseling."

"We aren't married," I said.

She gave me a withering a look.

"Look," I said, "maybe *I* need counseling, but I'm not sure *we* do. It's my own hang up, Leyla. I'm working on it."

"Are you?" she asked.

"Well, it's only been a week since we talked about this," I said. I admit, it even sounded lame to me.

She looked out over the lake. It was a gray day, and the heaving water lay like pewter out to the horizon. When she looked back at me, she had tears in her eyes.

"I can't help thinking that I'm the one who screwed this up." She wiped at her eyes. "We had a good thing going, and then I was so ready to believe the worst about you. Well, I don't anymore, Jonah. I believe the *best* about you. But now *you* are thinking the worst about *me*."

"I'm not, Leyla."

"Then can you even try and explain what the problem is?"

I thought about it. All I knew was that there was some kind of hesitancy, a slowness to give in to what I knew I could feel for Leyla, if only I let myself.

"I don't want to say it wrong," I said. "Maybe we should agree on some date, on that day, or sooner, I will tell you about it."

She shook her head, and covered my hand with hers. "I'm sorry, Jonah," she said. "I don't mean to push you. Let's talk about something else." She took a deep breath, and seemed to mentally shake herself out of something.

"All right," I said, "how about I tell you how Dan Jensen asked his wife Janie to marry him?"

She pursed her lips. "I suppose."

"I thought chicks loved engagement stories."

She flipped her hair back. "So now I'm just a chick?"

"Possibly a babe," I said. "But definitely not a broad."

"Are you going to tell the story or not?"

I pursed my lips. "I suppose," I said. She hit me.

"Okay, okay," I said. "So Dan and Janie have been dating for a while. Things have gotten pretty serious, and she can just tell it's only a matter of time before he pops the big question."

Leyla nodded sagely. "Women know these things."

"Anyway, he takes her to this really fancy restaurant in Duluth."

"What restaurant?" said Leyla.

"I don't know," I said. "One of those really fancy places, you know with thirty-dollar entrees."

"You don't know which restaurant it was?" she asked.

"No. What's the difference? It was –"

"You're telling me an engagement story," she interrupted, giving me with a withering look, "and you don't know which restaurant they went to?" For some reason, she seemed to be on the attack. "What was she wearing?"

"Wearing? Are you crazy? How could I possibly know that?"

"If you were a woman, you would know it."

"I am definitely not a woman."

She smiled a sudden and mischievous smile. "I have noticed that, actually."

"Do you want to hear this story or not?" I said.

"I suppose."

"You are walking on thin ice, lady," I said. "Okay. I don't know what anyone was wearing, and I don't know the actual restaurant, but it was the kind of place you go to ask someone to marry them."

Leyla offered the faintest hint of a sniff.

"If I may continue?" I said. "So all through dinner, Janie is expecting something. Dan is acting nervous. She's chewing her spaghetti carefully in case there's a ring in it."

"They paid thirty dollars a plate for spaghetti?"

"Okay, so I don't know what they ate either – or what they drank, for that matter. Do you really want to hear this story?"

"I'm enjoying the story," she said blandly.

"I don't know whether to laugh or cry," I said.

"It's about time someone gave you some of your own medicine." After a moment, she added, "go on."

"So Dan is a bit nervous. He keeps acting like he's going to say something important, and then ends up just asking for the ketchup." Leyla opened her mouth. I held up my hand quickly. "No, they did not put ketchup on their spaghetti, or even have ketchup, or spaghetti, for that matter. The point is, he's not asking the question, but she thinks he might be trying to work up to it."

"You're doing fine," said Leyla. "Someday, maybe you'll even be able to make your living in public speaking."

"Thankfully, people like you don't interrupt when I'm preaching," I said.

"Go on."

I waited.

"Please," she said, her eyes sparkling. "We're having so much fun, aren't we?"

"One of us is, anyway." But, truthfully, I was glad to see her back on an even keel. I took a breath. "Anyway, they leave the unnamed restaurant, after having eaten anonymous meals, wearing unidentified clothes. The question has not been asked. They go down to the shore to watch the sunset."

"The sun doesn't set over the lake."

"They go down to see the eastern sky darken," I amended, "and to watch as the silvering waters softly fade into the still, clear evening."

"That was nice," said Leyla admiringly.

"I am a wordsmith," I said modestly. "Anyway, down there at the beach, they sit on some rocks. They are holding hands, and Janie is positive this is it. Dan's hand is kind of shaking, and he keeps clearing his throat, but he keeps not asking the question." I took a sip of water. "So now she's starting to get nervous too. She can't believe the moment is finally here. All of a sudden, he says, 'Janie!' very sharply, like that. She jumps almost two feet. She stares into his eyes and says, 'yes?' And he says, 'Janie!' but he's not really looking at her. It's like he's looking past her. 'What is it?' she says. And he says, 'Janie! There's a skunk! Run!'"

Leyla titled her head at me and got a quirky, puzzly expression on her face. "There was a skunk? A real skunk?"

"A real skunk," I said. "This part, I know the specifics. So they leap up and start running. They are both muddled and flustered at this point. As they are running, Janie shouts at Dan, 'Will you marry me?' The skunk doesn't notice them until now. When Janie shouts and he sees them running, he turns around and lets loose on them."

"Wait," said Leyla. "Janie asked Dan?"

"Yep," I said.

"And then they got sprayed by a skunk?"

"Spaghetti or no spaghetti, that's exactly what happened," I said.

TWELVE

My mom called from Washington State that evening. We exchanged the normal greetings.

"Did you get the package I sent you?" she asked.

"I showed it to Alex Chan – my lawyer," I said. The orange kitten raced into the room and screeched to a halt in front of me, puffed up like a blowfish. I wiggled my foot at him. I had been unable to locate any owners, and no one else seemed to want him. It was too cold at night to kick him out.

"That wasn't estate stuff," Mom said. "I just sent it to the church out of habit."

"I know. Alex said it was just old case files of Dad's." The cat pounced on my foot, and then curled around it, attacking it with all four paws and his teeth. I winced and poked at him with my other foot.

"Did you read any of it?"

"Not yet," I said. "It's been kind of crazy around here.

"What's been going on?" she asked.

When you've been shot by a bank robber, it is a major moral choice to decide whether or not to tell your mother. Kind of like when you break a neighbor's window with a baseball.

I told her. After all, I'm supposed to be one of the moral bastions of the community.

She was quiet for a long time. The cat chewed on me in the silence.

"I'm OK, Mom. I hardly even limp now, and it's only been like a week."

"I think you should read the papers of your father's I sent," she said.

"Are you saying they have something to do with the bank robbery?" Abruptly the kitten released me and went tearing out of the room at full speed. Somehow, he managed to make galloping noises on the floor as he did it.

"I don't know," Mom said. "But I know he had a case a lot like that just a few years ago. Check it out."

We talked some more. When we hung up, Mom was still worried about me, but that was probably just because she was a mother.

I found the envelope and opened it. I pulled out the papers, extracted the first few, and set the others and the envelope beside me on the couch. The kitten came in, climbed up onto the couch and collapsed on the papers.

Since I was about ten years old, my dad, the police detective, had talked about some of his cases with me. If something was particularly interesting or unusual, he told me about it. He didn't really know how to talk to children, and I remembered him seeming a little uncomfortable when I wanted him to play kid-games with me. But once we started talking about his cases, we had common ground, and it was one way we had become close. Twice in his career, Dad had discharged his weapon. I knew this, but I didn't know much else. He never talked about those cases.

The papers I had weren't the official files, of course, but they were his notes, and sometimes photocopies of other evidence. Some of them were a trip down memory lane for me, and I recalled old conversations with my dad about this or that case.

After about twenty minutes I found the one Mom was talking about. I began to read carefully. Suddenly, something smacked the paper in front of me aside and two big eyes were staring at me out of a fuzzy orange face.

"I'm reading," I said.

He crouched on my chest and wiggled his bottom, like he was going to leap and attack my face. I reached for him, and he seized my hand instead. Several painful minutes later, I resumed reading. Fifteen minutes after that, I called the Grand Lake police department.

"This is Jonah Borden," I told the dispatcher. "Please leave a message for Chief Jensen to meet me at Lorraine's tomorrow morning."

I hung up and went back to the file. After another half hour, and a few more tussles with tooth and claw, I went to bed with a purring puff ball. But this time, the presence of the kitten did not relax me. All night, I tossed and turned, dreaming over and over again that I was shooting a man who wouldn't die.

THIRTEEN

The next day I had breakfast at Lorraine's. I was eating the Superior Skillet, which lives up entirely to its name. It comes in a skillet, so that part is right. It contains hash browns, country sausage, mushrooms, onions, peppers and eggs done however you want. The whole thing is topped with cheese, hollandaise sauce and a dash of cayenne pepper. It also accompanied by two pancakes. If you're going to die of a heart attack, I say, do it right.

I was on my second pot of coffee when Chief Jensen came in.

"A little late this morning," I commented as he sat down in the booth opposite me.

"Had a B & E to deal with first," he said.

"Breaking and Entering? In Grand Lake? What is the world coming to?"

He grimaced. "Turned out to be Jimmy Lenske, breaking into his mom's store. She locked her keys in last night, and he was trying to help her."

"Don't worry about it," I said. "You've still got the bank robbery."

"Just 'robbery,'" he corrected me, accepting a cup of coffee from Lorraine herself. I was pretty sure she gave it to him for free. On the other hand, with the amount that I drank, she probably lost money on my coffee too. "They didn't rob the bank, remember – just the customers."

"How's that going?" I asked. I had more than a passing interest.

"I know you're uptight about Ethel's money," said Jensen. "We're doing our best."

"Which is?"

"We got nothing."

I sipped some coffee. A comfort in every trouble. "I may have something," I said.

"Jonah," said Jensen, "this is police work, detective work. I know you are the police chaplain, but that doesn't make you a detective."

"My dad was a detective," I said mildly.

"That doesn't make you a detective either."

"But my dad – the *detective?* – did some *detective* work on our bank robbers."

"Just 'robbers,'" he said absently. "I thought your dad was dead."

"He is. But I think he came across the same gang about two years ago, shortly before he died."

Jensen sipped his coffee. Just to be sociable, I sipped mine. "How do you know it's the same gang?" he said at last.

"Gang of robbers in northern Washington," I said. "Police figured there was maybe five or seven altogether. They went into bank lobbies, usually four at a time. Dressed in black with ski-masks. They made the customers lie down, and then robbed them, leaving the bank itself alone. Usually came in on paydays or big deposit days for cash businesses."

"Ours could be copycatters," he said.

"They hit only small towns, remote counties, so the police manpower would be limited. And because they left the banks themselves alone, no FBI."

"Still no reason they aren't copycats."

"One of them was smaller than the other three. After a few jobs, the small guy got trigger happy, started shooting at security guards. No one else, just the guards. Couple people got killed."

Jensen's blue eyes became very still. "Anything else?"

"Not much," I said. "They were operating in the far north, like here. Could have run for Canada when they were done."

"What happened to them?"

"The state police got involved. Started staking out likely targets at likely times. They got lucky, and the gang did a bank while they were there." I sipped some more coffee. God's gift to Lutheran pastors, and to anyone else who saw the light.

"Jonah," said Jensen, "you don't have to make a big production out of it. Tell me what happened."

"There was a firefight. One of the robbers was killed. They figure after that, the gang kind of broke up, like the James gang did after the failed raid down in Northfield, way back when."

"You're rotten at this," said Jensen. "I can see there's more. Come on, I thought you wanted my help."

"The guy who shot the perp was my dad."

Dan was silent for a bit. "That is truly weird," he said at last. "They get anything on the dead guy?"

"Oh yeah," I said. "He was from Duluth."

FOURTEEN

On Friday night I went to the WW. 'WW' stood for Wally's Walleye Bar & Grill. It was an old establishment in downtown Grand Lake. They served walleye fingers, which were good, and hamburgers, which were also good. They also served alcohol, which was good, in my opinion, if taken in moderation, but it was rarely consumed in moderation at the WW.

I slid into my regular high-backed booth, and Ally, a petite, blond waitress in her thirties, came over.

"Hi, Jonah," she said, smiling devastatingly. "Want anything tonight?"

"I'm working," I said. "Coke on the rocks, and a cup of seafood chowder."

"You got it," she said, turning away and drawing the eyes of about a third of the male occupants of the room.

Before she could get back with my drink, Bud Richards slid into the booth across from me. Bud was big and burly with a pot belly, but still a manly, strong-looking man.

We talked about the Vikings for a few minutes, and he gave me some pointers on catching fall crappie. There was a lull in the conversation.

"Jonah," said Bud at last, "you ever wonder if it's all just a crap shoot?"

Across the room, I saw Ally raise a glass of coke and look at me, and then Bud. I shook my head slightly.

"What do you mean?" I asked Bud.

He waved his hands. "You know, life. Everything. I mean, maybe it's all just random, and there's no point to anything we do."

"Why do you care?" I asked.

He stared at me. "I didn't expect you to say *that*. I mean, *shouldn't* I care?"

"I'm not saying if you should care or not. But you seem to. So, why?"

He looked into his beer for a moment. "I dunno."

"Look at it this way, Bud. If it's all just a meaningless, random crap shoot, then there's no reason why you – a product of that randomness – should care that there's no meaning."

"I've had a few beers already," said Bud, nodding at me confidentially. "I'm not sure I follow you."

"The very fact that you wonder about it all, strongly suggests that there is meaning to life, and that you were made to find it."

"Oh."

"You ever see a lion in a small cage?" I asked.

"Sure," he said. "Como Zoo, in St. Paul, when I was a kid."

"What was it doing?" I asked.

He thought. "Pacing around like it was restless."

"Exactly," I said. "It was probably born in a zoo. That cage was the only life it ever knew. So why did it pace around like that?"

"Because it wanted to get out?"

"Sure, but why?"

"Oh, I get it. 'Cause lions weren't made to be caged up?"

"Right. That lion was restless because it was made to live free in the wild. And even if it never experienced that life, at some level, it was still seeking that. It was made for more. In a cage or not, it still has a lion's heart, a lion's desires."

"So you're saying, I wonder about life, because I was made for more?"

"Exactly. The very fact that the possibility of meaninglessness bothers you suggests that you were made for a meaningful life."

We chatted some more, and after a while, Bud left my booth. Ally came with my coke and seafood chowder.

"You looked like you were in the middle of one of your sessions there," she said.

"Yeah. People need to talk sometimes."

"I know I do," she said. "Got a minute?"

"No one here but you right now," I said.

"I'll take a quick break," she said, and slid into the booth. While I ate, she told me about her latest boyfriend. She was a single mom, probably too attractive for her own good, and she had experienced a string of bad relationships.

Mostly, I just listened and offered support. After about ten minutes she thanked me, and gave me a kiss on the cheek, and went back to work.

Over the next two hours, the bar got noisier and more full, and several other people stopped by to talk and share their problems. I liked to think of it as my public confession booth.

At about eleven, I was getting tired, and ready to head home. I looked over at the bar and saw Jasmine and Tony Stone. He was sitting on a stool with his elbows on the bar, his legs spread wide. Jasmine stood next to him. They both looked relaxed and comfortable. I wondered again what the problem was with their marriage.

He glanced up and saw me looking at them. He bent down and murmured in her ear, no doubt to make himself heard over the loud music that was playing.

I stood up and reached for my coat, but someone grabbed my arm first. It was Jasmine.

"Well hello, Pastor Jonah," she said. She was wearing tight black leather pants and a close-fitting red tank top. She exuded a kind of animal attraction.

"I didn't expect to see you here," she said.

"I'm sort of the bar chaplain," I said. "How're you guys doing?"

"Rotten," she said. "He brings me here, and then sits all night eyeing the other girls."

The bar sound system began playing "Smooth" by Santana. Jasmine grabbed my hand. "Let's dance," she said.

"I don't think so," I began, but her grip was surprisingly strong, and she seemed to know about physical leverage and how to use it. Before I could figure out how to gracefully break free, she had pulled me over to the tiny dance floor at the back of the room. True, I could have broken her hold, but it would have taken enough effort to make a scene. She slid her arms around me and pressed her body tightly against mine, moving with the rhythm of the song. I hadn't experienced anything like this since tenth grade, when Natalie Hensen gave me a dance that fired my adolescent dreams for years afterward.

I tried to push her away, but she tightened her arms. "You're strong," she said in a little-girl voice. "Please don't hurt me."

"This isn't appropriate," I said. For some reason I was having difficulty with my breathing.

"I know, isn't it fun?" She rolled her hips against me, and leaned in, and I could feel all the ways in which men and women are different. At one level, of course I liked it. But at a more fundamental level, it reminded me of my dead wife Robyn, and I felt violated to be so close to the body of another woman whom I barely knew. A second later, I also remembered that she was married, too. I chided myself for not thinking of that first.

Abruptly, she flipped herself around, and backed into me, raising her arms and dancing, pulling my hands down along her sides and hips. I felt incredibly awkward and foolish. I could feel my face burning.

"Jasmine," I said, stepping back, "This is all wrong, at so many levels." I could tell that many people in the room were watching us. I'm sure Tony Stone was.

She stepped up and slid her arms over my shoulders again. "Would you fight Tony for me?" she whispered, her lips tickling my ears. She slid her hands down to my butt. I reached back and grabbed them, and mercifully, the song ended.

"I could ditch Tony," she said. "We could go someplace."

"We're done here," I said. "I don't want to see you, except with your husband, in my office."

Her eyes were unreadable. "You really don't want to?"

"Want to or not, I won't," I said. "You may have just ruined any small hope I had of helping your marriage. No way Tony will talk about anything with me after this."

Now she looked speculative. She waved her hand. "Oh, I can get Tony to come back, don't worry." She gave me another long, thoughtful look, and then walked toward the bar and her husband, glancing back at me once.

My face was red, and I felt like everyone in the room was staring at me. I felt dirty, and had an almost overwhelming desire to go home and take a shower. As I gathered my things to leave, I thought at least one thing was clear: whatever the exact issues were, there was no doubt that the Stones had a deeply troubled marriage.

FIFTEEN

On Saturday morning, Ethel Ostrand called me up.

"What if I don't have enough money to pay for my funeral?" she asked me.

There are, of course, a number of possible answers to a question like this. Most of them, I consider to be funny, which means they are probably in poor taste. Finally, I settled for a truism.

"Ethel," I said, "I promise you, you don't need to worry about paying for your funeral."

I took a sip of coffee. More than one person had observed that I drink a lot of it, and that it may possibly have side effects someday, so I was experimenting with instant coffee, on the theory that I wouldn't like it, and would quit drinking so much. So far, it wasn't working. It just reminded me of camping, and waking up to pleasantly chill mornings in the outdoors and how drinking instant coffee is a really excellent way to begin a new day. Or, in the present case, to continue it. The cat didn't seem to like it, though. As a rule, I was sharing all my food and drink with him, but coffee hadn't caught on. All the more for me.

"Do you need anything right now, Ethel?" I asked.

"I need groceries."

"All right, do you have a list?"

She read a me a grocery list over the phone. There wasn't much to it, but since she lived alone and was not particularly active, I assumed she probably didn't eat that much. Maybe, I thought, I should teach her the finer points of cooking well for the single person. After all, since I'd been single for five years, and she for almost twenty, there was a lot she probably still had to learn.

Her groceries added up to one large paper-bag full. When I got to her house, I put them in her kitchen for her. I noted approvingly that she still had plenty of other food on hand.

"Anything else, Ethel?" I called from her kitchen. She was busy with something in her bedroom.

"No thank you, Pastor," she said.

I noticed a few bills on her kitchen counter – gas and electric. Searching around, I found some scrap paper and a pencil. Quickly I wrote down the information and stuck the paper in my pocket. I came out of the kitchen and found her in the living room. She reached out a plump, vein-ridden hand to me, holding two twenty dollar notes.

"No," I said. "This one's on me. I owe you that, and more."

"You don't really owe me pastor. I was mad at you, and it *was* mostly your fault I lost that money, but you aren't the one who robbed me."

"Ethel," I said. "Do you have any doctor bills or anything like that?"

"I don't really think it's any of your business, pastor," she said.

"It isn't. But I want to help pay your expenses until we recover your money."

She looked at me, and her glasses reflected the light so I couldn't see her eyes. She sighed.

"I'm fine, Pastor, really."

After I left her place, I ran by the utility companies and paid her bills, asking them to contact me next month about what she owed then also. I fretted a little that there must be other bills I hadn't seen, but I couldn't do much more without her cooperation. Afterwards, I went home to study and drink more coffee. The cat studied with me, purring and plopping down on every book I opened.

"You're a great help," I told him.

We had a brief dispute about the suitability of lying on my computer keyboard, but eventually I made my point clear, and he settled for the books only. At one point, he tried the coffee again, sniffing at the mug I had put out for him, but he rejected it. Cats are smart, but not that smart, I guess.

Halfway through the third cup, my cell phone rang.

"Did you remember you have an appointment this morning?" asked Julie, my secretary, without so much as a good morning.

"Fine, thank you," I said. "And you?"

"Don't try to make me feel guilty. You forgot, didn't you?"

"Have you ever heard of enabling?" I asked her.

"I'm not sure." She sounded suspicious.

"Sometimes, when someone is addicted to alcohol or drugs, the people around him kind of help him to stay addicted. It's not intentional, they just do things to compensate for his problems, and keep him from suffering the consequences. This allows the pattern to continue."

"You never answered my question," said Julie.

"I think you are enabling me," I said. "But I do appreciate it. Deeply. Now, see if you can figure out the answer to your question."

"Things at Harbor Lutheran would fall apart without me," she said defensively.

"Now you get it," I said. "I exist primarily so that you feel needed. It too, is part of the whole enabling system."

"You are a very frustrating man, Pastor Borden."

"I aim to please. By the way, Julie..."

"Yes?"

"Thank you."

She snorted and hung up.

Now that I had been reminded, I remembered perfectly well that Angela the feminist was coming back for another appointment, and what's more, she was bringing her husband. I still had time to make it to the church by foot.

~

When my wife Robyn had died, we were young, and life insurance was cheap. The result was that when I moved to Grand Lake, I paid cash for my land and cabin up on the ridge, about two miles or so from the lake. The Superior Hiking Trail passed nearby on its two-hundred-and-seventy-mile trek from Duluth to Canada. I had cut my own trail through my property to reach it, and by this path I made my way north, and then took another cutoff trail east down the ridge into town, coming out near Harbor Lutheran Church. I took five minutes at the lookout above the town, blinded by the blaze of fall colors against the impossibly bright blue of Lake Superior in the September sunlight. All art is merely a poor imitation of the work of the One Creator. I could be wrong, of course, but I'm not.

I made it to the church with five minutes to spare. After I opened up the doors and turned the lights on in my office, I thought I'd better make a pot of coffee for Angela and her husband. My keen memory recorded that Angela was a partaker of the third Lutheran sacrament.

When the coffee was done, it was only natural that I should taste it, to make sure it was acceptable. It was. Angela walked in halfway through the first cup. She had ditched her hippie outfit for expensive jeans and a long-sleeved orange shirt with frills at the sleeves and down the front. As before, her expression was troubled and serious. Beside her, was a man in his late thirties, clean shaven with messy brown hair and dark brown eyes of the type that I always thought women would find sensitive and appealing. He also wore jeans, and brown boots, with a light colored blue denim shirt that might have been either pretty cheap, or very expensive, depending on whether he'd bought it at Wal-Mart or a boutique.

I got up and greeted Angela.

"Pastor Borden," she said. "This is my husband, Philip."

"Phil Kruger," he said, sticking out his hand. It was hard without noticeable calluses, but his grip was limp, like a man who doesn't really know who he is. His brown eyes met mine, briefly, and then slid away. There seemed to be too much tongue in his mouth. He kind of left his lips parted, and I could see it in there. It was vaguely sensual, in a way that was gross to me; maybe Angela found it attractive. Or maybe that's why she'd had her affair.

We exchanged the normal pleasantries, and then got seated in my office. I was happy to see them sit together on the love seat. Angela seemed to sit very close to her husband, which was another encouraging sign.

"Philip has agreed to come and see you," she said, unnecessarily. "I haven't spoken with him about – what you and I talked about last time," she said.

"Is that what you want to talk about now?" I asked.

"What do you think?"

"Let's just start at the beginning, and see where things take us," I said.

Angela seemed much less rigid in her opinions than she had been when she met with me on her own. I invited her to share her reasons with Phil for wanting marriage counseling. Phil and his sensual mouth sat there looking insecure, and when I thought about the secret his wife was keeping from him, I felt a little sorry for him.

"Really, I don't have any complaints," he said, patting Angela's hand, which he was holding. "But I want her to be happy too, and I'm willing to do what it takes for that to happen."

"I just sometimes feel like you don't recognize who I am as a person," said Angela. "I am a woman. I am powerful. I'm not just an accessory to your life."

Kruger looked at her with an expression of quizzical concern. "I know that, Angela," he said, respectfully, and patted her hand again. She slapped his hand away. "Don't patronize me," she snapped.

Kruger looked at her strangely, but he kept his cool, and the moment passed. All in all, when the session was winding up an hour later, I thought the prospects for their marriage were good. There was still the matter of Angela's affair to negotiate, but I felt like with a solid beginning, they might be able to handle that.

"Listen," I said, looking at my watch, "time's about up for today. It isn't productive to do this for much more than an hour at a time. Except in certain circumstances."

They looked at me. "What do you mean?" said Angela finally.

"Well, I am putting together a little sailing cruise in a few weeks. I'll have two couples along, and we'll spend three days or so, out on the water together. We'll use the time together to work on some marriage issues. I wondered if you guys would like to be one of the couples."

They looked at each other. A little smile played near Angela's lips. It was good to see. She was normally so serious.

"Actually, that would be wonderful," she said. Phil nodded. "My previous therapist offered something like that, but Phil didn't connect very well with him."

I'll bet he didn't, I thought. Phil nodded again. "It seemed like a great concept, but the timing and circumstances just weren't right."

I wondered if Phil suspected the affair. I gave them the cost and the other details. "Well, you two think about it, and give me call. Let me know by next Wednesday, if you can," I said.

They thanked me and then left, hand in hand. Angela looked over her shoulder at me, gave a small smile and waved. It seemed to take ten years off of her, and transformed her from a somber, even gloomy individual into a vivacious woman in the prime of life. It made me feel good about my work, which just goes to show you how stupid I can be sometimes.

SIXTEEN

I preached an outstanding sermon on Sunday. Less than five people fell asleep, and a few others went to the extraordinary lengths of making eye contact and nodding at me as I spoke. After church, the Olsens invited Leyla and me to Sunday lunch at their house.

Leyla and I seemed to be back on an even keel of friendship. I always enjoyed spending time with her, and she seemed able to enjoy it once again as well. There was a still a spark that slumbered between us, but for now, both of us were able to ignore it. So, we accepted the invitation for lunch.

John and Kim Olsen were about my age, which is to say middle thirties, with, apparently, two hundred children. Actually, it was only four kids, but what they lacked in size, they made up for in noise and energy. I bought fresh eggs and fresh milk from their farm every week.

In the middle of the living room of their white, clapboard farmhouse, there was a little exercise trampoline, three feet in diameter. A small girl of about three bounced on it, unceasingly chanting,

"Daddy...Daddy...Daddy..."

"Lindy, Lindy, Lindy" said John, smiling at the little girl, whose name was Belinda. His response had no effect, and she continued bouncing and chanting the entire time that John and I talked about the weather, the Vikings and the Almighty, while we waited for Kim and Leyla to finish dinner preparations.

When everything was ready, three other miniature humans came rolling in like a freight train, yelling at the top of their lungs that the British were coming. John scooped Belinda off the trampoline to accompanying shrieks of joy.

"The British are coming?" I asked mildly.

"We are studying the American Revolution," said Kim. She home-schooled Mandy and James, their two oldest. The third child, four-year-old John Jr., apparently had apprehended the ride of Paul Revere by osmosis. This was not uncommon with home-schooling, according to Kim.

"Would you pray for us, Jonah?" asked John. For some reason, wherever I go for dinner, people always feel the need to ask me to say grace, as if it is better done by a professional or something. Or maybe my reputation as a cook had them scared, and they felt the need for divine support.

In the case of Kim Olsen, God had already blessed the hands of the cook. It was like a kind of minor Thanksgiving, with roast chicken and stuffing, roasted red potatoes and carrots, home-canned green beans and fresh corn on the cob. All delicious. In situations like that, it is a liability to be a pastor, because people naturally don't expect you to eat like a pig. Never one for social niceties, I ate like a pig anyway.

"Hungry, are we?" asked Leyla.

"Just want Kim to feel appreciated," I said.

After lunch, John and Kim settled the little ones in front of a movie, and the four of us had a pleasant conversation over coffee and apple pie.

As we were leaving, I remembered the cat. I said, "Say, do you mind if I take some leftovers home?"

"I'm honored," said Kim. "You're such a chef yourself. That means a lot to me."

Proving that even old pastors can learn new tricks, I kept my mouth shut about the cat. "It was delicious," I said truthfully.

Afterwards, I drove Leyla home. "What is this music?" she asked.

"I'm kind of on a Steve Miller kick," I said.

"Huh."

"The Steve Miller Band was big in the '70s," I said.

"But you were small in the '70s" she pointed out.

"Yes, I was. But the Internet evens everything out. Most of what I listen to, I discovered on the Internet."

"*Jungle Love* really sort of ruins your pastoral image."

"I listen to Tchaikovsky too. And Bach, Beethoven, all those guys."

"Steve Miller, Beethoven and the guys."

"You were afraid to say Tchaikovsky, weren't you?"

She hit me.

"Hey, I'm driving."

"That's right, buddy. You haven't got time to be mocking me."

Take the Money and Run started playing.

"Oh, I love *Sweet Home Alabama*," said Leyla.

I let it play a bit longer.

"This isn't Sweet Home Alabama, is it?" she asked, after Steve and the boys started telling the story of Billy Joe and Bobbie Sue, and how they robbed and shot a man, and then took the money and run.

I shook my head, smiling.

"You could have said something," said Leyla, pretending to be hurt, "instead of letting me feel stupid."

"I was instructed to shut up and drive," I said. "And specifically not to mock my very entertaining passenger."

She hit me again. We were silent for a minute.

"This is an awful song, isn't it?"

"Well, the lyrics glorify senseless violence perpetrated by shiftless drug addicts and resulting in immoral, illegal, selfish gain. But musically, the song doesn't get boring for almost thirty seconds."

"Why did you download this?"

"I remembered that it was some sort of classic hit, and I listened to less than thirty seconds before I made the decision."

Leyla smiled broadly. "It's good to see that you don't always know exactly what you are doing."

I looked over at her sharply. "What's that supposed to mean?"

"I don't know, Jonah, it's just that you're so – confident. It's part of what makes you attractive, but it can also be irritating sometimes. You're a terrific cook, a trophy fisherman, perceptive, smart, a great preacher." She paused. "An outstanding kisser." She looked at her hands for a second. I didn't stare at her, because I had to drive the car.

"Anyway," she said, waving her hands in the air now, "sometimes people just want to see that you aren't good at *everything*. Or that you aren't always right about everything."

It was my turn to smile broadly. "You wish I was a bad kisser?"

She tossed her hair. "You know what I mean. Some people can be just too perfect."

"Sure," I said. I had no idea what she meant.

She looked at me a moment. "You really don't see it, do you?"

I shrugged. "Maybe I just don't even try to do stuff I won't be good at. But I think it's more likely that you are just overcompensating for letting me down in my moment of need. But you don't need to, you know."

I paused. "I leave the toilet seat up."

"Too much information."

"There's another one – I give too much information."

She sighed dramatically, and looked out the window.

"I hate Jane Austen flicks."

She turned back to me. "Okay, now *that* is a serious imperfection."

"Happy to oblige," I said.

SEVENTEEN

Monday was my day off, and since the Wisconsin trout season went until the end of September, I went south on sixty-one early in the morning. To my left as I drove, the dark sky slowly faded into a soft pearl, which soon became stained with streaks of pink and red and then gold. At last, the sun shouldered its way above the blue horizon, blasting the ridges to my right with light and warmth, and tearing open the dark sky above me. Sunrise over Superior. I didn't get up for it every day anymore, like I used to when had first moved here, but it still touched me in a special way. It takes a cold-blooded person indeed to watch a Superior sunrise on the North Shore on a fine day, and not have any desire at all to give thanks to a Creator.

Bach accompanied the sunrise and stayed with me down most of the length of highway sixty-one into Duluth. I have found that coffee and donuts do not noticeably decrease the quality of that great composer.

I caught a piece of Duluth early rush-hour, but it wasn't too long before I had slipped over the high bridge to Superior, and was on my way east toward the Tamarack. With twenty minutes to go, I called Chief Jensen.

"Hey, Dan, it's Jonah," I said, when we were connected.

"Hi, Jonah," he said. "What can I do for you?"

"Don't suppose you had a chance to check up on any of the stuff we talked about last week, have you?"

"Did you know," he asked, "that some people regard 'what can I do for you' as nothing more than a polite greeting?"

"You never were that polite," I said.

"We are not your private detective agency. We are the public servants of the citizens of Grand Lake."

"Exactly. You are my servant. So, what'd you get?"

"You don't even live in Grand Lake, Jonah. You're technically part of the county, not the city."

"So you got nothing?"

"Zip," he said. "Actually, it was kind of weird. I got less than you got."

"What do you mean?"

"I mean, if I didn't know you better, I'd think you'd made it all up. I couldn't find any law-enforcement records to corroborate what you told me from your dad's notes."

"Seriously?"

"Seriously. It was like none of what you told me ever happened."

I started to protest, but he broke in. "I figured I owed you a little slack, since you were right about that thing last year. So I did a quick Google search. I found a few old websites and links to newspaper reports. There wasn't a lot, but it does look like there was a robbery and firefight in a town called Lynden. Details were pretty sketchy, and there's no way you could get the same information out of it that your dad's notes had, but it's something."

"What's up with that? You know I'm not making it up."

"Could your dad have been making it up?"

"Dan, would you make up a case file like that for the fun of it, especially if it involved an actual man you killed?"

"You know, that's the funny thing. The newspaper report I saw gave the name of the guy who was shot, the one you said was from Duluth. Charles Holland. I tried our system and got nothing on him – no priors or anything. At least not on any Charles Holland who is now dead. I started to feel funny about it, and called down to Duluth public records. There's a few Charles Hollands born in Duluth, of course, and a few living there now. I don't have time to turn over all the stones, but so far, there doesn't seem to be any connection between the Charles Holland that your dad said was from Duluth and any actual guy by that name from there."

"But you saw the newspaper report. So he must have existed."

"Doesn't mean he was from Duluth. The website didn't say anything about that."

"Even if he wasn't," I said, "his history, his contacts – that would be the natural place to start in investigating this group, wouldn't it?"

"That would be the place to start investigating the *Lynden* robbery. But so far Jonah, you are the only one who thinks there's a connection between the robbery at Lynden and the one in Grand Lake."

"It wasn't just Lynden. There were several robberies in northern Washington, and they were all just like the one in Grand Lake."

"That's exactly what I was not able to find out."

"C'mon, Dan, I know I can be a pain sometimes, but the bank was robbed in Grand Lake, on your watch. You aren't wasting your time by pursuing this."

"Never said I was. But I've got to go where the facts take me. You have your intuitive thing that you do, and you're good at it. But intuition doesn't do so well in a courtroom. Good police work is mostly just footslogging through the facts and letting them speak for themselves. And right now, they ain't saying anything about a connection between the First National robbery and your dad's old case."

I hated to admit it, but Dan was actually making pretty good sense. It's just that I am so seldom wrong. Maybe Leyla was right, and I needed to be taken down a notch or two.

I thanked him and hung up, just as I pulled into the parking area above the gorge of the Tamarack.

Trout fishing is the universal specific, guaranteed to ease whatever stresses or worries you. I wasn't extremely worried, but I was anxious to get Ethel Ostrand's money back, and I figured it wouldn't hurt me to get a little pro-active stress relief.

A while back, I had been bribed and threatened in this very parking lot, by people who had followed me there in an old green Honda. Today, a black blazer drove by shortly after I got there, but no one stopped.

I pulled on my old wool army-surplus sweater, and then slipped into my neoprene waders. My fishing vest went over the top, and then I grabbed my rod and took the trail down into the gorge.

Stepping into a clear, remote trout stream on a bright morning with the whole day in front of you is about as good as it gets this side of heaven. There are just a few other things as good or better, but in the moral code which I subscribe to, those involve marriage. Since I wasn't married, I went trout fishing as often as I could.

It was one of those days that reminds you that God is real and he is good, although maybe the fish felt differently about that than I did. They were voracious. I wasn't, so I let each one go with a warning, and sometimes a digital photo or two.

In September, night comes fairly early in the far North, so I quit by four, leaving myself a little daylight to spare. When I got back to the car, I stripped off my stuff. The parking area was empty and no cars were going by, but I always worried about strangers driving by and seeing me in my long Johns while I changed back into street clothes. I know it's silly, but there it is.

With my wardrobe properly assembled, I dialed my cell phone.

"Lund Investigations," said the answering voice.

"Hi, Tom," I said. "You may not remember me, but you helped me out on a case up in Grand Lake last year. I'm headed through Duluth in about forty-five minutes, and I wondered if I could meet you for a little bit."

"Grand Lake? You the pastor guy I followed around with that oily Chicago thug? The guy they arrested for murder and then who blew the whole case wide open?"

"That's me," I said, trying to sound modest.

"Yeah, OK," said Tom Lund. "Let's do it in my office. See you there in forty-five minutes."

Tom Lund was a tall, lean, broad-shouldered man with a thick blond mustache and short cropped blond hair. He wore a Duluth Royals ball-cap, which covered up the fact that he was going bald on top. He looked kind of like a blond version of Tom Selleck in his Magnum PI days.

Lund's office was in the Canal Park district of Duluth, two blocks south of the main strip, in an old brick building that was being renovated. His decorating style was something I would call "masculine minimalist." Each of the two rooms in his suite had four white walls and an old steel desk. The reception area held a security camera in one corner of the ceiling and a locked steel file cabinet. The old wood floors were clean, but bare. His inner office, in addition to the desk, had a window, two chairs and some files piled in one corner.

"I see you've been upgrading," I said, pointing to files in the corner.

"I knew you were coming, so I cleared off the chair," said Lund.

I sat in the indicated chair.

"I need you to look in to something for me," I said.

"Any money in it for me this time?" he asked.

"It's a bank robbery," I said. "There's a reward."

He shook his head. "I like you. I appreciate your style, and you are a refreshing antidote to the traditional pastor stereotype. But I don't work for free, or on speculation."

"Refreshing antidote to the traditional pastor stereotype?" I asked admiringly.

"I've been taking night classes. Might become a lawyer."

"An old lady lost her life savings."

He shrugged. "I'm becoming a lawyer. That means I'm in the process of losing my ability to care."

"How much?"

He told me, and I winced.

"How 'bout this," he said. "You pay me, and if I get any reward, I pay you back up to half of what you've paid me."

"Why only half?" I said.

He looked at me for a long time.

"You did threaten to have me knee-capped once," I said. "Surely you owe me something for that."

"I would not have knee-capped anyone, and you know it," he said. "Besides, I paid that debt already."

There was a moment of silence between us. I have no shame, so eventually Lund spoke.

"OK, I'll take my fee, and if I get any reward money, I'll donate it up to the amount of my fee to the charity of your choice. If the reward is more than my fee plus the donation, I keep the rest."

"Done," I said.

EIGHTEEN

The Stones had another appointment. I wasn't keen to see them, but Jasmine seemed very restrained this time. Her thick, dark hair was tight in a kind of grown-up pony tail. Tony was mostly the same, solid as a pile of bricks, but he looked a little more concerned than he had before.

After we had exchanged greetings, Jasmine spoke, before I could say anything else.

"I'm really sorry about the other night."

"Are you talking to me, or to Tony?" I asked.

She glanced quickly at her husband. "Both," she said. "I get so frustrated sometimes, and I guess I was just blowing off steam, or trying to get a reaction or something."

"Did you?" I asked.

"You tell me," she said with a little bit of a leer. Stone elbowed her. "Sorry," she added immediately.

"Look," I said, "I'll be honest. I can see you two have issues, but I still don't quite get your relationship. Then, with the other night, I'm not sure I can provide you with the best help right now. I have the number of two really good marriage and family therapists in Duluth."

Tony stirred. I realized he looked like a pile of bricks because he was a very solidly built, muscular man.

"Look, Pastor, we are very sorry. We have both agreed that we really want to work on this. Duluth is a long drive, and we both already know you and trust you. What happened last weekend won't happen again."

I sipped some coffee. I hated to turn people away who really wanted help. "Did you hear me when I told you that I really don't understand your relationship, or even the nature of your problems?"

Jasmine laughed. It sounded genuine. She laid a hand on Tony's arm and said, "Pastor, even *we* don't understand those things." She squeezed his arm. He looked at her and nodded.

"Listen, we heard that you are doing a counseling cruise on a sailboat in a few weeks. We wondered, if it wasn't full, if we could get in on that. I think that might help us all to clarify things."

I wasn't sure I wanted to be stuck on a boat with them and no way to escape. On the other hand, they sure seemed to be candidates for something to shake them up. I thought that some interaction with Angela and Phil might even be good for them.

I know now how wrong I was. But right then, what I said was, "All right."

NINETEEN

If Ely, Minnesota, isn't at the end of the road, at least you can see it from there. It is one of the prime jumping-off points for trips into the Boundary Waters Canoe Area and the wilderness that fills both sides of the Canadian border for hundreds of miles around.

I had once been in the Ely public men's sauna with Robyn's father, before we were married. There was a no-clothing rule, and it was an embarrassment that still haunted me at times.

This time, however, I wasn't in Ely for either the sauna or the wilderness. The main street down the hill in town was quiet and empty, ghostly as only a tourist town can be in the far north in late September.

I turned off to the left and found a white house on a neatly-kept street lined with large maple trees. Lawns were all mowed, probably for the last time of the season except for a final mulch once the leaves had all come down.

It was cool, with a high overcast and plenty of wind, as I knocked at the door of the house. After a few minutes, a well-dressed, attractive woman in her late fifties answered the door. She was about five foot three, with dark hair gracefully streaking into silver. She wore a dark pantsuit and sported dangling silver earrings.

"Jonah," she said, reaching up to hug me. She planted a kiss on my cheek. "So good to see you."

"You too, Ma," I said, returning the hug.

After a moment she stepped back and held me at arm's length. "When are you going to stop calling me that? It's been five years."

"Does it bother you?" I asked.

"Of course not," she said, waving me into the house. "But I worry about *you*."

We went into the kitchen, which boasted a comfortable array of wooden cabinets, well done brick on the walls, and an island with stools situated around it. She poured me a cup of black coffee without asking.

"I'm doing OK," I said. "Actually, I'm here to talk to you about that." I sipped some coffee while Robyn's mother sat patiently.

"You know," I said, "I have a lot of memories in this house."

"You've been coming here since your senior year in college," she commented.

"I proposed to Robyn right here in this kitchen," I said. She smiled at me warmly and said nothing.

"It's a funny thing, Susan," I said, using her first name for the first time in many years. "You know, you plan for forever. You think things will never change, or at least, not things like that."

She sipped her own coffee and nodded sadly. "I never expected to outlive both my husband and my daughter."

I looked out the window. Susan had an array of bird feeders in her back yard. There were still plenty of birds around who appreciated the free lunch. "For a long time after, it still felt like Robyn was with me." I turned back to her. "You know? I mean, I would even talk to her sometimes, like she was there, watching me."

She nodded again. "I know exactly what you mean. I did the same thing, not so much with Robyn, but with Rob."

"But about a year and a half or so after she died, then it was like she was really gone. Her *presence* was gone. That's when I was so lonely I ached every day. It felt almost physical sometimes."

Susan's brown eyes brimmed with unshed tears. She put her hand on my arm, but said nothing.

"But after a while of that, it finally started to ease. I moved out here, you know, shortly after Rob died, and finally one day, I realized, that though I'll always love Robyn, I was done grieving. Moving out here kind of helped me move on, which is funny, because I did it so we could help each other in our grief."

"You *have* helped me Jonah. More than you know. You've been like a real son to me, the best son-in-law a mother could ever wish for."

We were silent for a while, comfortable in each other's company without speech, without other distraction.

"I've met someone," I said at last. I couldn't meet her eyes.

"Jonah," she said, touching me again, "look at me Jonah."

I turned toward her. "I am so pleased," she said. "You're still young. You should have someone to share your life with."

"I'm not sure we are to that point yet," I said. "But she's the first person I've been really interested in since Robyn died."

"Tell me about her."

"Well, she's pretty – I think so, anyway, and she was a weekend reporter at Channel Thirteen in Duluth until last year. She's got a great sense of humor. She's warm and caring, and we can be very comfortable together."

"How long have you been seeing her?"

"Well, it's complicated," I said.

Susan sighed, loudly.

"It really is," I said defensively. "We started seeing each other last year, during that Daniel Spooner-Doug Norstad mess. Things were going great. But when they arrested me for Spooner's murder, she believed I had done it. She even did a story on me that suggested I had."

"Wow," said Susan.

"Yeah. Anyway, she felt terrible about it afterward, and there were some things from her past that maybe explain why she was willing to believe the worst about me."

"So you've forgiven her?"

"How could I not? I have been forgiven for so much more."

She nodded her approval. "So what's the problem?" Susan was always a very perceptive woman.

"Well, there are two. The first is that even though I have forgiven her, I still struggle a little to trust her. I don't know if she'll really be there for me if the chips go down again."

"You expecting to be accused of murder again soon?"

"You know what I mean. In marriage, you have to have each other's backs. You have to be the one person in the world that your spouse can count on, no matter what. There are all kinds of places where that kind of trust comes into play."

"True," she said.

"Anyway, I guess it'll take some time to figure out if I can trust her again."

"You said there were two things."

"Like I said, I have laid Robyn to rest – physically and figuratively. I am at peace about it. But thinking this way about Leyla still feels a little funny, almost a bit like a betrayal."

"Are you talking about Robyn, or about me?" asked Susan, looking at me closely.

"How do you do that?" I asked.

"The same way you do," she said. "We both have the gift."

"So, to spell it out, yes, I feel a little bit like I'm betraying you."

"Jonah," she said. "You began to be part of our family all the way back when you and Robyn were dating. You remained part of us after she died. It's been almost twelve years altogether. You aren't going to ruin our special bond, no matter what you do."

"It's just, I mean if Leyla and I – I'll have another mother-in-law too."

"So?" she said. "I promise you, I'll always be your Ma."

"What about holidays?"

"You've taken a few of those with your own mother, remember? I didn't wither away, did I? I have my brother and sister and their families too."

I got up and walked around the island and hugged her. "I love you, Ma," I said.

"I love you too, Jonah," she replied. "Now I want you to be free to let this relationship with Leyla go wherever it is supposed to go. And sometime, if it gets that point, bring her up here to meet me."

TWENTY

Driving home, the sun burst through the high clouds and lit the fall colors into bold golds and reds. There is a beauty to the Minnesota forest, but in the autumn it becomes edged with a maudlin poignancy for the approaching death that is winter in the far North. The trees on Highway One are mostly jack-pine, dark, and less than forty feet tall, interspersed here and there with birch and maple.

I flipped on my iPod and sank into the limpid lyrics of Charlotte Ryerson, which went perfectly with the wild, sad land around me. As a songwriter, Ryerson seemed to choose each word with care, placing it precisely, like a master jeweler setting gems in a tiara. The title track of her CD was *Moth Around the Moon*, and it described a lover whose love went unrequited, at least in full measure. Eventually, she got over her love, and, too late, the man whom she had loved realized what he had been taking for granted. *He* ended up as the unrequited lover.

Suddenly, I had an urgent desire to see Leyla, to spend time with her and work things out. I glanced down at my phone and saw that I had no service, which wasn't surprising in this remote stretch of Northland. Reflexively, I looked up into the rear view mirror. There was one black blazer, but he was patiently keeping his distance.

The blazer stayed with me all the way back to the North Shore, which irrationally irritated me, because I liked having Highway One through

Superior National Forest all to myself. Ah well, imperfection in this world only reminded me I was made for another.

A few miles short of my house, my phone rang. I glanced again in the mirror before making a grab for it, but the rear-view mirror was empty. I answered the phone.

"Pastor Borden? This is Red Hollis."

"Hi, Red," I said. "Everything coming along OK for the cruise?"

"Actually Pastor, that's why I called you. I just found out that my brother is very sick. Leukemia. I think I need to clear out my schedule for the next several weeks, and be there for him and his family."

"I'm so sorry," I said. "Is there anything I can do?"

"Well, you could say a word to the man upstairs for him, but other than that, I don't think so."

"I'll do it," I said.

"Here's the thing, Pastor," said Hollis. "I hated to let you down on the cruise. So I want to find you a replacement captain, and have you go without me, anyway."

I turned into my driveway. Hollis said he had sailed several counseling cruises, and I couldn't imagine Mike Schwartz, a good counselor, would have used him more than once if it hadn't worked out. In my mind, it wasn't just a matter of finding a sailor. A sailboat is a pretty small place. I needed someone who could fit into a counseling environment without intruding.

"Listen, Red," I said "I appreciate you going through the work, but I don't know. I mean he has to be a certain kind of guy."

"Oh, I'll get the right kind of guy," said Hollis, far too quickly and sincerely.

I slid the car into my garage and turned it off. "I'm not so sure. We could just cancel and try again next spring. It's not like I can't help these couples without a sailboat."

He cleared his throat over the phone, which hurt my ears. "Ah. I, uh...well the truth is, Pastor, I was kind of counting on the income."

I wasn't inclined to feel sorry for the financial plight of someone who owned a yacht. But the truth is, I didn't really know what kind of position he was in. While I sat thinking, he broke in again.

"Tell you what, I'll make it work somehow with my brother. I mean, he might be fine for a while."

"How about a compromise, Red?" I said. "Give me a chance to find a captain I'm comfortable with."

"You don't have much time. The cruise is in two weeks."

"I know. But I have someone in mind. If he can't do it, then maybe I can meet whoever you find, and make my own judgment. As far as I'm concerned, the sailing is a side issue. If the captain doesn't mesh, or doesn't know how to be there without intruding, the whole thing could become pointless."

"I know what you're saying, Pastor."

"Can I try my option first?"

Hollis blew out his breath, which again hurt my ear. "OK, give it a try. But get back to me right away."

"I will. I'm the one who would be letting people down if it doesn't happen, remember?"

"Yeah, OK," he said. "One more thing. "We'll be sailing out of Bayfield. I couldn't get a boat in Silver Bay."

"You mean a slip?"

"Yeah, sorry. I couldn't get a slip in Silver Bay."

"OK, I think that will be fine," I said.

"All right, Pastor. Thanks."

We hung up.

TWENTY-ONE

I hit the close button to my garage, and stepped into my back hallway. The hall ran past my utility room and office on one side, with my bedroom and a spare bathroom on the other. It opened into the great room, with large double-story windows looking across my deck, and down the ridge toward the lake.

I felt a sudden twist in my stomach. Someone was sitting in one of the chairs on the deck, watching the afternoon sun die on the water.

All violence and fear of the previous year came rushing back, along with the memory of the masked man trying to break in more recently. My heart began to pound.

Quietly, I slipped back into the garage. I fished a key from its place and unlocked my gun cabinet. I picked out my 12 gauge and fed three shells into the tubular magazine, but left the chamber empty.

Kicking off my shoes I crept back into the house. My fireplace divided the great-room windows in half, and I used it as cover between me and the person on the deck. From the hearth, I risked a quick glance outside. The stranger was sitting in an Adirondack chair looking at the lake. He wore a dark-blue nylon windbreaker and dark-blue ball-cap. It was hard to tell with him sitting down, but he looked kind of big.

I side-stepped to the sliding door, jerked it open and, leaping onto the deck, pressed the muzzle of the shotgun against the back of the intruder's neck. "Don't move," I said.

The man jerked involuntarily and then sat very still. His hands were tucked by his sides, in the pockets of his jacket.

"Very slowly, put your hands where I can see them. Slowly."

"Pastor Borden?" he said. Cautiously, he turned his neck until I could see that it was Tom Lund, the private investigator from Duluth.

I felt a little odd about being addressed as "pastor" by someone I had been holding at gunpoint. Suddenly, I also felt very shaky. I lifted the gun and pointed it into the air while I ejected the shells and put them in my pocket.

"Tom," I said, collapsing into a matching wooden chair. "What the heck are you doing here? And where is your car?"

Lund blew out a long breath. "That hasn't happened to me for a long time."

"Sorry," I said. "It's not a daily thing with me, either."

Lund rubbed his neck and rolled his shoulders. Abruptly, he stood up and stretched his back. "Feeling a little paranoid, are we?"

"You remember Risotti, the thug from Chicago? He sent some guys over here after me, during that Doug Norstad business. I've not taken kindly to strangers on my deck since then." I leaned the shotgun against the railing and then said, "Sorry about that though."

The private eye shook his head. "As much my fault as yours. Maybe I should have just called you."

"Why didn't you? I mean it's a beautiful drive from Duluth to here, but it's also kinda long."

"So's my story," said Lund. "You got a beer or something?"

"Ah," I said. "You heard I was gourmet cook, and you came up here to learn some tips for impressing the chicks."

"The only chick I want to impress doesn't need me to cook, but if you are offering supper, I'll take it."

"You married?" I asked.

"Yep," he said. "Best decision I ever made."

"What about her?"

"Her too," he said without pretension. This surprised me. Pleasantly.

"You sound happy."

"Perfect, no. Happy, yes."

I led the way back through the sliding doors. Going toward the fridge, I said, "I don't keep beer around. But I've got some hard apple cider."

"Hot apple cider?"

"Not hot, *hard*. Kind of like Mike's Hard Lemonade."

"You really ruin the pastor thing for me."

"Don't worry, I won't offer you weed or anything. Most people just have inaccurate stereotypes about pastors. You want the cider or not?"

"I guess I'll try it."

I got him a bottle of Woodchuck's Cider from the refrigerator, and one for myself. The cat came in. I had been trying to think of a good name for him, but so far one had eluded me. I poured a little of my cider into a saucer and he lapped it up.

"You sure that's good for him?" asked Lund, swallowing some of his own and nodding at the cat.

"Why not? John Adams attributed his long life to his daily pint of hard cider."

"Who's John Adams?" said Lund, burping.

"One of the Founding Fathers of the United States. He signed the Declaration of Independence. Went to France with Benjamin Franklin. He was our second president."

"Ben Franklin went to France?"

"Never mind," I said.

Tom Lund sat on a bar stool at the counter that separated the kitchen from the great-room. I went around to the other side to make supper.

I peeled an avocado, and put a few slices on a plate. I sprinkled them with lemon juice, salt and garlic powder and then put it on the counter between us, sliding him a fork.

"What's this?" He sounded suspicious.

"Just try it."

"Did Ben Franklin eat this too?"

"Yep," I said. "It's what gave him such a good memory."

He tried a piece. "Hey, that's all right."

I set a piece out for the cat, but he looked offended.

I started to slice up a large chicken breast I had thawed earlier. "So, you gonna tell me why you're here?"

"Yeah, hang on." He patted himself like he was looking for something in his pockets. "Do you have pen and paper? I want to write down your cell number, so I can just call you next time."

I frowned. I thought I had given him my number when I hired him to look into the identity of the dead Washington bank robber. "Why don't I just call your phone, and then you'll have it?"

"I'm kinda old fashioned," he said. "I like to have things written down."

I shrugged. "OK." I slipped the diced chicken into a cast-iron skillet with some olive oil and crushed garlic, and then grabbed some paper and a pen out of a drawer in the kitchen, and slid them over the counter to Lund.

"All right, what's your number?"

I told him, starting on an onion. When I had sliced large pieces of that and some red peppers, I added them to the chicken in the skillet. Lund was quiet while I sliced a zucchini and a yellow squash into chunks and added them to the pan. I sprinkled cumin, cayenne and chili powder on it and stirred it. Finally, I looked up at Lund and found he had slid the paper back across the counter, and was pointing to it.

I opened my mouth, and he said, "So what do you think of the Vikings' chances this year?"

"About the same as always," I said mechanically, reaching for the paper Lund had written my phone number on. "They'll start like Super Bowl champions. After a mid-season collapse, they'll barely scrape into the playoffs and lose in the first round."

On the paper, Lund had not written any phone number. Instead, it said, *someone may be listening to us.*

I stared at him. "What about you?" was all I said. I quickly scribbled *bugs?* I pushed the paper back to him. Everything about the scene seemed suddenly surreal.

"Oh, same as you. But it'll be fun to watch," he said. He glanced at the paper and nodded. He started to write something else, while also saying, "We don't have a real receiving corps. Now if we had old Chris Carter in his prime on this team, we might go somewhere." He pushed the notepaper back to me. It said, *let's eat and then take a walk.*

I nodded. While the chicken and vegetables cooked, I fried up a couple of corn tortillas. We ate the chicken fajitas topped with cilantro, sour cream, avocado and salsa. I put some on a plate for the cat too. He picked through the veggies and ate the chicken, sour cream and a little bit of the tortilla. Not much of a refined palate, I guess. Lund and I talked some more about the Vikings and then the upcoming hunting season.

When we were done, I said, "Want to stretch your legs? It's almost dark, but it's not far from here to a pretty nice lookout down the ridge."

"Sure," he said casually. "Better bring flashlights just in case."

I pointed at my shotgun, which I had leaned up by the front door when we had come in from the deck. Lund shook his head.

When we were outside and about fifty yards down the trail along the ridge, Lund spoke.

"Sorry about that. Might be nothing. But something pretty big is up, and I don't want to take chances."

"You seriously think someone put listening devices in my house?"

"I don't know. But I do know that it's possible."

"I have an alarm system."

Lund shook his head. "Doesn't matter. There's ways to do it without even going in the house. But if they wanted to, they coulda gone in anyway."

"Who are 'they?'"

"Don't know for sure."

"Why don't you tell me what you do know?"

It was almost full dark under the trees. When we came out onto the rock ledge that overlooked the lake, it was easier to see.

Lund looked at the water, steel-gray, fading into a dark blue twilight at the indistinct joint of the horizon.

"I'm being audited," he said.

I felt a surge of anger and disgust. I realized that while Lund seemed like a good guy, I didn't know him very well. He could be one of those borderline-paranoid conspiracy-theory types, the sort of guy who maintains that the moon landings were faked. "You got me to play cloak and dagger, and sneak off into the woods, just because you screwed up on a tax return? Man, you had me going there for a minute."

"You asked me to find out about this Charles Holland guy, the one your dad supposedly shot in Washington State." Lund's voice was calm and level, but I sensed that he was restraining his own anger.

"So?"

"So, I looked into him. I had to pull in some old IOUs, but I also ended up owing favors to half the administrative assistants between here and Seattle."

"And?"

"What I *didn't* learn was almost more interesting than what I did. Mostly, I learned that this guy is buried very deep, and someone very powerful does not want him dug up."

"What do you mean?"

"I mean I found out your dad shot a man named Charles Holland. I found out Holland was originally from Duluth. Just to find out those two things took a lot of conniving, bribing and cajoling. And then everything dried up. If I were to accept what I learned at face value, I would tell you that according to my investigation, Charles Holland was born in Duluth, shot in Lynden Washington thirty years later, and did nothing at all in between."

"What about employment records, friends, family, stuff like that?"

"Gee, maybe you should go into private investigations for a career change."

"You sound like Dan Jensen."

"The chief, here in Grand Lake?"

I nodded.

"I knew I liked him, minute I saw him. Point is, I couldn't find out anything at all about any part of Holland's life except his birth and death. I'm starting to think I'm incredibly talented to even have found out about those."

"Don't pull a muscle patting yourself on the back."

"There's more," said Lund seriously. "When it dried up, it was kind of sudden. Everyone just quit talking to me. I'd give them the birth and death information, but it was like suddenly the guy never existed. No one knew anything about him."

It was now full dark, but the lake still shimmered, lighter under the dark sky to the east.

Lund let out a breath slowly. "Then, my license got pulled."

I looked him. "What?"

"They pulled my private investigator's license. Just suspended it for a couple days. I know a guy, and we got it straightened out, but I don't think it was an accident."

"Because now you're being audited."

"That's right. There's someone who doesn't like me poking around, and he's got strings to pull to send me the message."

"Are you sure the audit couldn't be a coincidence?"

"And my PI license?"

"Could be."

"In my business, I'm not real big on coincidences. Two of them together really sets off the alarm bells. There's really three coincidences, if you count the fact that all of sudden no one knew anything about this Holland guy."

"What, you think there's a conspiracy between the police forces and administrative assistants of two states to cover up the past of a guy who is already dead and in the grave?"

"No. I think there's one or two people who don't want this line of questioning pursued. Whoever they are, they have the muscle to get people to shut up and to give me legal hassles. The individual secretaries and cops probably don't know what it's about – they only know that their boss told them to shut up about Holland. And the bosses probably don't know why either."

"And someone told someone to pull your license and audit you."

"I don't know about the audit, but I pretty much know for sure that's what happened with my license."

Sometimes I wished I chewed tobacco. Now seemed like good time to chew thoughtfully, and then spit. "Why would someone try to cover for a guy who's already dead?"

"It wouldn't be about him. It would about someone who is still alive, who has connections to the dead guy."

Again, I wanted to spit. Or swear admiringly or something. I settled for scratching my cheek, which an imaginative person might have called "unshaven."

"So where do we go from here? I mean all this stonewalling makes me think we're on to something."

"Yeah," said Lund. "But what? This feels a lot bigger than simple bank robbery."

"Simple bank robbery."

"You're the guy supposed to be good with words. You know what I mean, though. Your average Bonnie and Clyde wouldn't be folks with any pull in the government to hush things up like that."

"Is it possible that it's just that no one really knows anything about this Charles Holland? I mean, we're pretty good about documenting birth and death, but maybe no one really knows anything else about him."

"I thought you said your dad was a cop. Unless this guy never went to school, never got a driver's license, never got a social security number, never went to the doctor, never used a credit card – there would be some record of his life."

"Any ideas on what to do next?"

"Not at the moment."

"Why did you drive all the way up here? You could have called me."

"This kind of stuff going on, they might have a way to listen in on a phone conversation, or bug my office, or whatever. Seemed safest to talk in person in a place like this."

"How'd you get here anyway? I didn't see your car."

"Parked down at the Superior Hiking Trail trailhead. Hiked up here."

"How did you know how to get here from there?"

"Give me some credit. I investigate stuff for a living."

"You really think my house is bugged?"

"Naw. But if they can get my investigator's license pulled, they could probably bug your house if they wanted to."

"Any reason they'd want to? I'm not the one doing the investigating right now."

"Like I said, I doubt your house is bugged. But it's better for me to be safe, you know?"

"I really want to make this right for the lady who lost her money," I said. "And the police don't seem to be getting anywhere."

"Well, maybe there's a reason they aren't getting anywhere. Maybe they're hitting the same thing I am."

"Can you justify me paying you for another week, to see if you can come up with another angle?"

I saw a flash of white teeth in the dark. "I think I can always figure a way to justify another paycheck. But seriously, yeah, give me another week. I'll play it straight with you if I can't find any way to use that time."

After some discussion, and against my sense of dignity, I drove away from my house and met Lund coming out of the woods a hundred yards down the road from my driveway. I took him down to his car, and then, feeling silly, pretended to do some evening grocery shopping to justify the trip away from my house.

When I went to sleep that night, I dreamed of spies watching me from the next room.

TWENTY-TWO

I met Alex Chan for lunch the next day. We were at Lorraine's. Though I normally only went there for breakfast, they did have a pretty decent Philly Cheesesteak sandwich. I had a milkshake and fries with mine. Lorraine's was my main source for serious cholesterol.

"Can the federal government choose to audit people for reasons other than tax issues?" I asked him.

"I'm not a tax attorney," said Chan. He was eating Lorraine's version of sweet and sour pork.

"So you don't know anything about audits?"

"Only in general terms. I'm pretty sure that audits are supposed to be chosen randomly, or because of irregularities in tax returns. They aren't supposed to use audits as a way to hassle particular people."

"But they could."

Chan shrugged. "They do. I'm sure of it. But it's impossible to fight them on it."

I thought for a minute. "You heard about Ethel Ostrand's money?" I asked.

"Sure," he said. "This is Grand Lake. You and I are the only two people who keep secrets in this town."

"Well, I've been trying to run a little side-investigation. I have some angle that the police don't seem to be able to chase. But we're getting some push-back, maybe from the federal government."

"You saying the federal government doesn't want you to investigate the bank robbery? You're nuts."

I told him a little about the investigation, leaving Lund's name out of it.

"Huh," he said when I was done.

"People pay you three hundred dollars an hour for that kind of insight?" I asked.

"I never said it was morally right," said Chan. "Besides, you aren't paying me anything right now."

"OK. I don't have unlimited resources. But maybe you could poke around a little for me and see if you can figure out what's going on."

"Sure," he said, taking another bite of rice and pork.

"How can you eat that stuff?" I asked him. "That isn't even remotely like real Chinese food. Generally, I love the food here, but they should never even have attempted that kind of cooking."

"I'm not really Chinese, though," said Chan. "Well, I mean, my grandparents emigrated from China, but my parents were so big on integration that they never even let me have Chinese food as a kid. I think they were kind of ashamed that they had married each other, and not real Americans."

"They *are* real Americans," I said.

"That's what I tell them," he said. "But anyway, they made me as generic American – especially non-Chinese – as they could. For instance, they'd be thrilled if I can get something going with Julie, because she's their stereotype of a good old fashioned American girl."

"Whoa there, Silver," I said. "Number one, starting a relationship to please your parents is a horrible idea. Number two, I don't like this talk of 'getting something going' with Julie."

"Why? Are you into her, or something?"

I grinned at the thought. "No, I'm not into Julie. Think of me more like her big brother. Maybe I'm a little protective."

"So I need your permission to date her?"

"Well, no. But I don't want to see her get hurt."

He looked at me intently. "In all seriousness, Jonah, I really like her. She's got…"

"Spunk?"

"Yeah, something like that. She's vivacious. And pretty."

"Just don't be flippant about this. Under all that verve, she can be a very sensitive soul."

"I'm not flippant," he said. "So," he added, "I hear you have a cat."

"Boy, word really does get around this town," I said.

"What's his name?"

"I don't know yet," I said.

"You've got to give him a name. An old Chinese proverb says it's bad luck to have a cat with no name."

"I thought you said your parents tried to raise you as non-Chinese as possible."

"OK," he admitted, "I made that up. But really, you should name the thing. How about Luther? You know, 'cause you are a Lutheran pastor and all."

"Alex," I said, "You're brilliant."

"So you're going to name him Luther?"

"No."

There was a short silence. "Then why am I brilliant?"

"He shall be called Melanchthon."

"Muh-what?"

"*Muh-lank-thon*," I said, sounding it out for him. "Philipp Melanchthon was Martin Luther's right hand man. He was a talented scholar in his own right."

"So if the cat is Melanchthon, that makes you…"

"Martin Luther, of course."

TWENTY-THREE

The Farmer's Credit Union of Moose Lake was robbed the next day.

I heard about it when I had lunch with Leyla at Dylan's. Even though the *Grand Lake Gazette* was published only three times a week, they did do special editions for significant news, and Leyla was an inveterate news hound.

"They robbed another bank, Jonah," she told me while I munched on a mozzarella, tomato and avocado sandwich on grilled Panini bread. I decided happily that I was on an avocado kick.

"Did someone rob the bank or the customers?" I asked.

"Sorry, the customers." She sipped some Coke. No diet for her. I appreciate a woman who can take her sugar and caffeine like a man.

"Why don't you start from the beginning?"

"It sounds exactly like the Grand Lake job."

"'Job?' What, are we in *Ocean's Eleven* now?"

"You can be a very frustrating person to talk to," she said. "I thought you'd want to hear this."

"Sorry. You thought right. I do. I just can't restrain my natural ebullience around you."

"Whatever." She tossed her hair.

"So someone robbed the customers, like in Grand Lake?"

"Yes. Two people, dressed all in black, armed with automatic hand guns. They came busting in, got everyone on the floor, and then robbed from the customers, but left the bank alone."

"*Two* people? There were three in Grand Lake."

"You shot one, remember?"

Suddenly I felt like I'd been kicked in the stomach. "You think he died?"

"Oh, Jonah, I'm sorry. I didn't really think of that. I don't know, of course."

"Do you think it was self-defense, my shooting at him?"

"I don't think anyone is going to file charges against you, Jonah, and I don't think you'd be convicted if they did."

I looked down at my sandwich. It was odd that food could taste so good, even when contemplating things so tragic.

"I didn't exactly mean the legal thing. I mean, was it justified?"

Leyla cocked her dark head and looked at me carefully. "Is it bothering you, Jonah?"

"A little. Yeah."

She took my hand. Hers felt slim and small, but somehow I was comforted. "You did what you had to do."

"That's what I'm telling myself. But is it true?"

Leyla took her time answering. "I wasn't there. I didn't experience what you did. But I know you. I know what drives you and what doesn't. I didn't know those things before – when I let you down. But I know them now, and I trust your heart. If you shot at those bank robbers, it was because you had to, to protect yourself, and even more, to protect Arne and the others."

I met her eyes. It wasn't something I could do for very long and still control my heart rate. "You have been very good to me."

She glanced away. "Well, lately, maybe." She looked back at me again. "Are you OK?"

I nodded. "Thank you." I got my hand back, and ate some more of my sandwich and drank some coffee. "So you think it's the same gang?"

"Well, the police in Moose Lake aren't talking yet, but it sure sounds like it, doesn't it?"

"What about Chief Jensen?"

"No comment."

"Are you kidding me? What's the matter with him?"

"I don't know, Jonah, he's always been pretty careful with the press. That doesn't mean he thinks this is a coincidence."

We finished our lunch. Leyla was heading back to the newspaper office. At the door, I grabbed her hand.

"Leyla. Thank you. I really mean it. You helped."

She turned and hugged me tight. "You're welcome, Jonah. You are a strange mixture of toughness and sensitivity. Both things are very good, but they seem to create tension in you sometimes. You are OK."

"Yes," I said. "I am. You help to keep me that way."

She looked at me, and her face seemed a little unstable. Her hand stroked my cheek, and then she turned and left.

~

Before going back to the church, I went by the Grand Lake Police Station. Dan Jensen was in his office.

"Jonah," he said, waving me in. "Want some coffee?" He shook his head immediately. "Stupid question, sorry." He got up and poured me a cup.

"I heard about the robbery in Moose Lake," I said.

Jensen nodded. "Figured you would."

"What do you think?"

"Sounds like the same group that hit the First National here. Same method, same goals."

"It's a little unusual to go into a bank and rob customers, but not the bank, isn't it?"

"Yeah. These are the only two robberies like it that I've heard of."

"Except the ones in northern Washington."

"Yeah."

"Dan, what's the deal with that? You find out anything else?"

"Haven't looked into it any more. I got enough going on with Grand Lake. Don't have time to go down that road."

"But going down that road might help you solve the Grand Lake robbery."

"Jonah, it's a dead end. Even if what you say is true, I can't get at the information I need. No one out there seems to know anything. No one in Duluth, either. I'm better off working it from this end. The Moose Lake robbery should help some. I've got a call in to the State Police too, but there's some kind of bureaucratic holdup."

"So you think it's the same group."

"Pretty big coincidence otherwise."

I sipped some coffee. It was awful. I had some more, anyway.

"Anything I can do?"

"I appreciate it, Jonah. Normally, if one of our officers shot a man, I'd have you talk to him, help him through it. But in this case, you're the guy that pulled the trigger. No hostages to deal with, no one to counsel. You're the police chaplain, not a detective. So, no, I don't know what you can do right now." Jensen took a sip of his own coffee. His face revealed nothing about how old and bitter it tasted. He was a good cop.

"You could pray that we catch the S.O.B's though."

"Okay," I said. "Dear Lord, please let Dan Jensen catch those sons-of-"

"All right, all right. Clean up the language before you put it to the man upstairs."

"You think He's never heard the word 'bitch?'"

Jensen looked uncomfortable. "I suppose he must have."

"I'm sure the Roman soldiers called him a lot worse than that when they were flaying him half to death. But it would have been in Latin, of course, so it would have sounded more educated."

Jensen half-laughed, still looking not quite at home in his skin. "Sometimes I don't know what to make of you."

"So you want me to change the subject?"

"Please."

"All right," I said. "Let's talk about those S.O.B's down in Minneapolis who play football for our state."

Jensen shook his head. "You don't really talk like that, Jonah. Not normally."

"Only when I can use it to make you squirm like this."

TWENTY-FOUR

When I went back to the church, Julie flagged me down in the main office before I could get to my study.

"You told me to remind you to find a captain for your sailing cruise," she said.

"Julie," I said, "if Steve Jobs had had you, he never would have invented the PDA."

"Steve Jobs invented public displays of affection? But he wouldn't have, if I had been his secretary? I'm not sure how I should take that comment."

"Personal Digital Assistant. Electronic calendar, you know."

"Oh. Who's Steve Jobs?"

"Former CEO of Apple computers."

"I don't think he invented PDA's then. But I bet there is a PDA app for the iPhone."

"Whatever. My point is, you are better than a computerized appointment calendar."

She batted her eyelids at me, giving me a hideously fake smile. "Why thank you, Pastor Jonah."

"Sorry. It came out wrong. I meant to say, I really appreciate you."

She gave me an old-fashioned look. "I'm not sure our relationship is ready for overt expressions of gratitude."

"So, you'd prefer if we continue with the sarcastic remarks and humorous put-downs."

"You got it."

"The thing is, you always get the better of me on that stuff."

She smiled sweetly. "Now you are starting to understand."

I threw up my hands and went into my office.

~

Mike Slade was a member of Harbor Lutheran. He was a lawyer, but I kind of liked him anyway. He picked up the phone on the second ring.

"Slade!" I said by way of greeting. Even though it didn't sound pastoral, it would be impossible for any heterosexual male – including pastors and Supreme Court judges – to call someone by their first name if they had a last name as cool as Slade.

"Hey, Jonah," he said. My last name was not as cool as his.

"I have an unusual proposal for you," I said. "I know you do some sailing." I told him about my upcoming sailing cruise and our need for a captain.

"Hold on," he said. "When was this?"

"About ten days," I said. I had the grace to sound sheepish.

"And what kind of boat?"

"A forty-foot overnighter," I said.

"We wouldn't have to share a bed, would we?" He sounded suspicious.

"I like you, Slade, but not that much. We'd each have a couch in the main cabin."

"Hold on," he said. "Let me check my calendar."

I held on for a few minutes. With a rustle, he came back on the line. "Jonah, I would have loved to help you out, but I am booked that week. Also, I've never really sailed anything that big. My own boat is just a step up from a Paper Tiger – just a day-sailing cat."

"Yeah, I've sailed it, remember?"

"*You* sailed it?"

"Well, for a few minutes. Leyla sailed it the rest of the time."

"Anyway," said Slade, "I'm bummed I can't help you. If the marriage counseling didn't work out, I could have done their divorces for them."

I laughed. "A full-service cruise."

"You got it."

I was disappointed too. I wasn't ready to take on a captain I had never met, and I really thought the cruise could have helped the Stones and the Krugers.

"Slade, you know anyone else who could do it? Someone who could kind of fit into the whole idea of a counseling cruise and all that?"

"Well, if you weren't on the outs with your news-chick, she'd be the ideal choice. She told me once she did a captain's course down in Bayfield – you know, for the big boats like you're talking about. And she's got the sensitivity and everything that you're looking for."

"Leyla."

"That's what I said. Too bad you guys aren't getting along. What's wrong with you anyway? Catherine Zeta-Jones could be Leyla's ugly big sister."

"Who told you we weren't getting along?"

"This is Grand Lake, Jonah. C'mon, you're a pastor here, for Pete's sake. Word gets around."

I surprised myself by saying forcefully, "Well, word is wrong. We're doing great. I'm not crazy, you know."

There was a small silence. Slade's voice, when he spoke again, sounded serious. "I am really thrilled to hear that Jonah. Seriously, it makes me happy to know. You two just seem right for each other."

"Thanks," I said. I wondered if Leyla would still be happy to hear it too. Maybe I ought to have told her sooner.

TWENTY-FIVE

I picked up the phone to call Leyla. I put it down again a second later. For the first time in many years, I felt truly vulnerable to a woman. The game had changed. I wasn't on the fence anymore. I had something to lose. I could get hurt, and I didn't like the feeling.

I decided to do some studying first. As it happens, I was in the Minor Prophets. Hosea was having trouble with his wife. He laid it on the line for her, and she betrayed him. God told him that was how God felt about his people who had turned away from him. Then he told Hosea to forgive his wife and take her back. In the same way, God was ready to forgive and restore.

It occurred to me that the way I was feeling now was how Leyla had been feeling about me for some time. Yet she had hung in there, her heart exposed. She had dared to be vulnerable. She had dared to wait, even when my response was neither immediate, nor what she wanted. I owed her the phone call. I owed her a little vulnerability of my own.

My hand shook, and I felt like a teenager as I dialed.

"Hi, Jonah," she said.

"I remember the first time someone with caller ID answered the phone by saying my name," I said. "It freaked me out."

"Welcome to the twenty-first century, darling."

"Thank you," I said. "And may I say, it is a more bearable century because of your presence in it."

"Why, thank you," she said. There was a pause.

"I was thinking I'd like to cook you dinner tonight. What do you say?"

There was another pause. "Okay, Jonah. I..." she was quiet.

"Go on."

"Never mind."

"I've got a minute."

"No, we can talk about it tonight."

"All right. Come by any time after 6:30."

~

Later, at home, I put on some tunes and went to work in the kitchen. Kari Hilpert came on, acoustic, mellow and heart-lifting. Something in her music brings life and light and hope. As I listened, I settled into peace, and to the joy of food preparation.

Tonight it was spinach lasagna, three layers, each one basted with my homemade Italian tomato sauce, spread with ricotta cheese, sprinkled with seasoned ground beef, and then filled with onions, green peppers and fresh spinach, topped off with mozzarella. In a fit of creativity, I found a zucchini in my fridge, sliced it up and added some to each layer. I briefly considered, and then discarded, the idea of an avocado as well. There are limits, after all.

Leyla got there at about six forty-five. I answered the door, and there she stood, looking fresh as a greenhouse carnation in February. Her dark hair fell in layered waves and tresses. She wore a dark blue pullover, and tan pants, and as usual her clothes fitted her perfectly, showing her figure to advantage, but not ostentatiously. She wore little, dangling silver earrings that looked like bells.

"Here you are, with bells on!" I said, a little breathlessly.

"Do you like them?" she asked, brushing her hair back a little more from her ears.

"You look like a million bucks," I said.

"Thank you, Jonah," she said. "May I come in?"

I realized that I was standing in the doorway, staring at her. "Sorry," I said. "Please."

She smiled at me and walked in. "Smells wonderful," she said.

Melanchthon, the newly named kitten, came tearing into the room. He skidded to a stop in front of Leyla and stood on stiff legs with bristling fur. His eyes were wide and wild.

"Oh," said Leyla. "Your kitty!"

For a heartbeat he stared at her, and then raced from the room, making a loud galloping sound with his tiny paws on the wood floor.

"He's cute," she said, laughing. "Did you name him yet?"

"Melanchthon," I said.

She got a frowny expression on her face that I thought was almost as cute as the cat.

"What?"

"Does no one learn about obscure sixteenth century scholars in school anymore?" I asked. "*Mel-ank-thon*. He was a Reformation scholar, a close associate of Martin Luther."

"Luther would be a good name for a cat," commented Leyla. She still looked vaguely disapproving.

"You people are all the same," I said, throwing up my hands. "He shall be Melanchthon. That's my final word."

"Okay," she said. "Don't blame me if he has social problems as a result of growing up with a weird name."

She smiled at me, and then went to stand out on the deck, looking into the twilit vastness of the lake, while I set the table. I set a match to the fire I had laid earlier, and then called her in. I felt like a schoolboy. I had lit candles, and we ate by them and the firelight.

Melanchthon crept cautiously back into the room. I scooped a small piece of lasagna for him and put it on a plate on the floor. He sniffed at it, and then began eating.

"Is that good for him?" asked Leyla.

"Why wouldn't it be?" I said.

She looked at me for a moment, and then smiled happily. "Why, Jonah," she said. "You've never owned a pet, have you?"

"I'm figuring it out," I said. "So far, it's working out."

We had Riesling with the lasagna. It was technically a wine that should have been paired with different food, but we both liked it, and neither of us cared much about wine-food pairing.

Afterward, we sat on the couch and looked at the fire. Melanchthon climbed onto the back of the couch and sat next to my ear, purring loudly. Leyla sighed, leaned back, and closed her eyes. "This is lovely," she said.

"Yes, it is." I felt like a teenager more than ever. I was trying to plan how to make my move. We were both on the couch, but there was some distance between us. If I stretched out my arm, it would reach around her neck, but not around her shoulders.

I was well into my third decade of life, and I had been married before, and here I was, struggling to get to first base with a woman who had already told me she was waiting for me to decide if I wanted to pursue a romantic relationship with her. Finally, I reached over and held her hand.

Her eyes popped open and, she looked over at me. I slid my fingers in between hers, so that they were intertwined, and I scooted over so our shoulders were touching. She looked down at our hands, and then back up at me.

"Jonah," she said. "We have to talk."

My heart sank. "Okay," I said. I had waited too long. She had moved on.

Slowly, she disengaged her hand. "Jonah, this is all wonderful. Too wonderful." She had a trick of looking beautiful and vulnerable and strong, all at the same time.

"This is exactly what I want with you. But it's too painful – to spend time with you like this, to have this, but not have it, if you know what I mean."

"I'm not sure I do," I said.

"I feel too vulnerable. I feel like maybe you're taking advantage of me. I can wait for you to make up your mind about me – for a little while. But I can't wait, and then act as if we're together, when we're not."

"We said we were friends with a future."

"That's right. And I don't cuddle on the couch, and do who knows what else, with someone I'm only friends with."

"*Who knows what else?*" I said. I thought I kept my tone mild, but she punched me in the shoulder anyway.

"You know what I mean. I want this with you, but not open-ended, not until I know you want the same thing."

"You want me to commit."

Leyla tossed her hair back. "Maybe some girls are afraid to demand that. But I'm not. I'll wait for you. But I won't be your idle amusement while you make up your mind."

"Okay."

She looked at me suspiciously. "Okay what."

I reclaimed her hand. "Okay, I commit."

She looked at me some more.

"We were friends with a future. I want the future to start now."

"Just like that?"

"No, not 'just like that.' I've been thinking and praying and working things through. I invited you here tonight to communicate that very thing to you."

"By holding my hand."

"Yes."

"I thought you were married before."

"What does that have to do with it?"

"Maybe men communicate these things by holding hands and making a move. But women need to talk about them."

"Making a move?"

"I'm not vain, but I've had my share of men trying get to first base with me – and beyond. I know what you were doing."

"For the record, I didn't plan to go beyond first base."

At last, she smiled. Her eyes were warm and full of mischief. "That's a good thing. You see, I've had this spiritual awakening over the past year, and you aren't getting anywhere near home plate until there's a ring on my finger, a dress in my closet, and cake in our freezer."

"I'll consider myself warned. And for the record, though parts of me might disagree, I feel the same way as you do about it."

Leyla turned toward me and slipped her arms around my neck. "Now that's all settled, there's nothing wrong with a little restrained second-base action," she said, and kissed me.

TWENTY-SIX

"Hey, let's not steal any bases," said Leyla, a little while later.

"Sorry," I said, catching my breath. "It's been a very long time, and I sort of forgot myself for a moment."

"Well, it's gotta be longer still, buddy."

"Edward Gibbon would approve," I murmured.

Her nose crinkled up into a puzzled expression. "I can imagine you saying that God approves, or my mother would approve, or your own mother, or even you yourself, and I would agree with you. But who is Edward Gibbon?"

"He wrote *The Decline and Fall of the Roman Empire*. He said basically that all civilization is built upon the resolve of women to insist upon marriage before sex."

"So, you're saying I just saved civilization?"

"I would not have let it go that far either." Honesty compelled me to add, "I don't think."

We looked into each other's eyes for a long moment. The moment got even longer. I began to lean toward her again.

Melanchthon chose this moment to launch a pre-emptive strike on Leyla's dangling earrings. She gave a little shriek and then collapsed, laughing. She grabbed the kitten and pulled him into her lap, stroking him. He clutched at her hand with his paws and began to gnaw gently on one of her fingers, purring wildly.

"So, how does saying no to sex, save civilization?" she asked.

I straightened up, and then stood up. "Thank you, Melanchthon. You want some water or something?"

"Sure," she said.

I went over to my kitchen and got us both some ice and water. "According to Gibbon, Roman society began to fall apart after marriage lost its value in the culture, and promiscuity became widespread. Divorce became common, families were fractured and then other social institutions also began to break down. Basically, without the dominance of what we call 'the traditional family,' cultures break down and eventually collapse."

"Isn't that a little bigoted? I mean, nowadays, a lot of people feel that there are many different variations of 'family' and all of them basically valid."

"History done right is a bigoted discipline."

Leyla took the glass of water. She sipped it and then winked at me. "This is good. We need a good intellectual discussion right now. So how is history bigoted?"

"I guess what I mean is, it shows things as they really are, or were, rather. Nowadays we maintain all choices for family units are equal. We try to pretend that all beliefs and practices are neutral in relation to each other. But history tells a different story. It shows us that not all beliefs and practices are equal in terms of their effects on people. Some things really are better than others. Democracy really is better than Nazism and Communism. Capitalism, for all its faults, really has benefited far more people than socialism. And, according to convincing arguments from people like Edward Gibbon, society really is better off when traditional marriage and morality are valued, as opposed to when they aren't. It isn't just a religious thing either – Gibbon was not a Christian himself. It's just the bigoted historical fact."

"Do you always think this way, or only when I kiss you?"

"We could find out," I said with an un-pastorly leer.

"Yes, let's," she said primly. "I just kissed you not long ago, so now let's try not kissing, and see how *that* works."

"Hey, speaking of marriage," I said, trying to hide my disappointment, and ignoring the mischievous twinkle in Leyla's eyes, "I need to ask you a favor."

She looked at me suspiciously. "That is a very weird way to set up a question," she said.

"Well, in my own small way, I too, am trying to save civilization. I do a fair amount of marriage counseling."

Leyla relaxed a little. "And?"

I told her about the marriage counseling sailing cruise.

"Isn't it a little late in the season for that?" she asked.

"Well, we're getting it ridiculously cheap, and these two couples really need the help. Plus, if they keep on like they have been, I could just save civilization by throwing them off the boat."

"Seriously Jonah," she said. "I'm a little worried about you at this time of year. The weather on Superior is nothing to mess with. Storms often come up out of nowhere."

"Then come along," I said.

"What are you saying?" She said each word very distinctively, looking at me in a way that I would describe as "levelly."

"I need a captain. The guy we had bailed out on us. You can handle one of those forty-foot yachts, can't you?"

"Where would I sleep?" she said.

"Why does everyone ask me that?" I said. "We'd each have a couch in the main cabin. The two berths will be for the two couples."

She was silent for a moment. "Jonah," she said after a minute, looking into the fire, "you didn't – you didn't make a move on me just to get me to say yes to this, did you?"

I reached over and palmed her cheek, bringing her eyes to meet mine. "Never," I said. "I am many things less than wonderful, but I would never do that to you, or anyone else for that matter. Regardless of whether or not you want to captain this cruise, I want to commit to you, to let our relationship go wherever God takes it."

"Good," she said. "I mean, I didn't think so, but...well, never mind."

"The past few months have been tough. I'm trusting you again. You need to trust me too."

"Okay. Can I think about the cruise?"

"Of course. But not too long. It's coming up pretty quickly here."

"Gee," she said, "you're coming up with all kinds of ways for me to save civilization."

"Just want you to feel needed," I said.

TWENTY-SEVEN

Two days later, over a cup of wild rice and chicken gumbo at Dylan's Cafe, Leyla accepted my invitation to captain the marriage counseling cruise.

"Where will I be when you do the counseling sessions? She asked.

"Well," I said, "we'll see what works out best. We may want to just talk informally while we're going along, or we might have formal sessions. I want to play that one by ear. Anyway, you may not be able to avoid being where we are."

"There aren't many private places on a boat that size."

"Exactly. And it wouldn't surprise me if the couples drew you into the conversation. I'd say, if you are drawn in, try to ask questions more than give answers. Mostly, if they are going to work things out, they need to be thinking things through for themselves. Questions help them to do that more than answers most of the time."

"That actually makes some sense," said Leyla, smiling and slurping some more gumbo.

"Don't sound so surprised."

"It's that whole macho-sensitive thing," she said. "Sometimes I get so caught up in the hunter-fisher-martial arts side of you that I forget the sensitive side."

"You forgot intelligent, good-looking, and above all, modest." For some reason, she kicked me under the table.

After that, things began to come together pretty well. I appointed myself maritime chef, of course, and happily stocked up on avocados.

I had one more land-based session with each couple before we went.

Phil and Angela Kruger seemed a little tense with each other again. After they were seated in my office, Phil looked directly at me.

"Is this really necessary, Pastor? I mean, we're going out on the boat in a week."

"Normally, I recommend counseling at least once a week, if not more," I said. "Plus, the sailing-counseling tour is not magic. I think it will help you guys, but you can't sit back and wait for some bolt of lightning from the sky. You need to be at work on your relationship *now*."

"Yeah, Okay, fine," grumbled Phil.

"Philip," said Angela, "this is an opportunity. Let's make the most of it. There are some things I want to talk about right now."

Phil look at her like she'd stabbed him in the back. He looked at me.

"Go on, Angela," I said. "If you have something to say to him, go ahead."

I figured she was feeling ready to confess the affair. Frankly, I wasn't sure if it was a great idea, considering her husband's current mood.

"I don't like how you patronize me, Philip," said Angela. I quietly let out a little air.

"What're you talking about, Babe?" he said. "I try to treat you like a queen, Angie, you know I do."

"I've asked you to call me Angela," she said. "And maybe I don't want to be a queen."

"Ten years, I been calling you Angie, all of sudden, this year it's got to be Angela? Plus, now Phil isn't good enough for you, and you gotta call me

Philip, like my second grade teacher or something."

"Philip is your given name. Angela is mine. They are nice names. Nicknames and diminutives are demeaning and are often used by authoritarian figures for the purpose of dominating others."

I said a silent thank-you to the Lord that it was difficult to turn Jonah into a nickname, and so I was protected from being demeaned and dominated. I think God might have laughed. He seems to have a better sense of humor than most of the people I know.

"I don't even know what that means," said Phil, sounding a little plaintive. "We used to be happy. We didn't worry about garbage like what we called each other, and who was dominating who."

"Whom," said Angela, and I felt I had to agree with her grammar.

"I think it's these crap feminist classes you're taking at UMD. They're putting ideas into your head."

Angela shot him a deadly look. "They have only confirmed what I already knew intuitively to be true," said Angela. She looked at me, and it sounded like she was trying to convince me, more than Phil.

"I'm sorry Angela," said Phil respectfully. "I didn't mean that."

She glared at him for a minute and he looked down.

"Anyway," she said at last, "you know I won't be taking classes anymore for a while." She sounded sulky.

"Hey, Babe," said Phil, putting his hand on hers. "I'm sorry you gotta quit. I know you liked all that crap. Maybe you can do it again someday."

"You're quitting your studies?" I asked Angela. On the whole, it seemed to me that her studies were not helping her come to grips with her issues, and she had to get the philandering professor out of her life, but I also knew that she derived a great deal of satisfaction from her feminist courses at the University of Minnesota Duluth.

"Yes," she said, looking away. "It's kind of a money-thing."

Phil gave a little smirk. I wondered if he had been less than honest with her about their finances, in order to get her to stop.

Phil got his face under control again. "Look, Angela," he said, "I know things are kind of tense with us right now. Just hang in there, OK? You know it will get better soon."

She smiled weakly and took his hand. "I know, Philip. It will be better soon, won't it?"

"Before you know it, Babe," he said.

"All right, listen," I said. "When you go home tonight, I want you to talk more about Angela's studies. But I want you practice telling each other only how you feel. Instead of blaming the other person, or accusing them, just tell them about your feelings. Instead of saying, 'you demean me when you call me Angie,' try something like, 'I feel very hurt and small when you don't call me Angela, like I've asked.' Get the picture?"

After some more conversation, they were on their way. They remained committed to the cruise, and I thought maybe we were getting somewhere.

TWENTY-EIGHT

My purpose for meeting with the Stones was to talk them out of coming on the cruise. After we were all seated in my office, I told them so.

"But why?" said Jasmine. "I think it could help us so much."

"We have problems, Pastor," said Tony Stone. "I think this cruise will help us. We don't know anyone up here. We don't have the support of a community, and you can give us that with this cruise."

They sounded like little kids asking for extra cookies. "Look," I said, "the truth is I still don't understand your marriage. You are like no other married couple I've counseled. I don't understand your problems. I don't even understand your *relationship*. I think I will be wasting your time and money."

Stone, normally so expressionless, had a queer look on his face, part heartsick, part something that almost looked like admiration. He began to stand up.

"Sit down honey," said Jasmine. "We need to tell him."

"*Tell* him?" Stone sounded shocked. "Jaz..."

"Yes." She turned to me quickly. "Our problems are all about sex."

Stone was staring at her. He slumped heavily back into his seat. She patted his cheek. "Oh, quit pretending, Honey. Obviously, Pastor Borden could see we were not being honest with him." She turned back to me. "It's just that we're kind of embarrassed, and we didn't know how to bring it up."

I rubbed the back of my neck, where I felt a slight headache beginning. "Well, OK, what seems to be the issue?"

"Can't we talk about this on the boat?" asked Stone. His voice was a little hoarse, and he cleared his throat.

"The boat isn't magic," I said. "I think it can be helpful, but I don't know why you think that will solve all your problems, if you can't begin to face them here and now."

Stone looked like he wanted to swear.

"OK," said Jasmine, with a defiant glance at her husband. "I'll start. How come men seem to think that having sex will fix everything?" Tony was staring at her again, his mouth gaping slightly.

"Because it will," I said. Now they were both staring at me.

"I beg your pardon?" said Jasmine after a minute.

"Tony thinks sex will fix everything, because for him, it probably will. It does for many men, though not all."

Stone began to grin. Jasmine seemed off balance for the first time since I'd met her.

"Look," I said, "I'm a Christian counselor. What I believe is that God made sex, and it was good. He made it specifically for marriage. Outside of marriage it is destructive. But in marriage it can be incredibly positive and helpful. In some ways, it's almost like magic."

They both chuckled, a little uncomfortably, I thought.

"This doesn't apply to all men," I said, "but it probably does to at least a majority. For those men, it is almost impossible to overemphasize the importance of physical intimacy. That kind of intimacy alone will resolve many conflicts – for the men, anyway – and it goes a very long way toward making them feel happy and content in their marriage. It's almost like magic. My suggestion to many wives is, you've been given your magical powers for a reason. Use them."

"But it doesn't work that way for most women I know," said Jasmine.

"That's very true," I said. "It's unfair, but men have *not* been given a magic potion that will make everything better for their wives. Physical intimacy doesn't do that for most women. So, Tony, you're still on the hook. It takes hard work and sensitivity."

"That's kind of strange," said Jasmine. "What's so helpful for men is sometimes hard for their wives, and vice versa."

"True," I said. "We often think marriage is about our spouse making us happy. But I suspect that in part, God created marriage as a means to force us to mature as human beings."

Both of them had perked up immensely at this discussion, and they peppered me with questions, and when we were done forty-five minutes later, I had changed my mind, and agreed that they should come on the sailing cruise.

TWENTY-NINE

Bayfield, Wisconsin, reminded me of all the quaint New England fishing villages I've never been to. It could have been the set for Amity, the town in the old movie, *Jaws*. The main street drops straight and smooth toward the lake and the town marina. On that early October day, the impossibly beautiful water sparkled to its endless horizon in the sunlight, framed between old brick buildings housing mom-and-pop stores, as well as touristy craft shops, a sprinkling of boutiques and a few hometown cafes. There were only a few masts still bobbing in the harbor, but they were enough to complete the picture.

"I love Bayfield," said Leyla, sighing. She had her legs tucked under her in the front seat next to me, both hands wrapped around a cup of convenience-store coffee. I shifted down as we dropped toward the harbor.

"There are some good trout streams nearby," I allowed. For some reason she hit me.

"Hey," I said, "I was agreeing with you."

"You could have fooled me."

"It's an adequate town," I amended, feeling generous.

"It's a good thing I have such manly shoulders," I said a moment later, "or all this unwarranted violence might injure me."

Truthfully, however, it *was* a gorgeous little town, and we were arriving early morning on a day that was singularly spectacular for October in the North Country.

"What a day!" I said when we got out of the car at the harbor and stretched. "It's got to be at least seventy degrees." Peak color season had passed, but there were still wide swaths of gold and red forest along the shoreline, all the more brilliant in their contrast with the blue water.

"It's adequate," said Leyla.

"I suffer because of my upbringing," I said. "I was taught never to hit girls."

Leyla stood with her hands behind her back, her long dark hair spilling in waves over her right shoulder. Her eyes glittered with mischief. "You could punish me with a kiss," she said in a small voice. For some reason, I became aware of my heart pounding in my chest.

"You *are* bad, aren't you?" I said. I moved towards where she stood, her head bent down now like a naughty school girl. Just then, a car pulled up next to mine. Through the windshield I could see Angela and Phil. I checked my movement, opting instead for pastoral decorum. Leyla grinned wickedly and winked at me.

I introduced Leyla to the Krugers. Phil seemed keyed up, his dark eyes sparkling and his sensual mouth active and smiling. He was wearing blue nylon pants, the kind some runners wear, and a dark, blue nylon jacket. Angela seemed excited too. Her outfit was almost identical to Phil's, only the jeans and sweater were clearly styled for the female form.

I shook their hands and introduced them to Leyla.

"Wonderful to meet you," said Angela, glancing from Leyla to me, and back to Leyla again. "Jonah didn't mention that he was married."

I felt a little twinge of awkwardness. I opened my mouth, but Leyla rescued me. "Oh, we're not married," she said. "I'll be the captain for this cruise."

Phil glanced quickly at Angela. She wrinkled her brow.

"Captain?"

"Yes, I'll be sailing the boat. Jonah isn't really qualified," she added unnecessarily, touching my cheek with the palm of her hand.

They noticed the touch, and I saw another glance pass between the Krugers. I cleared my throat, feeling strangely embarrassed.

"Leyla and I are also, ah, seeing each other."

Phil gave a kind of shrug. "Well, this will be terrific," he said.

"It will," I said, hoping I sounded convincing. Now that we were here, I thought it could be a very long weekend indeed, if the Krugers and Stones didn't cooperate.

Angela looked around, took a deep breath and sighed. "I have really been looking forward to this," she said to no one in particular.

"Well," I said, "let's go find the boat."

There weren't that many boats still in the water by that date in October, and we found her easily enough. *Tiny Dancer* was painted in a loose freehand font on her stern. In fact, it looked almost like an amateur paint job. I wondered about that. My impression of nautical matters is that there was a great deal of superstition involved. Wouldn't someone consider it bad luck to have the name of your boat painted in such a sloppy fashion? Even so, if it didn't bother Red Hollis, it was no business of mine. Maybe he'd painted it on there himself out some *other* nautical superstition. Some sailors are funny that way.

She was a nice-looking yacht and didn't seem all that tiny to me. Leyla said she was a forty footer. The cabin, with tiny windows, stood up only a foot or so from the rest of the hull, but ran almost the whole length and width of the vessel.

"Looks like there will be plenty of room below," said Leyla

approvingly. I took her word for it.

Ropes and pulleys ran all over the deck and the top of the cabin. There was one mast that towered into the bright blue autumn sky. Near the base of the mast, a pole extended horizontally – the boom. It was wrapped with some kind of bulky blue canvas cover. At the bow of the boat, a steel cable climbed to the top of the mast. Around that cable was wrapped a sail.

"That's the foresail, or jib" said Leyla, seeing me looking at it. She was looking around too. She pointed to the base of the foresail where a kind of wide, flattened pulley was installed.

"That will make things much easier," she said. "It makes it much simpler to control the sail."

"Yeah, I was just thinking how nice it was that we had one of those," I said, dodging a blow from Leyla. "I thought sailing was supposed to be a simpler, old-fashioned thing," I added, looking at the spider's web of ropes draping the vessel, "I've seen computers less complicated than this."

"Oh, it's not so bad," she said. "It's basically the same as that catamaran we go out on sometimes. Just bigger, that's all."

At the rear end of the boat (*aft* as I learned it is called) there was an open cockpit. It didn't seem all that large. Behind that, was the wheel, about two feet in diameter, apparently made of steel tubing. It was attached to a small pedestal that also held a compass, an engine throttle and a GPS unit. The walls between the outer hull and the inner cockpit were very thick.

At the front of the cockpit was a doorway that was blocked by boards and padlocked shut.

Leyla walked to the marina office to pick up the key, while I went back to the car for our bags. Phil and Angela also picked up their luggage. I have many failings. Among them is great pride in my ability to pack small and light. Leyla, apparently, did not share the same pride. For a moment, I felt slightly embarrassed about the amount I was forced to carry, until I noticed that the Krugers had even more.

As I went back for the second time, a black SUV with tinted windows pulled up. Jasmine and Tony Stone got out. Stone looked, as always, like his name. His face was flat and expressionless. Like Phil, he wore blue jeans, but he wore a gray University of Minnesota Sweatshirt. There was a small, old-fashioned pager on his belt. He nodded when he saw me, and then went without a word to the back of the blazer for their luggage. Jasmine was animated as always, but in a businesslike way today.

"Do you have everything set?" she asked.

"I think so," I said. "The boat seems to float anyway." I started to move toward the back of the blazer. Jasmine stepped into my path, stopping me.

"Tony is very particular about our stuff. I wouldn't offer to help him, if I were you."

"Farthest thing from my mind," I said without thinking. "I mean," I added when I realized how that sounded, "I had other things I was thinking about."

Jasmine smiled and laid her hand on my arm. She stood a little bit closer to me than I felt comfortable with. "It's okay, Jonah," she said. "We're very grateful that you are willing to help us." I could smell her perfume and for some reason that was unsettling. Her black hair was pulled back into a tight pony tail held with a lavender band, and she wore a matching outfit of lavender-trimmed blouse and pants.

When I got back to the *Tiny Dancer* with the second load, I found Leyla had opened up the hatch. I stepped from the dock to the deck around the cockpit, and then down into the cockpit. Two more strides took me to the hatch and companionway. There were four more steps down, and by the time I reached the bottom, I was pleasantly surprised. I could stand up fully without banging my head. In front of me was the saloon, or, main cabin. It was a long room with a padded settee on each side. It was neat and well-appointed, with polished wood paneling and cupboards. It even seemed a little spacious, like a large and unusually wide camper-trailer. On the right hand side slightly toward the front, the settee was formed into a wide U around a table. The table had a little lip on all around it, presumably to keep things from sliding off the edge when the waves tilted the yacht. Directly to my right was a small, but neatly ordered, galley, complete with stove, refrigerator and sink. The counter formed the back of one arm of the U-shaped settee. I looked over my shoulder and saw a narrow door aft of the galley. I swung it open to find the tiniest toilet-shower room that has ever been built. I bet the Pilgrims had bigger facilities on the *Mayflower*. I swung back to the left and found another door that seemed to lead toward the back of the boat. I opened it to find the small stern cabin. I could stand up in the area right next to the door, but the bed was underneath the floor of the cockpit. Sleepers would lie with their faces only a foot or two from the ceiling. The outside wall had two long narrow windows. The inside wall, I assumed, separated it from the toilet.

There was another cabin at the front of the boat, under the bow. It was, not surprisingly, v-shaped. Once again, at that point, the cabin no longer protruded above the deck, and the sleepers would be tucked in fairly close to the low ceiling. There was a skylight above the bed, which apparently could be opened and used as a hatch.

In the main saloon, on the port side, aft of the straight settee, was a little desk. Like the table, it has a small lip all around it. Above it, set in the wall, was a bank of electronic equipment. It held what looked like a CB radio and possibly a GPS unit, or maybe a depth finder, I wasn't sure which. There was also an ordinary stereo of the kind you might find in a car. The CB radio was on, a mechanical, computer-generated male voice droning out a weather report. It sounded promising.

Leyla came down the steps into the cabin. She turned to the radio and switched it off. "Well, the radio works and the weather sounds good." She turned to me. "What do you think?"

"It's kind of like a camper," I said.

She regarded me with a long, level gaze.

"A big camper," I amended.

The look did not waver.

"A big, fancy camper," I added, "with sails."

"This could be a long trip," she said for some reason. "We've got these berths," she said, turning and gesturing at the settees, "which one do you want?"

"I guess I'll take the one on the left," I said.

"I beg your pardon?" said Leyla.

"Sorry," I said, "port."

"That's better. We might as well make this as authentic as possible. When we are facing forward, left is port. Right is starboard."

"Aye-aye Cap'n!" I saluted.

She eyed me with twisted lips. I returned her look with wide-eyed innocence. "A *really* long trip," she muttered, turning away.

There was a little flyer on the table. It read, "Welcome aboard the *Zephyr*." It was some kind of pamphlet for a rental yacht, which was apparently quite similar to the *Tiny Dancer*.

"Hey look at this," I said to Leyla. "Whoever was on here last was thinking of renting a different boat."

Leyla looked at the flyer. "I don't see why," she said, shrugging. "It's exactly the same model of boat." She looked more closely. "Basically identical in fittings, actually."

"Maybe the owner of the *Zephyr* charges less than Red Hollis," I said.

It took about half an hour to get everyone's luggage stowed. Both the Stones and Krugers insisted on handling all of their own bags, so I was occupied stowing my things, and then Leyla's, in cupboards in the main saloon. After that, I transferred our food from the coolers in our vehicle to the galley on the *Tiny Dancer*.

When we had completed everything, Leyla called us all together in the cockpit outside. I introduced her to the Stones.

"OK," she said. "I need to go over some things. You may have heard that at sea, a captain functions as supreme dictator of his ship."

"Or *her* ship," said Angela, a little more loudly than was necessary.

"Yes," said Leyla. "The point is, there is a reason for that. At times, decisions may have to made quickly, and actions may have to be taken immediately or we could experience major disaster." She paused. "I mean, life-ending kinds of disaster. I don't expect that sort of thing to happen. But if we do get into a tight situation, you have to do what I say immediately, without arguing, or questioning, or something very bad could happen. Are you with me?"

We all agreed that we were with her. At this point, my phone vibrated, signaling I had a text message. I ignored it steadfastly, paying close attention to the captain. I generally enjoyed paying close attention to her.

"Another thing. We use certain terms in sailing, like port for left, and starboard for right. Using these terms while we are on board will keep everything clear so that we all understand each other in an emergency, and even for just sailing the boat." She glanced significantly at me. I looked up at the mast.

"So, just so you know what we're doing, and you can help sail if you want to, and so you won't be confused in an emergency, let's go over the terms."

She went over port and starboard again. The very front of the boat was called the bow. Anything toward the front was "forward." Anything toward the rear was "aft." The very back of the boat was called the "stern."

Leyla also showed us where the life jackets were stowed, under one of the cockpit benches. "It if gets rough," she said, "we'll want to wear these whenever we are in the cockpit or on deck." There were short metal railings around the bow and the stern. Between them on each side stretched metal cable life-lines, running through stanchions set along the sides of the boat. There were two cables, one at about shin height, the other maybe thigh high.

Tony Stone was regarding Leyla with a level of attention that was a bit more than polite. Jasmine noticed this and elbowed him so hard, he grunted. I pretended not to notice the sound, or the look she gave him. It all reminded me that I had my work cut out for me, and it was not going to be all fun and games out on the lake.

If only I had known how true that was.

THIRTY

It was about eleven o'clock when we set sail. Well, technically, we didn't set the actual sail until after, but we left the marina at that point. Leyla turned a key and the big diesel engine rumbled to life below decks somewhere. I unhooked the ropes that tied the *Tiny Dancer* to the dock, and then jumped back on board. We chugged slowly backward out of our berth, and then slowly forward out of the harbor into the wide channel between Bayfield and Madeline Island.

To my surprise, we were towing a little dinghy on a long rope behind us. "What's that for?" I asked Leyla.

"If we anchor in a bay, we can use that get to shore without swimming," she replied. I nodded. "It has other uses too," she added, "but we won't need it for that."

"Doesn't it slow us down?" asked Phil.

"A little bit, maybe," said Leyla, "but we aren't racing here, and it doesn't slow us much. This isn't like a speed boat – it isn't going to bounce around in our wake like a water skier."

"It'll slide smoothly through the soft, silky water," I said. Nobody paid any attention. I thought about repeating it louder, but ultimately went for the dignity of silence.

It was still a perfect day. The lake was as blue as the eyes of a blond Norwegian child, mirroring the perfect sky. They were both the kind of

SUPERIOR JUSTICE

blue that you only see on fine fall days – never in summer or winter. On shore, it had been almost seventy-five degrees. Out on the water where the wind blew, it was probably closer to sixty, but for autumn on Lake Superior, that was spectacularly and unusually warm. The trees on the shore were mostly leafless or brown, but there were vibrant stands of dark pine, offset by the stately muted hues of orange oaks. If this atmosphere couldn't help the two couples work through their differences, I didn't know what could. The setting was picture perfect.

That sparked a thought. "Camera!" I said out loud.

"Me, too!" said Jasmine.

I went below, and she followed. I opened one of the cupboards in the saloon to dig out the camera. Jasmine hovered for a moment, and then Angela came quickly down the four steps of the companionway, stumbling as the boat shifted in the swell of the great lake.

"Are you OK?" I asked, turning and reaching out towards her, rocking a little on my feet as well.

She waved me off. "I feel a little woozy is all," she said, grimacing. "I guess maybe I'm not a good sailor. I think I'm going to lie down for a little while." She continued past me to the bow cabin. An unpleasant thought popped into my mind. This would hardly be a weekend of marriage restoration if they were lying around sick the whole time. I realized, feeling a little sick in a different way, that I hadn't even brought any motion-sickness medicine for anyone.

Jasmine disappeared into her cabin under the cockpit. She emerged a second later, shaking her head ruefully. "I can't believe it. We forgot our camera."

"Don't worry about it," I said. "I'll give you copies of everything I take. If you want to take some shots yourself, feel free."

She glanced at me. "Do you have a video capture mode too?"

"Sure," I said. "Knock yourself out."

"Okay," she said. "I'll borrow it later."

Back in the pristine Superior air, I took some shots of the lake and the brilliant fall colors of the shore.

I turned to capture an image of Leyla behind the wheel. She stuck out her tongue as I clicked the button.

"Nice," I said. "Maybe that one should go on the Internet."

She laughed, her hair billowing in the breeze and eyes sparkling. Then she set her face in a more somber expression.

"OK, do it again."

As I snapped the second picture, she deepened her expression into a severe mock-frown.

"Seriously!"

She was laughing again. "All right, this time I promise." But I had already taken two shots of her laughing at the wheel. I felt a strange joy as I smiled and said, "Never mind."

I turned and took some candids of the Stones and then Phil Kruger, lounging on the deck in front of the mast.

Jasmine saw me and offered a stunning smile for the camera. Tony Stone just looked at me without expression.

"Hey, Tony," I said, trying to loosen him up, "we need to at least pretend to be having fun. How about a smile?"

He looked quizzically at Jasmine, and then back at me.

"I am smiling."

I gave up and turned the lens toward Phil. He seemed very tense, and his smile for the camera was patently forced.

Suddenly, the engine note changed, as Leyla dropped into idle. The boat slowly lost way, and sat, heaving in the swell with the engine ticking over.

"All right people," said Leyla. "Let's do some sailing."

My plan, which I had talked over with Leyla, was to take the afternoon to relax and enjoy the sailing, and not start in on the group sessions until we anchored for the evening in some secluded bay. Phil came back to the cockpit, to get out of the way.

Leyla reached over the port side of the deck and pulled on a rope. As far as I could see, it didn't do anything. She removed a kind of winch handle from a bracket in the cockpit and handed it to me, pointing at a big round pulley sort of thing that was fasted to the deck just outside the cockpit on the starboard side.

"Stick that in the hole at the top of the winch," she said.

She then grabbed another rope and wrapped it around the pulley a couple times.

"Now crank," she ordered."

I began cranking. The line tightened, and as it did, the front sail began to unwind off the forward stay and open up toward the starboard side. The wind began tugging at it, and it made a loud flapping noise.

"Faster," she said, and I cranked faster. The sail slowly unfurled, and then the wind caught it full, and I could feel the pressure of it on the boat. The rope pulled tight. Leyla leaned around me and did something with it, and then leaped back to the wheel. The boat turned its shoulder, shifted a little, and then leaned over and began to push through the water. Leyla reached over and abruptly the noise of the engine ceased.

"We're sailing!" cried Leyla exuberantly.

The first thing I noticed was the absence of noise. Except when I was hiking or skiing, going from one place to another required an engine and, therefore, noise. But here we were, sliding through the clear waters of Superior, and there was no sound but the gurgle and slap of the waves on the hull, and breeze in our ears. Over the past year I had sailed several times with Leyla, but it still delighted me to realize that we were moving, powered by nothing more than the wind.

Jasmine made her way to the bow, glancing down at the skylight that opened into the bow cabin. She sat at the very front, looking out at the waves and the shore.

Stone sat in the cockpit looking around. It seemed like he was enjoying himself, but with him, it was hard to tell. Phil Kruger sat opposite him, on the starboard side, which happened to be the low side at the moment. He looked around and fidgeted, drumming his fingers on the gunwale, shifting his weight. He seemed keyed up.

Finally, he stood up. "I'm gonna check on Angie," he said.

I resisted the urge to say "Angela," and settled for nodding. He went below. Tony Stone looked up, suddenly alert. He glanced at the bow where Jasmine sat, facing into the oncoming waves. Then he looked at me like he was about to say something. I waited expectantly. It wasn't unusual for reticent people to want to talk about marital issues in privacy. He drew a breath, and then Phil Kruger came back up into the cockpit and the moment passed. Stone looked away like he never had intended to say anything.

"How's Angela?" I asked Phil.

"Okay, I guess," he said. "Probably more tired than anything." He stretched. "So how deep are we here, anyway?"

I glanced at the depth finder next to Leyla. "Around two-hundred feet, looks like."

"About a mile along here, and it will be three hundred and fifty feet."

said Leyla, gazing off into the distance. "Past Outer Island it stays around six or seven hundred feet. The deepest part is more than thirteen hundred feet."

"Deep enough to drown in," said Phil.

We sailed in silence for a few more minutes. There was a muffled sound from forward. The skylight over the bow cabin rose slightly and stayed there.

A minute later, Angela came up the companionway.

"How are you feeling?" asked Leyla.

"I'm fine now, thanks," said Angela. She finished wrapping her hair into a ponytail. "I opened up the skylight to let in air. I hope that's okay."

"It is in this weather," said Leyla. "If the weather gets bad, we may have to close it."

"We listened to weather on the way here. It sounds good."

Leyla shrugged. "It does." She jerked her head over her shoulder. "But if that catches up with us, we'll have to run for shelter."

I looked astern. We were out of the shadow of the blue hills near Bayfield. In the distance far to the west was a dark smudge the covered the bottom quarter of the sky. It seemed to be coming from the northwest.

"Should we be concerned?"

Leyla shrugged again. "Angela's right. I checked the weather on the on-board radio when we first got the boat. Sounds like they aren't expecting anything. The trouble is, sometimes things happen that they don't expect." She looked directly at Angela again. "So, you are feeling okay?"

Angela nodded. "Fine. It was probably just nerves or something."

I was surprised Angela would be that nervous. Maybe she was afraid of the water. Maybe she felt there was a lot riding on this trip.

"Well, if you all agree, I'd like to hoist the mainsail too, and show you what real sailing is all about."

We all agreed, and Leyla swung the bow into the wind. She reached over and snapped a rope loose from its clamp. The jib in front spilled all of its air, and flapped idly while we heaved in the waves. Leyla began to direct us to pull some lines and loosen others

Stone cranked on the pulley I had used earlier, while I worked the line that pulled the sail slowly up the mast. Leyla made some adjustments, and slowly the big white sail began to tighten and catch the wind from the northwest. Next we worked the jib, and within about five minutes both sails were full. The *Tiny Dancer* drove her starboard shoulder into the water and leaped forward.

Before, we had been sliding sedately through the water. Now we began to move much faster. The wake boiled behind us, and we swooped gently from one wave to the next. It felt almost like flying. One of the stays began to vibrate, making a low humming sound. As our speed picked up, the bow began to kick up spray as it plowed into the waves ahead. Jasmine had already returned to her place there, and she whooped as the icy water caught her. She stood at the very front, one hand on the front stay and the other flung out wide. Her dark hair streamed unfettered in the wind.

Leyla and I glanced at each other. We both knew, without saying it, what Jasmine felt. The fresh wildness of Superior at her best is almost like a drug. I glanced at Tony to see what he thought. I almost did a double take as I saw him grinning and wiping spray from his face.

Phil was nodding to himself like he was pleased. But it was more like he was pleased that we were making progress, rather than that he was enjoying the ride. Angela still seemed a little tense.

"Is that Madeline Island?" asked Phil, pointing to our starboard.

"That's right," said Leyla. "We're almost clear of it. The first one we passed to our port was Basswood, and we are almost clear of Hermit over there."

"And that one is Stockton?" asked Phil, pointing to a low line of trees rising some distance almost straight ahead.

"That's right," said Leyla. "I was thinking we might anchor in Julian Bay on Stockton. With this northwest wind, that should be a perfect spot."

"I was hoping to see the lighthouse on Outer Island," said Angela.

"You guys have done your homework," said Leyla. "We'll have to see how the wind holds up. It's a good fifteen miles more – maybe two or three hours at this speed. If it stays like this, we won't have to tack, and we'll probably have enough time before sunset. But no promises out here."

"I'd really love to try," said Angela.

"Okay, then," said Leyla. She reached for a rope and used it to pull the mainsail boom closer to the center of the boat. We heeled over even further to starboard and the increase in speed was perceptible. She had me crank the jib sheet also, and again we could feel the change in the boat.

Like true Minnesotans, we all stayed out, enjoying the sunshine and what passed for balmy warmth on Superior. No one in the North wastes a nice day, any time of year. From time to time, Leyla made little adjustments in our direction, and with the tightness of the sails. After a while, Jasmine had to use the bathroom, which, on board the boat, was called the "head." Angela abruptly got up and went with her. I have often observed that females feel the need to go to the bathroom in groups of two or three, but there was simply no way they would both fit into the tiny facility together. I guess some habits die hard. They both returned a few minutes later. As they stepped up into the cockpit, Stone raised an eyebrow at his wife. She just shrugged slightly and gave a barely perceptible shake of her head.

At last, I reluctantly concluded that we should probably eat soon.

"I'm going to go get a snack together, and then make lunch," I said.

"Need any help?" asked Jasmine.

I shook my head. "Stay out here and enjoy it."

I went below into the tiny, neatly kept galley area. I took two avocados out of the cupboard where I had stored them earlier and glanced around for a small knife. Not finding one, I began to open the drawers in the galley. The first one held a big roll of gray duct-tape, two pens and some other odds and ends. The second one held eating utensils. I found a knife and peeled the avocados, slicing them into medallions. I sprinkled them with lemon juice and garlic salt, and arranged them on a plate with crackers and slices of cheese.

"What *is* this?" asked Stone suspiciously when I ascended to the cockpit and offered him the plate.

"Why does everyone say that?" I asked. "Haven't you ever had an avocado?"

"I've had guacamole."

"Think of this like sophisticated guacamole." I handed him the plate to pass around.

He reluctantly took a piece of avocado, put it on a cracker with cheese, and took a bite. He chewed, and then nodded. "That's actually OK." From Stone, that amounted to a rave review. I went back down into the cabin to get drinks and napkins.

As I reached the bottom of the companionway, the boat lurched violently to starboard. I caught myself on the galley counter. She straightened fairly quickly, and I heard whoops and laughter from the cockpit. I assumed some kind of rogue wave had hit us. As I regained my footing, I noticed that one of the port forward cupboards was open, and my duffel bag was hanging partway out. I went over to it, and put my hand under it to shove it back in. I felt something solid and almost metallic through the fabric. Puzzled, I lifted the bag down to the floor. I couldn't think what I had packed that might feel that way. I opened the zipper. Some of my things were missing and at one end of the bag was a heavy metal box that I had not placed there. My heart began to pound. I carefully lifted the cover an inch or so and peered inside. When I did, I went cold all over.

 I was looking at a bomb.

THIRTY-ONE

It's true, I had never seen a bomb in real life before. But I have seen enough movies to know that either this was a real bomb, or someone had gone to impressive lengths to scare me. Either way, the implications were staggering.

I carefully replaced it and secured my bag gently on the lowest shelf of the cupboard. I took a few deep breaths, shook my head and went up the companionway.

The others looked at me curiously.

"Couldn't find the napkins?" asked Jasmine.

My heart dropped in sudden fear, but I replied smoothly, "Just wanted to check on everyone after that lurch."

"Rogue wave," said Leyla.

"We're all fine," said Jasmine.

I went over to Leyla where she stood at the wheel. I put my arms around her from the side and whispered in her ear.

"Don't act surprised, just be normal. I want you to keep everyone on deck for a while. Get them involved in a sailing lesson, or tell them it's a nautical tradition to stay above board or something."

She looked quickly at me, and then back straight ahead. She smiled and nodded. I paused. "I love you, Leyla," I whispered.

She turned back and looked at me longer. Her eyes were soft and troubled. She touched my face and said softly. "And I love you, Jonah."

I went below, promising drinks and napkins soon. I turned to the radio. There were two of them. One was clearly a normal stereo of the type you might find in a car. It was mounted flush in the wall underneath one of the storage cupboards, above the desk. Above the stereo was the marine radio. It was maybe ten inches long, and about four inches high. In the middle there was a small dark LCD screen, with some buttons underneath it, apparently for navigating through an electronic menu. On the left was a clearly marked power button, underneath a small speaker. The hand-held microphone plugged in next to the power button and hung on a hook on the wall next to the unit. To the top right of the LCD was a volume knob. Underneath that, in the middle, was a red button behind a switch guard marked "DSTRS", and below that was a channel selector knob.

I found the volume and turned it all the way down. Next, I pushed the power button. The LCD turned green and the number three showed on the screen. I assumed that this was the channel number, like a CB radio. Slowly, I turned the volume knob until I could just hear the weather report that was apparently broadcast continually.

I knew there was a channel that was used to broadcast emergencies, but I didn't know which number it was. I turned the channel selector and felt a series of subtle clicks. The number on the screen didn't change. The weather report continued quietly. I turned the channel knob again. The LCD still read "three," and the same report droned on.

I took the microphone and held down the talk button. "SOS, SOS, SOS" I said clearly, but quietly. "Vessel in trouble near Outer Island." Maybe I was supposed to say "mayday." I had the idea that was for airplanes, but just in case, I repeated that three times also. When I held the talk button down, the weather report continued uninterrupted. I had a vague idea that this was wrong, that my talking was supposed to silence the other broadcast, at least on my end.

I tried switching channels again, but nothing changed. The number steadfastly remained on three, and the mechanical weatherman droned relentlessly on. Time was passing. I didn't know how long it might be before someone wanted to come below. I didn't know how long Leyla could keep them distracted.

I flipped up the switch guard, and pressed the DSTRS button, which Leyla had told us was for emergencies. As far as I could tell, nothing happened. I tried talking into the microphone again, but the weatherman still didn't stop. I paused. Something about the weather broadcast wasn't right. I knew that they used recordings until something changed, but this sounded like exactly the same report I had heard in the marina when we first came on board, several hours ago. I noticed that nothing identified the date, and it cut off and repeated before it gave any information for tomorrow. That didn't seem right somehow.

Madly, I began pushing buttons, trying to call up the radio menu, anything except the weather report. Nothing worked. I shut off the power and put it on again. Still just the same old generic weather. I pushed the distress button again, and then turned down the volume. In desperation, I turned on the stereo below it. It was tuned to an AM station in Ashland, still receiving, though with a lot of static. In vain, I tried the microphone, but I knew it wasn't hooked up to the AM/FM radio.

I began to feel desperate. Someone had planted the bomb, or the fake bomb, and I had to find out who and why before they got suspicious and came below. I went to the cupboard, and found my cell phone. I turned it on, but it couldn't find a signal. It showed I had a text message.

Reflexively, I checked it. It was from Dan Jensen. It read, *"Finally got a lead on Charles Holland. Has a sister, Angela, and one other brother, unidentified still, suspected of being part of the gang. Gang struck again this AM in Ashland WI. We'll get them soon."*

I went cold. *Angela*. Surely it wasn't *this* Angela. But if it wasn't, who had brought the bomb on board? Ashland was not far from Bayfield. They could have robbed the bank there and easily made it up to the Marina to take off with us.

I tried again to use the phone, but it was out of range. I had brought Leyla into the middle of Lake Superior with a gang of murderous criminals. It was time for plan B.

THIRTY-TWO

I went back to the cupboard that held my duffel and removed the bag. The AM radio began relaying the news. The bank robbery was the top headline, of course. I paused for a moment. The bow-cabin was closest. I went forward and pulled one of the Kruger's bags out from under the v-shaped bunk. It held Angela's clothes, including undergarments, and I was embarrassed, but not enough to stop. I grabbed a second bag and unzipped it. I stopped and sat back on my haunches.

Several hundred thousand dollars in cash will do that to you.

The Krugers had another bag of cash as well, and some handgun ammunition. I quickly thrust questions of how's and why's into the future and went to work. I was dimly aware of the boat heaving and swooping on the waves; maybe the swell was getting bigger. The news report started talking about the murder of a professor at the University of Minnesota, Duluth. The man in question was a professor of counseling and women's studies. He was shot to death the night before in his home.

When I had everything shipshape up front, I made my way back to the Stones' cabin, flipping off the radio when I reached the base of the companionway. Jensen's message hadn't said anything about the Stones, but obviously Phil and Angela and had partners. My heart was in my stomach. At that moment, Jasmine came down the companionway, followed by Angela.

"Do you need some help?" asked Jasmine.

"Sure," I said. "You can help me carry drinks" I felt wooden, sure my face would betray me.

I went to the cooler in the galley and removed cans of soda and handed them to the women. I considered telling them I would be right up, but I thought that might be pushing my luck. I grabbed two sodas and some napkins, and went back up into the cockpit in front of them.

Tony was standing at the wheel.

"Leyla's been teaching us how to sail," said Jasmine, handing her husband a can of Diet Coke. We were level with Outer Island on the port side. Directly in front us lay only the lake, a vast freshwater ocean. Most of the islands were low smudges behind us. We couldn't see Michigan or Minnesota, and the Bayfield massif was merely a dim smear. But when I saw the towering clouds to the west, I gave a silent prayer of thanks. The sunlight was fading even as I watched.

"I've got bad news," I said, looking meaningfully at Leyla. I jerked my thumb at the western sky. "I just heard that is turning into a major storm. We need to run home for shelter."

"Are you sure?" asked Angela. She sounded very concerned.

"It sounded pretty serious," I said. I looked at the towering wall of clouds behind us. By a massive stroke of good fortune, the weather appeared to be cooperating with my desperate ploy. The sun was behind the clouds now, and Superior heaved gray sullen waves at us, each one seemingly bigger than the last. Here and there, the wind whipped the top of a wave into white foam.

"It's not worth taking the risk," agreed Leyla.

"How did you hear about it?" asked Angela. "On the radio?"

"That's right," I confirmed.

Angela's face went dark, and I knew my mistake at once. Of course they knew the radio didn't work – they must have rigged the weather report themselves. And then just like that, Angela and Phil were holding guns. Big, black automatics.

"I'm sorry," said Angela, "but we won't be going home."

Leyla stared at the guns, standing motionless with her can of Coke poised between her hands in the act of opening it.

Stone gave a quick glance at Jasmine, nothing more. Jasmine took a breath and let it out. She seemed almost relieved. I was puzzled. I expected them to produce weapons as well.

I looked over at Outer Island, maybe two miles away to port. In normal water, I could probably make it. I wondered if Leyla could. But Superior was already well below fifty degrees Fahrenheit; sometimes it was as low as thirty-nine by this point in the year. Water that cold stole your breath, slowed your reactions and drained the life out of your body. The waves were now rearing up to five feet or more. I probably couldn't last for half a mile.

Stone caught my glance and almost imperceptibly shook his head. I turned back to Angela.

"Angela," I said gently and calmly, hoping my face didn't betray me, "we can still talk about your marriage. You don't need this cruise so badly. But it isn't safe to stay out here in the storm."

She gave a short, harsh laugh. "Don't try that crap on me. You found something, or figured it out," she said. "Because I know the radio report didn't say anything about a storm."

My heart sank. Everything might depend on them believing that I knew nothing up until the moment they pulled their guns. "Yes, it did," I said. "The AM news station in Ashland said it. There was a lot of static, but I heard it clearly enough. You can go listen right now." I prayed that the past few minutes hadn't taken us out of range.

"AM news?" asked Phil quizzically.

"Damn it!" said Angela. "Richard forgot about the regular stereo."

"What are we gonna do about the storm?" asked Phil.

"Well, it's too late now," said Angela. "We'll have to keep on anyway. Actually, it'll help to sell the story."

Stone started to turn toward Angela. "Listen," he began.

"Shut up!" snapped Angela. "Keep your hands on the wheel until I tell you otherwise."

She smiled without mirth. "I guess I am the captain now. You will all do what I say without question."

"Angela," I said. "I don't know what –"

"You shut up too," she said, gesturing with her gun.

"Can you drop us off on Outer Island?" asked Jasmine. She was looking at Angela intensely. Angela looked back. It struck me as a weird exchange.

"Sorry," said Angela after a moment. "Can't be done."

There was no talking for a minute, and the sound of the boat plowing into the thickening water was loud. Spray flew continuously from the bow, showering us like a light rain. The darkness was growing, and the boat began to push farther to starboard as the wind from the west strengthened.

"Turn a little to starboard," Leyla instructed Stone.

"Shut up," said Angela. "I'm giving the orders."

"Fine," said Leyla coolly. "If he doesn't do it, we'll all be in the water in about three minutes. The cold will kill us long before we can reach land. We'll be dead within forty-five minutes." She was so calm and brave and fragile and beautiful, I didn't know if I wanted to cheer or cry.

Angela looked at her, and Leyla met her gaze calmly. At last Angela nodded reluctantly. "Do it," she said. "For now." She stepped over to Stone and held the gun up to his side. "But not too much."

Tony nudged the wheel a little. We leveled out a little bit.

"We need to shut the hatch over your berth – in fact, any window or skylight that is open."

"Philip, go get the GPS," said Angela. "While you're down there, make sure everything is shut up tight."

"We already have a GPS," said Leyla. "Right here."

Phil hesitated. "Go!" snapped Angela. He went down the companionway.

I tensed. There were four of us and only one person with a gun. Stone caught my eye, and then without moving his head, flicked his eyes towards his left shoulder where Angela stood. Angela saw me looking at him. She stepped smoothly away from Stone and put her left arm around Leyla, holding the gun high where her jaw met her neck.

"One of you stupid testosterone junkies might be willing to take a bullet," she said. "But are you willing for her to?"

I sagged, weakened by the rush of unused adrenaline. Stone's mouth tightened. Jasmine stood tense, not moving except to brace herself against the swoop and dive of the boat.

A little later, Phil emerged, holding a small GPS unit. "I turned it on," he said. "The course is all set."

"Show it to her," said Angela, jerking her head at Leyla.

"What about it?" said Leyla as she looked at the screen.

"That's where we are going," said Angela. "You need to follow that course, or your boyfriend will start losing body parts."

"I can't run the boat with you attached to my side," said Leyla. I decided it was cheering that I most felt like doing. I was awed by her calm strength and courage.

"Phil," said Angela. "Get the other one."

Phil smirked and slipped behind Jasmine, wrapping an arm around her front. He held the gun up to her head. He seemed to be holding her pretty tight.

"Easy," said Jasmine. She sounded more irritated than anything else. Angela looked at him sourly. "Don't get distracted," she snapped. She looked first at Stone and then me. "Now behave boys," she said, and released Leyla.

The boat was heaving more violently than before and the sky above us was now already completely gray. Angela lost her balance and half-fell onto the starboard cockpit bench. I started to move but Phil said sharply, "Easy, or Jasmine gets it."

"This is only going to get worse," said Leyla. "We can't make it through the storm like this."

"Sorry, sister," said Angela. "We are going through this storm, whether you like it or not." She gathered herself together. "We need to immobilize them," she said to Phil."

"You will die with us," said Leyla. She was calm, but she had to speak quite loudly now to be heard above the sound of the wind and waves. "It is suicide to carry this much sail into a storm like this." The wind was whipping her thick dark hair around her face. Her dark eyes were steady and serious. There was depth and strength I had never guessed at in Leyla.

Angela hesitated. "OK," she too, spoke loudly to be heard over the increasing tumult. "What do we do?"

"We need to start by taking down the sails. Then, we really should run for cover."

The *Tiny Dancer* heeled far over to starboard again as sudden blast of wind slammed into the big sail. I held on to the port side railing as we passed fifty degrees of slope. I glanced quickly toward Phil, but he had simply taken Jasmine to the deck, lying with his left arm around and underneath her, the right hand holding the gun to her temple. I thought he was holding it kind of loosely, but it wasn't worth risking her life to try and get to him. Slowly, the heavy keel pulled us back more or less upright.

"You two go below," called Angela to Phil. I'll check with you every five minutes. If I don't check in, then kill her." She looked at me and then Stone. "Do you understand?"

"Got it," I said shortly. Stone nodded. Jasmine went down into the cabin, followed by Phil, who didn't seem to be covering her very closely. Angela braced herself in the front port corner of the cockpit. She waved her gun at us. "Now get to it."

First, Leyla opened one of the cockpit lockers, and handed life jackets to all of us. She hesitated when she came to Angela, but Angela reached for it, so Leyla let her have it.

After we had secured the life vests, Leyla took the wheel from Stone, and called out instructions to us. We all had to lean to port, and crouch and hold on to things in order to keep our feet. I loosened a rope to port while Stone cranked the mainsail closer to the boat. We started heeling over again, but Leyla turned more to starboard and we leveled out a little more. "Get up to the mast," she called to me. I climbed out of the cockpit to port, and scrambled forward, holding onto the cable railing, and then the ropes until I was kneeling at the foot of the mast. Stone came around on the starboard side. I freed the rope that kept the big sail fully open. Stone and I reached up and grabbed big handfuls of canvas, pulling toward the deck. As the sail came down, the starboard pressure decreased even more. We were still swooping up and down waves that now approached ten feet high, but we no longer felt like were falling over so much to starboard. Following Leyla's shouted commands, we pulled the sail all the way down, and then secured the canvas in a rough, untidy bundle around the boom. Leyla let the boom out a little to starboard so it would be out of the way of the people in the cockpit.

The waves had whitened all around us. I wasn't completely sure if it was raining or not, but we were soaked with either rain or spray. The temperature had dropped twenty degrees, and the cold began to numb my fingers.

"Wave! Wave! Wave!" screamed Leyla. I caught a brief glimpse of a white-streaked gray wall climbing in front of the bow. I dove for the mast and got one hand on it before the water hit me.

THIRTY-THREE

The water was smooth and slow and very heavy. It was like a giant had poured the contents of a large swimming pool out onto the *Tiny Dancer*. The cold was deadly. My breath exploded out of me with the shock. I clutched at the mast with my left hand, but I couldn't reach all the way around it. I couldn't lift my right hand against the massive flow of icy water. My hands had been numb and freezing to start with. Slowly, my fingers slipped, plucked off one-by-one by the inexorable force of Lake Superior. Dimly, I heard a scream behind me.

I couldn't breathe. Suddenly, I lost my hold entirely and slid helplessly backwards. Something slammed into my chest. I felt a sickening weightlessness, and then landed with bruising force on my face inside the cockpit.

"Jonah!" Leyla screamed. "Jonah!"

I forced myself up to my hands and knees, hacking and coughing. Leyla was kneeling beside me. The wind was howling now, and there could be no doubt that water was falling from the sky as well as whipping up from the waves. It was as dark as dusk. The cockpit was half full of water, but it drained out quickly through drainage holes made for that very purpose. I recalled vaguely that they were called scuppers.

"I'm OK," I said weakly.

"Watch the wheel!" shouted Angela sharply. She was completely soaked, but she remained braced in the corner, her gun held steady. Leyla stood up shakily and returned to the wheel.

"This is crazy," she called. "We're all going to die unless we get out of this." She was taking small steps and straining at the wheel as it bucked in her hands.

Angela shook her head. "I have every confidence in you. Follow the GPS course."

I sat back on my heels. Stone was also as wet as if he'd stepped fully clothed into a bath. His legs were dangling into the cockpit, while his arms were still tightly intertwined with the rope that went from the traveler on the deck, up to the boom. As I watched, he let go and slid down to a sitting position on the starboard bench.

He glanced at me. "That was close." If I was given to imagination, I might have thought he looked mildly concerned. Suddenly, I was very glad he was with us on this trip. I returned his look.

"Yeah. Fun though."

The corner of his mouth twitched. I swear it did.

Stone patted his soaking blue jeans to make sure everything was there. He patted again and then looked down. He glanced all around the cockpit, then stood up and looked at the deck forward. He sat down again and started to swear vehemently.

"What's up?" I asked.

"I lost my pager."

I was puzzled. Surely a pager should be the least of his worries at this moment. Human nature is funny though. Sometimes we focus on peripheral details to avoid dealing with the big problems right in front of us.

Angela smiled like she was sharing my thoughts. "Your pager is irrelevant now. You aren't going to work, even if you're called in."

Stone took a deep breath and then shrugged.

A big gust slapped the foresail, and we tipped far over to starboard again. I held my breath while the waves pounded at us, keeping us over. As slow as spring thaw, we came up again, dragged by the great counter-weight of the leaden keel.

"We should switch to diesel and bring down the foresail too," said Leyla. "This wind, it's safer with no canvas."

"Do it!" snapped Angela.

"We can do this from the cockpit," said Leyla. "Jonah, take the wheel."

I did. Immediately I understood why Leyla had been moving about. The wheel was like a live thing trying to jump out of my grip, first pushing down to starboard and then leaping back up the other way. I fought to hold it steady, taking little steps to keep my balance against the plunge and roll of the boat and the kick and buck of the wheel.

Leyla reached around me and turned a key. Through the increasing roar of the storm, I could feel, more than hear, the engine throbbing to life. She pushed the throttle lever forward about one third of the way.

"Keep it there," she shouted. I did my best. Then, with Tony Stone's help, she cranked the foresail until it was completely rolled up on the forestay.

"Now the dodger," she shouted, shaking her head. "I should have had that up the whole time."

The folded-up dodger was apparently what had struck me in the chest when I was swept back into the cockpit. Leyla and Stone unsnapped the retaining straps, and with some difficulty pulled up a canvas hood that was stretched across a metal frame. It looked a little bit like one of those manually operated convertible tops on an old car, except it was backwards, folding out the windshield first, then a yard or so of canvas roof, leaving the back open.

There was something wrong with it, however. The metal frame appeared bent, and I realized that it was probably my body that had done it. They wrestled with it for a few minutes. Finally Stone was able to get the starboard side strapped tight into place. Immediately, the noise in the cockpit abated a little bit and the spray slammed up against the clear plastic windshield instead of onto us. But the rear port side of the hood flapped insanely in the wind. Stone stepped over to where Leyla struggled with it.

While they were trying to get it secured, Angela rapped on the closed companionway door. I glimpsed Phil's face as he opened it. They exchanged a few words, and the door shut again.

Leyla and Tony finally settled for tying down the port side of the dodger with a bit of rope secured to one of the many cleats lining the gunwale. It still flapped and shuddered, and water flew through that side fairly easily.

"It will have to do for now," said Leyla in the slightly quieter air of the cockpit.

"Speed up now," said Angela. Leyla looked at her without comment and then leaned in front of me and pushed the throttle all the way forward. The result was not spectacular. "These engines aren't made for speed," she said.

A minute later, there was a rap on the companionway door. Angela moved over to Leyla and put the gun against her head.

"You know the drill," said Angela to Stone and me. "Behave if you value her life."

Phil emerged from the cabin a few moments later.

"All secure?" she asked him.

He nodded. He stared for a moment at the wind and the waves. "This is getting worse."

"A lot worse," I said. "Superior is a man-killer. We need to run back for cover." I glanced behind me, towards where the islands should be, but nothing was visible except big waves and driving rain.

"Shut up Borden," said Phil. He walked over and stood by me. He pushed the power-button of the *Tiny Dancer's* GPS. Then he looked at the handheld unit which Angela had passed to him. He programmed the boat's GPS to match his. He watched for a few moments, looking first at one screen, then the other. Finally, he nodded.

"Now," said Angela. "We have an appointment to keep, so we are going to follow the course on this GPS. You all will have your turn steering." She turned to Phil. "Show us how to do it," she commanded.

We braced ourselves against the heaving waves as Phil explained how to hold our course to the destination indicated on the GPS.

"Whoever is in the cabin will have our handheld unit," said Angela. "If we see you going off course, we'll hurt someone. If it happens a second time, someone will die."

"Where is this?" I asked. "Where are you taking us?"

"Nowhere," said Phil. "It doesn't really concern you."

I was no GPS expert, but it looked to me like we were heading into the middle of Lake Superior in the teeth of an autumn storm that had only just begun.

THIRTY-FOUR

The waves were piling up and white spray seemed to fly everywhere. Sail or no sail, the wind from the northwest pushed us a little to starboard, while fifteen-foot waves tossed us around like a toy. Every so often we hit one wrong, and it crashed across the deck, burying our bow underwater for a few heart-sickening seconds. But each time, the *Tiny Dancer* heaved herself up like Archimedes slowly getting out of his bathtub. The water washed around the dodger for the most part, though some of it still flowed into the cockpit, only to drain out the scuppers. The sky was black, and the steadily increasing wind roared and plucked eerie tunes from the rigging.

Angela waved her gun at Leyla. "Take the wheel. Someone will relieve you in two hours. If we start moving off course, we'll castrate your loverboy first, and only afterwards send someone up to correct you. You understand?"

"Stay on course," said Leyla grimly.

"Philip," said Angela. He went down the companionway. Stone started to move after him.

"Wait!" snapped Angela. "Let him get to the bottom and out of your way first. You try anything, and that pretty little girl down there won't be so pretty anymore."

We waited a beat. "Okay." She waved us forward with the gun.

Stone waved me ahead of him. I was one step from the bottom when the boat lurched just a little more than it had on the previous wave, and he came crashing down on top of me. We fell to the cabin deck with him on top, bruising me to breathlessness.

A bare millisecond after we landed and were still, he coughed softly and sighed a little bit. I strained in shock, but I couldn't see his face. Then I heard a loud click and Phil was standing, legs low and spread apart to brace against the roll of the boat, his gun about one foot from Tony's head. I couldn't see Angela because Stone was on top of me, but I heard the barely controlled rage in her voice.

"Do you have a death wish?"

Stone lay still on top of me. "I lost my balance is all," he mumbled. He coughed softly again, but didn't move.

"Get up," said Angela.

Slowly, with what seemed a great deal of trouble, Stone got himself off me, but not without pushing and poking me and using me as if I was some kind footstool to assist him. My breath began to come back. I rolled over onto my hands and knees, and then sat down with my back against the galley wall. Stone clambered to his feet and Phil grabbed his arm, shoving him into the straight settee on the forward port side.

"Now you," said Angela, who was down in the cabin. The door behind her was shut. I got up slowly, making a show of feeling my aches and bruises. "To the other settee." She gestured to the starboard U-shaped bench that went around the eating table. "Hands on the table, always visible," she said. I put my hands on the table and sat down with my back to the forward bulkhead, facing the stern. Jasmine was standing next to me, her hands on either side of the great steel mast-pole, secured by plastic cable-tie type handcuffs.

Stone glanced at her. "I lost my pager, Jaz," he said. He sounded like it was the end of the world.

For a moment, her face looked shocked and worried, but quickly her expression became bored again. "Now is not the time to worry about work," she said.

"He just about went overboard," I said. "Both of us did. The wave probably ripped it off his belt. It's at the bottom of Superior now."

She stared at me, and then looked at Tony.

"The pager is the least of your worries," said Phil. He pointed to me. "Move around," indicating that I should sit at the top of the U with my back to the starboard wall. It was a pretty good strategic arrangement. Jasmine stood just out of Stone's reach, against the mast-foot. She couldn't move from the mast in any case. My hands were visible on the table, and it wasn't possible to make any sudden moves – I was encumbered by the table, which extended over my legs, almost to my stomach. No way was I getting out of there fast. Stone was out in the open, but too far from anyone to make a move. He still looked a little groggy from the fall.

"We've heard about you, Borden," said Angela. "We know you are a killer, but so are we. So sit tight back there. I don't think that even you can move fast enough to get anywhere before we shoot you."

"You shoot me, you might put a hole in the boat," I said. "You'd be killing yourself."

"Hollow-point bullets," said Phil. "They spread out on impact. Made to stay inside the body they hit. Do a lot of damage to the target, but not to anything behind it. If we'd used them before, maybe you wouldn't be walking so well right now."

"Shut up Phil," snapped Angela. But I could see the gleam of Stone's eyes under his lowered brow.

"You –" I paused to feign incredulity. "You were the bank robbers?"

Angela stepped over to Phil and slapped him on the face. "You're an idiot, Philip, as I've told you before. They don't need to know anything."

I looked closely at Phil, but the slap did not seem to shock him. He took it as if it were a normal way of relating. "Sorry, Angela," he mumbled. I could see the red flush spreading across his whole face, not just where her hand had struck him.

There was a long silence that stretched out even longer until it simply became the way things were. The sound of storm was louder down here. The boat creaked and groaned as she heaved through the water. I could hear banging and thumping from above, and I assumed that various ropes and pulleys were being slapped against the deck by the angry waves. The engine beat stolidly through the deck. I slowly began to warm up.

"Can I take off my jacket?" I asked. "My legs are cold, and I want to cover them."

"Nice and slow. Stand up where we can see what you are doing."

I couldn't really stand up straight. But I slid my back up the wall with my knees bent, and slowly, awkwardly removed my coat. My helpless position and easy movements seemed to satisfy them. After it was off, I held it up in my hand. Angela nodded. I sat back down and spread it over my legs under the table. I fumbled a little bit.

"Hands back on the table," said Angela.

I put them back in view. I let my head droop with shock and weariness. My shoulders slumped in defeat. But inside, I was buzzing. When Stone fell on me and coughed, he had whispered "FBI. Wait my signal." And when he was getting up, pushing and pulling on me, he had stuffed a knife into my jacket pocket.

THIRTY-FIVE

Time passed. Phil sat on the outside stern-end of the U-shaped settee to my left, facing forward. Angela settled on the companionway steps, the whole cabin in front of her. *Take the Money and Run* was flowing through my head endlessly. I got the irony, I hated it, but I couldn't stop looping that song over and over again. The pitching and rolling of the *Tiny Dancer* was getting worse. All of us had to brace ourselves constantly against violent movements of the boat. I moved a little, to try and keep my muscles loose, but it didn't help. I had been cold and wet, and now sitting still had begun to make me stiff and sore. I leaned back against the hull and glanced around aimlessly.

"What are your plans for us?" I asked Phil.

"Shut up," said Angela.

"That's nice," I said. "But I'd like more specifics."

No one said anything.

"Chatty group," I said. I looked at Stone, sitting against the opposite settee. His head was down, but he was nodding imperceptibly, like maybe he wanted me to keep talking. I glanced sidewise to my right at Jasmine, and she too gave the tiniest nod.

"So, a sailboat seems like a slow way to get where you want to go." I could have been talking to a trout I had just caught.

"So." I stretched again. "You guys are the bank robbers that have confounded everyone on the North Shore. Pretty clever modus operandi –

small banks, small police forces, no FBI." I was careful not to look at Stone when I said that. Still no response. I was used to preaching to tough crowds, but this was ridiculous. I swallowed and gathered myself before my next comment.

"You have your flaws, though. You tend to get your partners shot, don't you? First my dad shoots one of you, then me. Pretty ironic, huh?"

With an inarticulate cry, Phil dove across the table at me. I caught a glimpse of him swinging his gun like a club, and then something very hard and sharp-edged struck me high on the left side of the head. I flung up my arms, and caught another blow on the forearm. Through the ringing of my head and the blood that had begun to flow down into my eyes, I sensed another blow. I twisted towards it, caught his arm and pulled it down, jamming his wrist between me and the edge of the table. I slammed it hard and he grunted and dropped the gun onto the floor under the table. I ducked under after it, but before I could reach the weapon, Angela's voice cut like a whip-crack. "Touch it and he dies."

Slowly I pulled myself up above the table top. Angela stood with her left hand around Stone's head, the gun screwed into his right ear. Phil was kneeling on the aft portion of the settee, kitty-corner from me, wringing his right hand.

"Philip, get the gun," said Angela, speaking as if to a slow child.

He backed off the seat, knelt to his hands and knees and scooted under the table. A moment later, I gasped as he struck me in the shin with the butt of the gun.

"Enough, Philip," said Angela. "We need him able-bodied."

Phil emerged from the under the table, chest heaving. My shin felt like I had kicked a coffee table with it as hard as I could.

"I wanna kill him," said Phil. "Can we just kill him now?"

"Shut up, Philip," said Angela patiently. She looked at me. "You killed his twin brother, so he doesn't like you very much, you see."

My face felt wooden. Blood dripped down my forehead. "So the man I shot died then," I said. "I'm so sorry, I didn't mean to." And I didn't. What kind of ordinary person ever would?

Phil just glared at me with pure hatred.

I thought about pointing out that if no one had been shooting at me, I would not have fired back. I might have suggested that if one didn't rob banks, one would be less likely to get shot. But I didn't think it was what I would call a teachable moment. And truthfully, I was too distressed about my own part in it to say anything more.

Angela took a smooth step backwards. "Come stand in the galley, Philip," she said to her husband. She grabbed his arm and pulled him over as he passed her and whispered something into his ear. He took a breath and nodded, and then moved behind the galley counter, covering me with his gun, leaving Angela to cover Stone.

I wiped at my bloody face. Angela got a washcloth from the galley for me, and I held it to my head, which began to throb.

It was not exactly quiet, with the roar of the storm, the beat of the engine and crash of water against the vessel, but somehow inside the cabin, things began to settle down again. Stone had not had time to act during the confusion – Angela was too quick. I didn't know what else I could do. I wasn't so sure about the future either. One of my captors clearly wanted me dead.

Stone hunched far over, bracing his elbows on his knees, his head hanging low. Jasmine slid her bound hands down the mast foot and sat on the floor, leaning her head on the brightly polished pole. I was tired and sore, but I didn't dare fall asleep while I waited for a signal from Stone. I started to get hungry.

Suddenly, without warning, the engine stopped. A moment later, it coughed and sputtered, then died again. We heard the fruitless sound of a starter laboring to give life to an engine that would not catch. Stone looked up, alert. I watched him.

Immediately, our movement in the water changed. Though it was rough before, our steerage had given the boat a certain rhythm, almost predictable. But now we bounced around any which way, and the movements grew more and more violent.

"What the – " said Angela, turning for the companionway as the door slid open and Leyla's form appeared, haggard, wet and cold.

"Now!" said Stone. Across from me, his right hand dropped smoothly to his ankle and then he stood up rapidly, holding a gun, straightening his arm toward Angela. "FBI!" he shouted. "Drop your guns." Time slowed down for me, as it always seems to in such moments. I threw my jacket into Phil's face. He fired blind twice, the boom shockingly loud in the confined cabin, but I was already under the table, squirming like mad for the walkway.

I emerged and looked up at Stone. He was hesitating as he noticed Leyla in the companionway above and behind Angela, in the line of fire. Angela herself was still half turned between Leyla and the rest of the cabin. Then a violent wave threw Stone off balance. Angela brought up her gun and fired four times in rapid succession. Leyla screamed.

The noise of the shots was like a physical blow. Stone's gun clattered to the floor, and he sat back down heavily on the settee.

My ears were ringing, though I still dimly heard the waves and wind in the background. Jasmine was calling Stone's name urgently. Leyla had sat down on the top step of the companionway. As I watched, water cascaded across her back, and she turned and pulled the doors shut.

Angela's weapon was trained on me. "Stay away from his gun." Her face was flushed and she was breathing fast. She was smiling.

"I'm kicking it to you," I said. I pushed it away from me with my foot and turned to Stone, who was half reclined on the settee to my right. His entire right side was a mass of blood.

"I can help," Jasmine said. "Let me go, let me help him."

Angela looked at her with hard eyes. "Why did he have a gun?" she asked.

Jasmine shrugged. "I never knew about the ankle holster."

Angela glared at her for a moment longer, and then turned to me. "You can help him. But if you find any more weapons on him, you just hand them carefully to me." I was aware of her gun, very near my head. She had a strange look of satisfaction on her face. She looked like I felt just after I landed a big fish.

The boat was plunging ever more wildly. It was hard to keep my balance.

"I'm trained in first aid for this sort of thing," said Jasmine. "Let me help."

Angela gave her a funny look. Jasmine cut her eyes quickly at me and then met Angela's gaze again.

"Tell me what to do, Jasmine," I said. Angela gave a shrug.

"What do you see?" asked Jasmine. "Where is he hit?"

Tony was conscious, but he wasn't speaking. His eyes were glassy and his breathing was labored. I gently pulled his jacket aside. There was a lot of blood. Some of it seemed to originate from his right shoulder. "Shoulder." I carefully explored more and found a long tear in his shirt and a gash across the right side of his ribcage where a bullet had plowed an ugly furrow through the skin without penetrating the body. "Flesh wound on the right side of the ribs."

Tony seemed like he was trying to whisper to me, but couldn't make the necessary noise. I leaned down with my ear to his lips. "High, right side of the chest," he said, barely breathing the words. "Tell them I've got a lung wound." I explored the area. It was covered in blood, from his shoulder, but I could find no wound. Stone grabbed my right arm, in front of my body, where Phil and Angela could not see. His grip was like iron. He pumped my arm twice, looked meaningfully into my eyes and then let go.

I made a show of looking further. "He's hit in the chest too," I said, pointing to his blood soaked shirt below the shoulder wound. "Maybe clipped in the top of the lung."

Jasmine took a deep breath. "Okay," she said. "We need clean cloths for bandages. Any dishtowels or anything?"

"I'll get them," said Leyla. Phil and Angela moved out of her way as she went to the galley cupboards. She brought the dishtowels forward and I took them. Following Jasmine's instructions, I bound up Stone's two wounds, plus his fake one. I was glad he was not hit in any vital spot, but his shoulder was an awful mess. He probably didn't have to fake the agony that he expressed as I worked on him. It took me much longer than it might have, because the boat was bucking like a prize rodeo bull.

"Since he wasn't hit low, we can give him a pain killer," said Jasmine. "But not Aspirin or Advil – those thin the blood." Under Angela's watchful eyes, Leyla got a glass of water and some Tylenol. Right before she brought it to me, Stone's head slipped down to his bloody shoulder. I lifted his head up again. His eyes were still open, and he gave me a nanosecond wink, more imagined than seen. I supported his neck and held the glass while Leyla put the Tylenol in his mouth. He took it, and then blew a flimsy red bubble of blood out of his mouth. Angela saw it, and so did Jasmine. Jasmine said in a strange dispassionate voice, "He's hit in the lung. He won't last long without surgery."

"He should have thought of that beforehand," said Angela, which seemed a little hypocritical to me. Jasmine looked at Angela. "Any need to keep up with this still? These other two aren't much of a threat, and I can't do anything like this anyway."

Angela shrugged. "I guess not."

"Good," said Jasmine. "Then get me out of these stupid cuffs."

Phil stepped over wordlessly, and cut Jasmine's plastic's handcuffs. She stood up and stretched, and then ran her fingers through her thick dark hair. She reached under her fleece, and pulled out a black leather wallet, opened it and tossed it on the table. It was an FBI badge, accompanied by her photo ID. "Glad to be finally done with that," she said to no one in particular.

Jasmine walked up to Stone and grabbed his face in one hand, pinching his cheeks like an angry mother does to a naughty child. She glared at him. "Now, you Neanderthal SOB," she said in low, bitter voice, "I'm going to enjoy watching you die slowly."

THIRTY-SIX

I stared at her. I could feel Leyla doing the same. In the last five minutes, Jasmine had been an ordinary civilian caught in horrible situation, then an FBI agent deliberately hunting her quarry, and now what? An agent turned bad, a criminal?

"What is this, Jasmine?" I asked.

"I'm quitting my job," she said sweetly. "They just don't know it yet. In fact, as far as they'll ever know, I am about to die in the line of duty, along with Tony here." She looked at me significantly. "They'll probably give me a posthumous medal – which I will be alive to enjoy."

"Jasmine," said Angela. "Don't talk so much."

Jasmine shrugged. "What does it matter now? The only serious obstacle was him." She jerked her thumb at Stone.

"We talked about this," said Angela. "Just wait until tomorrow."

"Fine. Suit yourself."

There were several long moments of silence in the cabin, while the storm beat upon the outside of the vessel. The boat shuddered. Leyla shook herself. "We've lost the engine. We need to put out a sea-anchor to straighten us out to the waves and slow our drift, or we'll be battered to pieces."

"Not so fast," said Phil. He pointed at Stone, who had closed his eyes and was trying to brace himself from bouncing around and aggravating his wounds. "He said they were FBI."

"Phil," said Angela in a sarcastic and pained voice, "try not to be such an idiot. We *knew* he was FBI. Jasmine was too. She gave him to us."

Phil was suspicious, but perhaps not overly bright. "Okay, but what if Borden was working with them, you know, wearing wire or something?"

"A *wire*, out here?" asked Jasmine incredulously. "A wire is a short-range transmitter. You have to be within half a mile. There's no one within two dozen miles of us. Besides, he wasn't cooperating with the FBI – *I'm* FBI, remember? I'd know."

"Maybe he was working with Stone, not you."

"Tony was my partner. We would have worked it together."

"You didn't work *this* together with him, did you?" asked Angela. "Are you sure he had no suspicions of you?"

"Doesn't matter now, does it? We've taken care of him. But if it makes you feel better, search Borden and Bennett. In fact, *I'll* do it."

Jasmine thrust me roughly against the closed door that led to the bow cabin. "Stay still, *pastor*," she said in a mocking voice. She patted me down lightly.

"Clean," she said. I breathed a sigh of relief. When I took off my jacket, I had hidden Tony's knife in my shoe, underneath my foot.

Angela searched Leyla, somewhat half-heartedly. "She's clean too."

"Okay," said Leyla. "We need to get that sea anchor out, right away."

"No," said Angela. "We need to keep on. Put up the sail again."

"That's very dangerous," said Leyla. "We could capsize, founder, all sorts of things."

"So make it safer," snapped Angela. "Can't you just put part of it out? What do they call that, 'shortening the sail?'"

Leyla's shoulders slumped. "We could do that I guess. But it's still pretty dangerous to carry *any* sail in this storm."

"Do it," said Angela. "And get us back on course to that GPS point."

"I need one other person to help me," said Leyla.

I could see they didn't like it. If one of them went, it shortened the odds below deck, though I had no idea how I would take out one person armed with a gun, let alone two. But if I went up with Leyla, they would have only one hostage below, a man they thought might already by dying.

"What are we going to do?" I asked. "There's nowhere to go, and you'll kill Tony and us if we try anything. We've seen that you'll use those guns."

Angela chewed her lip for a minute. "One of us could go," said Jasmine. "But that leaves one of us cold and wet and slow. Why be more uncomfortable than we have to? Borden is right, what are they gonna do?"

"Okay, go," said Angela. "When you are done, Leyla comes in and Borden stays out to steer."

I took my jacket from the galley counter. There were two holes in it from when Phil fired his gun.

We staggered up the stairs, and stepped into the cockpit, pulling the doors shut after us.

The wind roared like a thousand tortured souls and plucked a deadly threnody from the rigging. The dodger offered little protection anymore, and the spray and rain were constant. It was like being doused with ice water every five seconds. Actually, we *were* being doused with ice water every five seconds. It was full dark, but I caught glimpses of the wild and angry waves. They were heaving twenty feet and more, creating an ever-changing violent landscape of hills and valleys. I had to hold on to the rails to keep my footing.

"How did you manage out here?" I shouted. "This is insane!"

"It's easier when we are under way," Leyla shouted back. "The dodger gives more protection then, and the waves are more predictable."

We both strapped life vests on. As Leyla directed, we freed the appropriate lines. She swung the starboard one around a winch roller as I handed her the handle. She began to crank. The rope tightened and then stopped.

"It's not working," she called. "It's hung up on something."

She tried again, to no avail.

"How important is this?" I asked, squinting through the deluge.

"Probably life or death."

"Okay," I said. My head was throbbing and my shin was aching. I was freezing once more, and icy water had seeped behind the life vest into the bullet holes in my jacket. I took a breath, grabbed the cable life-line, and put my foot on the cockpit bench.

"Jonah!" shouted Leyla. "What are you doing?"

"Going to fix it," I bellowed back.

We stared at each other for a moment, water streaming down our faces. "You said life or death."

Her shoulders slumped in resignation. "Let's at least rig a rope," she said.

We found a rope and secured one end of it to one of the cleats in the cockpit. I spent the next three minutes trying to tie a bowline around my waist. I had almost no feeling left in my fingers. When I was finally secure, Leyla pulled on it to check it. It held. She pulled again and I stumbled into her arms. We held each other tightly for a long moment.

"I love you, Jonah," she said into my ear. "Be careful."

"I love you too," I said, and climbed out of the shelter of the cockpit.

It was worse on deck. I had been wrong about the dodger offering no protection. As soon as I stood up, the wind slammed me forward and I sprawled onto my knees, my hands scrabbling for something to hold onto. I slid to the starboard edge, and grabbed the lifeline. Here, higher up on the boat, the pitching, corkscrewing motion was like that of a roller coaster designed by an unimaginably manic personality. The wind battered at me and the spray felt like bullets of ice pelting me all over. I could feel the tension on the rope around my body as Leyla slowly gave me slack. Reluctantly, I let go of the cable lifeline and felt for the jib-sheet – the rope we needed, that was jammed somewhere. Inching forward on hands and knees, I felt along the line for tangles and obstructions. After roughly ten feet, the sheet ran through a line organizer that routed about a half dozen ropes around the deck. My fingers were numb and the moments jarred by in agony as I tried to make sure that the obstruction wasn't in the organizer. I spent another twenty seconds trying to make sure that I followed the correct rope out of the forward side of the organizer; twenty seconds of lashing wind and freezing water and pitching blind through the darkness.

At last I was reasonably sure I had the right rope, and I continued forward. A few feet further on, I found that the wind had tangled the jib sheet with another rope, I couldn't tell which one. I held on to the lifeline with my right hand, while with my left I plucked at the knot. I could barely feel it through the numbness of my fingers. I was closer to the bow now, and waves regularly swept up over the deck here. I felt like I was sitting at the edge of the tide at the beach, except that the shore was heaving and jostling like a crazed water-buffalo.

I was making no progress on the knot. There was a little lip at the very edge of the deck, maybe an inch or two high. I think I had heard Leyla call it a toe-rail. I turned my back to the lifelines, kneeling down and bracing my toes against the toe-rail. Now I could use two hands on the knot.

Another wave swept over the deck, covering my thighs. It lifted my feet from their brace as the deck canted down behind me, and I slid quickly and easily over the edge, underneath the lifelines.

THIRTY-SEVEN

I caught myself on the toe-rail. Holding on with my left hand, I flung my right upwards and grabbed onto the lifeline. The cold metal bit into the palm of my hands as it took my weight. My chest was at deck level, while the rest of me hung there, my feet dragging in the water below. A second later, I was submerged all the way above my waist as the starboard forward quarter dipped down and a wave foamed across the deck from the port side to splash into my face. The cold was like physical blow striking my entire body at once. Abruptly, I was heaved up and out of the water again, only to be dipped once more like a grotesque fondue item in a feast of the storm-gods. Only, instead of cooking me, the fondue was slowly freezing me.

Twice, three times, I was submerged to my chest and then hauled back out. My hands were so numb, I couldn't tell if my grip was firm or not. I was panting for breath that was repeatedly stolen by the cold. On the fourth roll, as the water came up around me, I took advantage of my suddenly lightened body-weight to swing my right leg up over the toe-rail. In my numbness I missed clumsily, merely kicking the side of the boat with my toes. As the boat rolled back to port, my body fell back down with a cruel jerk against my arms. It was getting harder and harder to clench my hands. The next time I went into the water, I was motivated by desperation. I drove my right leg high and forward like a peripatetic roundhouse kick. I pulled my heel back to meet the toe-rail, and found I had thrown my leg all the way over the bottom cable of the lifeline. I wrapped my leg around and held on. The roll to port lifted me out of the water, and I tumbled back inside the lifelines, on deck once more.

I sat for a moment, holding on to the lifelines, panting hard. Finally, scrabbling in the dark with numb hands, I found the tangle. It was near the skylight hatch that was over the forward cabin. I could see the light from the main cabin filtering faintly through the closed door and then up to the skylight. I knelt with my legs on either side of the skylight and gripped hard with my thighs. Working feverishly with the last remnants of feeling in my fingers, I finally freed the loops and twists that held the jib sheet. I pulled on it twice to signal Leyla and felt in return when she pulled it tight to keep the rope free of further encumbrances.

Feeling old and lame, I found the lifelines and crawled back to the cockpit. I slithered in face first and lay on the floor, breathing hard.

"Jonah!" said Leyla, kneeling next to me. "What happened?"

"Almost went overboard," I said. "I'm OK, just tired and cold and wet."

"Can you help with the jib?"

I pushed to my feet, and cranked the line while Leyla held the wheel.

"That's enough!" she ordered sharply. "We aren't going to use the whole sail. We'll keep most of it furled."

Ahead in the darkness, I could make out the white form of the sail. I felt the life in *Tiny Dancer* again as she came under way.

Leyla slowly took her around to port, headed back for the GPS waypoint, and we heeled over to starboard as the wind came more abeam of us.

"Let it out just a bit," commanded Leyla, and I did. "Now come here."

I went over to her. She took a hand from the bucking wheel and pointed at cluster of dials on the pedestal in front of her. "This is an autopilot. I used it when we were on diesel, and spent most of my time out of the wind, up close under the dodger."

"Why didn't you tell you Angela about it?" I asked. "You could have come in out of the cold."

I felt, more than saw her shrug. "I don't know. I was worried about what she would do if she didn't think she needed us to keep running the boat."

That was a sobering thought, but also a wise one.

"The auto-pilot runs on electric power. That wasn't an issue when the engine was on, but without the engine, it starts to drain the battery, especially with the work it would have to do to keep us on course during this storm."

"So we shouldn't use it anyway?"

"Maybe for a short time you could turn it on, and get out of the wind for a few minutes." She proceeded to show me how to use it.

"Do you want to see if Angela will let you change into dry clothes first?" she asked.

I thought about what was in my bag. Chances were that Angela would either stand and watch me get my clothes, or else get them for me. "Never mind," I said. "I'll be fine."

Leyla looked at me doubtfully.

"Maybe you could bring me some hot coffee, though."

She smiled and kissed my cheek. "That's my Jonah. Coffee fixes all ills. One more thing," she added. "We need to keep all hatches and the companionway shut all the time. If a wave came over and started pouring into the cabin, the weight of the keel, plus the water, would pull us under. We'd drop like a rock."

"Okay," I said. I stepped behind the wheel, and Leyla went below, shutting the door behind her.

It was not peaceful. The wind screamed through the rigging, the waves battered us again and again on the forward port quarter. Spray and rain splattered noisily onto the plastic windshield of the dodger. The part of the dodger that was bent and not fitted correctly was on the port side – the side where all the wind and weather was coming from. About every five seconds, I was sprayed in the face by the water that made it over and through. At least I knew it was clean. You could take water straight out of the middle of Superior, put it in bottles and sell it. Well, you could if it was legal.

The wheel jerked and shook in my hands, and I had to make constant small corrections to keep us on course, and to keep the wind from knocking us too far over. It was wild and wet and cold and dangerous, and after five minutes I realized I was singing a hymn, a fierce grin of joy on my lips. Here, where my very life was in the balance, I felt fully alive and at peace. My heart was full of love for Leyla, implacable determination to stop Angela, Phil and Jasmine, and strangest of all, gratitude to God. I shook my head in wonder as I realized that I hadn't even had my coffee yet.

I touched the GPS to check my course, and backlight illuminated the screen. There was a graphic display that showed our course and position. It was all blank around us, reflecting the vastness of the lake. I looked carefully at the unit, not wanting to screw it up and have Angela ask me why I had done so. I touched the menu button and quickly figured out how to change the detail level on the graphic display. After I zoomed out several times, I could see that our course was a long gentle curve moving from northeast to straight north, ending in the middle of the western arm of lake Superior, probably thirty-five miles from the nearest land. We were about forty miles from the end of the path, and it would take us all night to get there. Presently, we looked to be about twenty-five miles off Michigan, and more than forty from Minnesota or Wisconsin. Even if I could see through the rain and dark, no land would have been visible.

I wondered why Angela wanted to go the middle of the lake. The surface of Superior is as big as South Carolina, and it drops to depths of thirteen-hundred feet. There was nothing but huge amounts of fresh, clear, cold water where we were going.

I fought the wheel and mocked the cold rain and spray, and thought. After a few minutes, Leyla came up with a cup of coffee in a covered travel mug, proving, as coffee always did, that there is a God in heaven, and he is good.

Leyla took the wheel from me, while I cradled the mug with both hands and stepped forward to shelter a little more behind the dodger.

"What do you think they want, Jonah?" asked Leyla.

"I'm not sure," I said. "That's what I was just asking myself."

"Angela seems to be in charge."

"Absolutely."

"She seems to have issues with men. Phil acts pretty cowed."

"I don't normally talk about counselees, but somehow I think confidentiality is off the table," I said. "Angela definitely has a lot of confusion in her life about men and male figures. We didn't get this far in counseling, but it wouldn't surprise me to learn she was abused by a man, or several, at some point in her life."

"So you think she'd be more inclined to listen me?"

"I don't know," I replied. "It could be. Probably more than me anyway, though before this, I thought we had developed a little bit of rapport in counseling."

I finished my coffee, and stepped back to the wheel. "Another cup?" I asked, handing her my empty one. She smiled and went below. I thought for a moment about Angela and her issues with men.

A few minutes later, the companionway opened and Angela herself came out. She handed me another cup of coffee. "I don't know if you and your girlfriend are up to anything, but you'd better not be."

I sipped some coffee. "We like being together," I said. "And we're just trying to stay alive." The boat jumped and rolled and the waves thundered around us. The only thing I could think to do was to try and dig around and unsettle her somehow.

"How is your struggle with guilt coming along, Angela?"

She laughed, short and harsh. "That was all a put-on, to sucker you into all this."

"But how did you know I would have a counseling cruise? I've never done that before."

Angela was silent. "I'm going below," she said abruptly. "Stay on course if you like your girl so much."

I considered my unanswered question. She had clammed up, like she was talking too much. Right before that, she had said this was all a put-on, a set-up to sucker me into this situation. That meant that from the beginning, she and Phil had planned to go on a sailing cruise – before I even had the idea for it. And my idea for it came from Red Hollis. Hollis was in on it, he had to be.

There were five bank robbers in Washington. My dad had killed one, Charles Holland. That left four. Apparently I had killed another, Phil's brother. That left Angela, Phil and – it must be – Red Hollis. Maybe Hollis was really Holl*and*, and he was the other brother that Jensen had mentioned in his text. But where was Hollis/Holland now?

I had goaded them earlier with the fact that both my dad and I had shot members of their gang. But, surely, that was too bizarre to be coincidence. They must have known who I was all along. Perhaps they came to Minnesota seeking vengeance for their dead comrade. My dad had died of a heart-attack, cheating them out of revenge in Washington. Maybe they robbed the First National Bank of Grand Lake deliberately when I was in there, trying to kill me. I shook my head. Silly. There's no way they could have known I was going to be there at that time, that day. So, at least at that point, they hadn't known I was related to the man who had killed one of their own.

Jasmine must have come into it later. I doubted she was one of the robbers. Maybe she'd caught them at some point, and they'd bribed her. Or maybe she went to them with some kind of knowledge she had, in exchange for a cut of the money.

I sipped some more coffee, and then put the mug back into one of the cup holders built in to the steering pedestal. Angela and Phil hadn't killed me yet, and that made revenge seem unlikely. And the whole boating set-up seemed a little bit elaborate for simple revenge. But maybe it was revenge, plus something else.

It wasn't really the time or place for quiet reflection. The wind screamed, pushing at the half-sail up front, plowing us through the mountainous waves, trying from time to time to shove us starboard-side into the lake itself. The wheel jumped and fought me like a rodeo calf. But our lives might depend on my figuring this out.

That thought arrested me for a moment. It had always been the smallest member of the gang who shot people, and Jasmine almost certainly had not participated in any robberies personally. That meant that Angela was the trigger happy one, the killer. Another thought crashed into me like one of the giant waves around me. The brief news report I had heard while I was trying to get the radio to work told of a man who was shot to death in Duluth. He was a university professor at University of Minnesota, Duluth. His name was Ethan, a professor in women's studies and counseling.

Just like the lover that Angela told me had been all made up. Another murder.

I thought about Jasmine's words. "As far as they'll ever know, I am about to die in the line of duty, along with Tony here. They'll probably give me a posthumous medal."

I knew Angela was a murderer. She must have realized that I would figure it out.

I chewed on it some more, beating my brain to work. I wished I had some Bach to listen to, to make me smarter. I began running Toccata and Fugue for organ in D minor through my head. Just before I got to the more pedestrian part in the middle, I had it.

Red Holland was the key. As far as anyone else knew, we took off into the middle of the world's largest freshwater lake. Accidents happen. We were going to disappear. Even if the authorities suspected Phil and Angela, as obviously they did, they would believe that we all died out here. Gordon Lightfoot with his famous song, *The Wreck of the Edmund Fitzgerald*, had coined the phrase, "Superior it is said, never gives up her dead." It wasn't just rhyme. It was true. Normally, when people drown, bacteria make the bodies decompose. The gasses released from that process cause the bodies to float. But Superior is so cold that the bacteria which normally feed on drowning victims can't survive. It was actual fact that drowning victims never floated in Lake Superior. So, no one would expect to recover our bodies in five hundred or more feet of water, miles from any land. Angela and Company would be assumed dead, along with the rest of us.

But what about Red Holland? He must be bringing a boat from Canada or someplace. So Angela and her gang would play dead, and escape to Canada. Meanwhile, there was no way she would let us live to tell others that she was still alive. We really were going to die out here.

I had to admire it. It was perfect, except for the part about us dying.

THIRTY-EIGHT

In a way, I felt relief in knowing what the stakes were. It was life or death, us or them. I still struggled to understand their plan. It would make sense if they were headed to Canada. Northwest Ontario, directly north of us, is probably the wildest, least populated area along the Canadian-U.S. border. You could drive for hours on the trans-Canada highway up there and see more moose than people. But sailing was about the slowest way to get there I could imagine. Unless they were being followed by the FBI or someone, the simplest thing would be to drive across the border. Grand Lake wasn't all that far from Canada, and I had been hiking up in the little mountains outside Thunder Bay several times. Usually, I was just asked a few questions, and then waved across the border when I got there. No one had ever searched my car for stolen loot.

I shook my head and allowed a blast of spray to strike me full on the face. Of course, they *were* being watched by the FBI. Obviously, Jasmine must have told them that. That would have kept them from just driving to Canada.

The companionway door opened, and Jasmine stepped out, swathed in rain gear and a life vest. She pulled the door shut and came over to the wheel.

"Two hours, my turn."

"Why did you do it, Jasmine?"

Not used to the spray and cold yet, she winced as we were showered with icy water. She wiped her eyes and shrugged. She glanced at the companionway door. She looked like she was about to speak. Then she shrugged again and said, "You'd better get below."

I stayed. "I figured out this was the gang doing the bank robberies around the North Shore. I think they also operated in Northern Washington, where my dad was a state cop."

"That's true," admitted Jasmine.

"But you weren't with them during the robberies."

Jasmine was silent.

"And why did the FBI get involved here? They robbed the customers, not the banks. Robbery is a local crime, not a federal one. I thought the FBI would stay out of it."

"If they hadn't got greedy and violent, we might have. But the Bureau had local police forces all over the area clamoring for our help. Finally, because they hit so many banks and were shooting people, we found a judge who gave the FBI a wink and nod to get involved. I think the technical argument was that this gang, though not actually robbing FDIC-insured institutions, was significantly harming banking and commerce."

"And then you decided crime pays better than law enforcement."

Jasmine peered into the darkness ahead of us, blinking in the continuous spray. "Don't make this harder than it is, Borden. Get below before Angela comes out here."

"You and Stone aren't married, are you?" I asked. Finally, their relationship was making sense.

"Your profile said you were brilliant," said Jasmine in mockery.

"I have an FBI profile?"

She shrugged. "Initially, you were part of the investigation. You had the Washington-North Shore connection like the rest of the gang. You met with Richard Holland in Duluth. So, we faked a marriage, and marriage problems, to get in with you and try to get close to Angela as well."

So Red Hollis *was* actually Richard Holland – the brother of the dead member of the gang, Charles Holland, and Angela's brother as well. That was my final confirmation.

"You didn't fake it very well," I said. "Yours was like no marriage I had ever seen."

She laughed. "And I got in close with Angela anyway."

"Too close," I said bitterly. "Just out of curiosity, when did the FBI know I was in the clear?"

"The FBI stopped considering you a serious suspect after that night at the bar – that dance." In the wild darkness I thought I saw her face darken like she was blushing. "We figured no one but a real pastor would react to me like you did."

She glanced at the companionway door again. "Get below now. I mean it."

I went.

THIRTY-NINE

Angela stood at the bottom of the companionway, with one foot on the first step. I turned and pulled the hatch closed behind me.

"Thought I'd jumped her?"

Angela shrugged. "I'm just careful, that's all."

The cabin was blissfully warm after the wild frigid wet of the cockpit. I saw that there was coffee in the pot in the galley. "May I?" I asked. Angela nodded.

Tony Stone was lying on the port settee, which was now stained with blood. He was propped up so that his chest was higher than his lower body, and someone had rigged a kind of canvas that kept him from falling out of the berth. He opened his eyes slowly and looked at me, and then closed them again. Phil was sitting on the starboard settee at the top outside of the U, with his back to the bulkhead wall of the bow cabin, facing the rear of the boat. Leyla sat across from him, looking forward. Her hands were secured together by plastic cuffs that looked like giant zip-ties.

"Give me your hands," said Angela. "Remember, Phil can shoot you before you can disable me and get to him too."

I remembered. Angela put a plastic figure eight around my wrists, but kept my hands in front of my body, leaving me free to drink coffee. We must take comfort wherever we can in hard times. She pushed me down next to Leyla, and then slipped into the galley. "Keep your hands on the table where we can see them."

"You OK?" I asked Leyla. She nodded tiredly.

A minute later Angela put a plate of sandwiches in front of us. It slid across the table, and stopped as it came to rest against a little lip built in the table for exactly that reason. The plate slid back and I caught it with my bound hands.

"Eat," said Angela. "It's going to be a long, rough night."

I took a bite of sandwich and chewed for a minute. "Could I get some avocado on mine?" I asked. Angela gave me a long look. "Actually, it's good just as it is," I said.

I began to wonder if I was wrong about their plans to kill us. You don't bother feeding people you want to kill. Unless, I thought unhappily, you don't want them to know they will be killed, and you want them to be strong and cooperative enough to sail a boat for you.

"Rest for a while," said Angela. "You'll be back out there soon enough." This seemed to confirm my fears. I was finally warming up, starting to feel my fingers and toes. I laid my head on my arms and tried to sleep.

I kept my eyes closed and my breathing regular, but mostly I thought about our predicament and what we might do. As I began to drift off to the rhythm of the waves, I had a thought that startled me awake. It took all my willpower not to sit up. After that, my mind worked furiously, and sleep was simply impossible.

It seemed like forever before Angela prodded me. "Move," she said. "Leyla's turn."

I opened my eyes, and carefully sat up. "It's OK," I said quietly. "Let her sleep. I'll go."

Angela curled her lip at me. "You think she can't handle it? Because she's a woman?"

"I think she can handle it better than anyone," I said. "But I care about her, and I want the best for her."

Angela regarded me for a few moments. "Look," I said. "The truth is, I'm not sleeping well. I don't mind being out there all night. She'll be safe, which will make me happy, and you'll have her hostage, which will make you happy. I'd rather be doing something than sitting here thinking about it."

"Okay," said Angela. "Go." She cut my plastic cuffs.

I pulled on a life-vest and went. Jasmine was huddled over the wheel, shuddering uncontrollably with cold. Under the circumstances, I decided I did not feel all that sorry for her.

"I'm on," I said. "You can get below."

Without a word, moving like a zombie, she relinquished the wheel and went down the companionway, closing the door behind her.

The first blast of spray was awful. It was like putting on a cold, wet swimsuit. Somehow I had forgotten how cold and miserable it was. It took exactly five seconds to remember. In fact, I felt even colder than I had before, after being in the warm cabin for so long.

The night was black and ugly and violent. The waves still reared up to port, half the height of the mast. They blasted through the defective dodger, they crashed across the deck and into the cockpit, swirling over the tops of my shoes until the scuppers sent the water back where it belonged. The wheel was as recalcitrant as ever, and the cold rain sliced in from the dark, angry sky.

I risked a quick look over my shoulder. I caught glimpses of wild white-tipped waves, but little else. Holding onto the wheel with one hand, I turned half-way around. A sudden heave sent me sprawling against the stern rail. I scrambled clumsily to my feet and grabbed the wheel again.

Checking the GPS, I made a small course adjustment. Then, still holding the wheel, I slipped to the other side of the steering pedestal, holding the wheel backwards, facing the stern. A few seconds later, I saw what I wanted. I breathed in deeply, unsure if I was relieved or terrified.

Stumbling and slipping, I made my way back to the right side of the wheel. I leaned forward and peered at the GPS again. Then, reaching to my left, I set the autopilot and turned the switch to on. Letting go of the wheel, I watched carefully. We slid down the side of a wave and swung to starboard. The wheel moved, as if guided by invisible hands, and we shifted back to port, holding a steady course. I watched it happen once more, and then swiveled around to face the stern.

The rope I sought was secured to a cleat on the stern. I knelt down and reached over the wide gunwale and grabbed onto it. Water sloshed over my calves as the remnants of a big wave slid slowly down the scuppers. I pulled and felt the weight of the dinghy we were towing on the other end. It seemed heavy, far too heavy. Even so, I could move it closer, and I did, slowly jerking the rope toward me, hand over hand. I spent a pleasant moment imagining that I was finally hauling in the giant fish of my dreams.

A few moments later, I could just make it out in the dim light. It was a zodiac-style runabout, with wide pontoons forming its outer shell, the kind made popular by Navy Seal commercials and movies. It rushed down a wave toward the stern of *Tiny Dancer*. I stopped pulling, and cast about in vain for something to stave it off. Just before the dingy struck, *Tiny Dancer* lurched up the next wave, and the little runabout fell behind again. I heaved a breath of relief. If the dinghy had struck us, Angela and company would have been on deck in seconds, demanding to know what I was doing, and the slim chance I was clinging to would be irrevocably lost.

I let the dinghy painter slip back through my hands, and the distance between us increased once more, but there was an emptiness in the pit of my stomach as I realized that my plan could not work as I had conceived it. The dinghy was back at the end of the painter now. I guessed it was maybe forty or fifty feet astern.

I had only one choice, and if I waited long to consider it, I knew I would lose my courage. I took firm hold of the painter, slid under the aft guard rail, and slipped into the next wave.

It was like being struck with a heavy blow, all over my body at once. My head was above water, but I couldn't breathe. My muscles felt like they were moving in slow motion through a vat of molasses. A wave submerged me for a minute, but my life-vest popped me back up a second later. I began to choke and gasp for air. The feeling was rapidly leaving my fingers, and I was afraid of losing the rope through sheer numbness.

Like a man in a nightmare, I reached out with all the speed I could muster – which equaled that of the most advanced geriatric patient in a nursing home – and pulled myself along the rope to the dinghy. Thankfully, the forward motion of the boat helped, so mostly all I had to do was let the rope slide through my hands, but this was made difficult by the numbing cold. I shuddered to think of how I would get back.

I came to a fork in the rope. Apparently two ropes were attached to the dinghy to keep it tracking well, and to prevent it from twisting or spinning in rough weather. I chose the rope that went to the left, which was actually the starboard side of the little boat.

Fairly quickly, I met the bow of the dinghy. Too quickly, in fact. It loomed above me in the darkness and I tried to duck, but I reacted so slowly that it still struck me in the back of the head. I held on, stunned for a moment.

Now I was being towed along with the dinghy, and there was a strong flow of water pushing against me, shoving me against the bow, splashing my face, trying to force me under the runabout. I struggled to turn so that my back was to the *Tiny Dancer*, and my face out of the water. It seemed like it took a long time, but finally I managed to get the rope under my right armpit and brace my left hand on the gunwale of the dinghy. I paused for a moment, panting. I couldn't catch my breath – the cold robbed the power from each heave of my lungs.

I scooted forward, throwing my left arm further over the wide pontoon gunwale of the dinghy. I scrabbled around with my hand, trying to find something to hold onto, but finally I had to settle for bending my elbow with the inside curve of the pontoon and clamping tight with my whole arm.

I tried to heave myself up and over the gunwale, but halfway through the motion, I knew I wouldn't make it. I grabbed desperately at the rope with my right hand, and caught it just before the movement of the boat put it beyond my reach. I was holding on, face down in the water.

Again, I painstakingly worked myself around until I had the painter under my right armpit. I swung my legs up to gain some traction on the side of the dingy, but the bottom was flat, and the pontoons were too high in the water to be of any use for leverage.

I felt weak. I knew I had to get out of the water soon, or my muscles would seize up and I would freeze to death in less than an hour. I heaved again, letting loose of the rope with my right hand, swinging my body up over the dinghy with everything I had.

It wasn't enough. My left arm slipped, and my left leg didn't make it over the edge. I slid helplessly along the smooth side of the little boat, my left arm slipping further and further out along the pontoon. Inexorably, the force of the water on my body pulled my arm up until my hand was on top of the pontoon, barely held there with all the pressure I could muster. Then, with a twitch of a wave, it came off.

With a gasp, I flailed wildly. My left hand connected with something solid, and graspable, and I realized I was holding on to the transom – the board that made up the stern of the pontoon boat. I wheeled my right arm high and forward like I was throwing a discus, and then I had two hands grasping firmly. With a groan and a heave of desperation, I snaked my legs and contorted my body and jerked my arms and finally I was lying in eight inches of water in the bottom of the dinghy.

FORTY

The eight inches of water quickly grew to twelve. I realized that my weight was pushing the bow upwards, and all the water was collecting around my body in the back of the boat. I pushed myself up to my knees and fumbled around until I found a bailer, tied to one of the benches. I scooped water out for several minutes until I no longer felt like I was sitting in a frozen kiddie-pool.

There was a bench across the boat immediately in front of me. Behind, me, fixed to the transom, was a small outboard motor, and to my left, next to me, a small gas tank. The weight of the motor and of the water was probably the only thing that had kept it from overturning in the tumultuous seas.

The movement of the waves was greater on the smaller vessel. I stayed on my knees and slid over the bench. Three feet ahead of me was a second bench, but unlike the first, it was enclosed all the way to floor. It was, in fact, some kind of storage bin, or locker, which is exactly what I had remembered.

The seat-locker opened up from my side. I found the lever and spread my arms to prevent anything from flying out in the wild weather. I pushed the lid up. It slammed down again immediately in the wind. Patience is a virtue. Virtuously, I pushed the lid up again, and held it there with my left hand. With my right hand, I rummaged around inside.

There were two life-jackets, which unhelpfully got in the way. Still virtuous, I explored the area carefully with my hand. I pulled up a hard plastic object and found I was holding a flare gun. I put it back. I found a flashlight next. Light would help me find what I was looking for, but it could also betray me. If, in the wild movement of the waves, the flashlight were to shine ahead to the *Tiny Dancer* and hit one of the windows of the companionway doors or of the cabin, I could find myself in serious trouble with Angela and company. I left it off. After that, I found the flare gun again, and then a package of three flares.

I felt a smooth flat surface, like a fish finder. My hopes began to rise. I pulled it out of the bench and shut the cover, and knelt over it. My hands were quite numb, but I pushed and prodded it until I hit some kind of a power button. As the backlight came on, I felt a bitter taste in the back of my mouth. It was another portable GPS unit, not the radio I had staked all of my hopes on finding.

I began to despair. There was no real reason to carry a portable marine radio in a runabout. It was just the only thing I could think of that might save our lives. I opened the lid, replacing the GPS unit, and almost immediately felt something long and thick and flat, like a big walkie-talkie. I pulled it out, and crouching behind the seat-locker, I flicked on the flashlight. It was a radio. We were saved.

FORTY-ONE

Only we weren't saved.

The radio didn't work. I twisted knobs and pushed buttons and slapped and banged, but I could not get that radio to do anything more than a doorstop would do. I risked the flashlight again, and examined it carefully, and tried all the right buttons, according to their labels, but it wouldn't turn on. I tried all the buttons in other combinations, but still nothing happened.

I snapped the light off and sat back on my haunches. Almost immediately, I fell backwards against rear seat, as a wave tossed the little boat around. Pushing myself back up, I wondered what I could do now. It had to be the batteries. Most likely, someone had left it there and not bothered to check batteries at the end of the season. I could bring the radio back to the boat, store it in the cockpit, and try and sneak some batteries from the cabin back up to the radio. Except that I would have to submerge the radio to get back to the boat, and though it was probably water resistant, I doubt it was made to actually go *under* water.

For a few moments, I felt no cold, no wind, not wet, nothing except blank despair. There was simply no way out. I held on to the bench beside me and stared out at the lights, wondering what I could possibly do.

I stared out at the lights. With ridiculous slowness it dawned on me that I was looking at lights in the middle of Lake Superior. There was a ship! Far off to starboard were the clearly visible fog-lights of a vessel, probably a large one. Immediately, I thought of the flare gun. But almost as quickly, I dismissed it. The bright flare would almost certainly shine through even the small windows of *Tiny Dancer's* cabin on this dark night. Angela would come up to the cockpit and find me gone. Once she realized I was in the dinghy, she would cut the rope and leave me to drift while *Tiny Dancer* escaped into the night. I could probably use the two remaining flares to make sure the ship picked me up, but Leyla and Stone would be out of luck.

From somewhere in the back of my numbed mind, a voice was screaming at me. Dully, I tried to pay attention to the buried thoughts. When I finally realized the idea that was clamoring for attention, I was horrified. But now that I had opened my conscious mind to it, the thought wouldn't go away. I didn't have much time.

Quickly, I located the GPS and turned it on. Desperately holding on to figures in my head, I punched in a destination. Then, with trembling hands, I loosened the knot of my right shoe, and slipped Stone's knife into my hand. I slid my upper body across the port-side pontoon near the bow and grasped the rope that formed the left side of the towing harness. Before I could think of any more reasons not to, I cut the rope.

Immediately, the dinghy jerked to starboard, as all the weight was transferred to the rope on that side. The force of our movement through the water pulled the starboard bow down, dragging the dinghy underwater. Gallons of icy liquid began pouring over the pontoon. I leaped for the rope, but before I got there, I felt a sudden jerk, and we were sliding backwards down a wave. The rope had snapped, and my decision was irreversible. Far more quickly than I anticipated, the ghostly form of the *Tiny Dancer* faded into the nothingness of the wild, black night.

FORTY-TWO

Immediately, I located the bailer and scooped a great deal of Lake Superior out of the dinghy. Then I turned to the outboard. One cannot live in northern Minnesota without coming into regular contact with outboard motors. They are a fact of life whether you like it or not, kind of like mosquitoes and people claiming to enjoy lutefisk.

The gas tank had a rubber hose running to the motor, which looked to be about ten horsepower. I opened the valve on the motor, pumped the bulb on the gas-line and then fumbled for the pull-start rope. I found it, braced myself and pulled. Unsurprisingly, the motor did not start. The little boat was riding up the sides of the giant waves, but often, just before we reached the top, part of a wave would break over us. I bailed for a few more minutes, and then fiddled around in the dark on the outboard until I found what I hoped was the choke. I put it on and then pulled again. Nothing. So far, I was not discouraged. This was how it went with outboard motors, chain-saws and weed-eaters. I pulled again, and then again, with no results. I began jerking the rope like a mad-man, putting all my strength into it, over and over again. Nothing, except that for the first time in what felt like my entire life, I began to feel a little bit warm. Now I began to get worried.

We slipped up another wave, only this one was bit steeper, and I felt us starting to roll. Flinging myself on the up-wave side, my face inches from the wall of water, I prayed my weight would hold us. The edge of the boat climbed to more than forty-five degrees, and then I quickly slid back into the middle, to prevent us flipping the other way as we rushed down the back side of the wave.

After about ten minutes, splitting the time equally between bailing and pulling on the starter cord, and occasionally abandoning both to keep the boat from flipping, I gave up. I looked to starboard. The lights of the big vessel were nearer. The wind and the waves were pushing me toward the ship. But before long it would cross my path, and then I would be behind it. It was now or never, and I prayed that the *Tiny Dancer* was far enough away so that they wouldn't see the flares. After a moment's thought, I prayed that the ship was close enough.

Fumbling around in the seat-locker, I found the flares and the gun. I pulled out the flashlight again too, and carefully loaded the gun. Then, pointing it at an angle that I hoped would get the attention of the ship, I fired.

The bang of the gun was much louder than I expected. A barely visible trail of smoke streaked into the sky, and then a red light flamed high in the air. It slowly descended, burning for about seven seconds, and then it was swallowed in sudden darkness.

The ship continued on its course, apparently unaware of me. I loaded a second flare, and fired that one as well. Then I loaded the third and waited.

The ship continued on. Now it was close enough for me to see that it was a big freighter, probably carrying a load of iron ore from the North Shore back east, or perhaps carrying western coal from Duluth to New York. I could hear the throb of its giant engines. It was maybe half a mile away. I fired the third and final flare like I was trying to hit the bridge. It arced into the air toward the ship, but because of the shallow angle, it quickly descended and hit the water a few hundred yards short.

My mind leaping at all the survival tips I'd ever heard, I pulled out the flashlight and flashed it at the freighter. Three short flashes, then three long, then three short again. I hoped that was right. I kept it up. I intended to keep on until the battery died.

At last, I heard a change in the rumble of the great engines. The ship heaved a little to its port, toward me. It slowed more noticeably and turned a little more too. Then, out of the darkness, a blinding light pierced the storm, stabbing into the wild waves in front of me and to my left. The light jumped around erratically, and I continued flashing my light, to help them find me.

The searchlight passed over me quickly, and I yelled in frustration. But it immediately returned, carving a small circle around me until suddenly I was in the middle of the light, blinded as St. Paul, by my salvation.

FORTY-THREE

The ship seemed to continue on past me, but the searchlight stayed on me, though with occasional jerks and jumps, caused, no doubt, by the waves. I assumed one didn't stop a six-hundred foot freighter on a dime. Dimly, I heard bells clanging. It seemed like I waited there forever in the blinding white light. I couldn't see much outside of my shining circle. The great shadow of the freighter seemed to loom closer, and the rumble of the engine grew. Twice more, I had to fling myself to the side of the boat to keep from capsizing. Just to keep busy, I bailed constantly. For a moment, I paused my bailing and slipped the portable GPS unit into the zippered pocket of my jacket.

At last, over the thin howl of the wind and the deep rumble of the ship, I thought I heard the high growl of an outboard motor. After a few seconds, I was sure of it. Finally, a large open boat roared up and stopped about twenty feet away.

"Ho there!" said someone whom I could not see through the blinding glare of the spotlight. It seemed like a stupid thing to say, in the circumstances, so I parroted it back. "Ho there!"

"We're throwing you a rope!" shouted the voice, more business-like now.

"OK," I shouted back. So I didn't have the best lines for the moment either.

I slid down the side of a wave, and the other boat disappeared for a moment. A second later, they were high above me, while I was in the valley. Something big and circular came flying out of the light, and I ducked instinctively. Almost in the same moment, I cursed myself and looked up again just as a round life-preserver smacked against the outside of the dinghy. I dove forward, grasping for it, but it had already floated out of reach.

I waited. "Again," I heard dimly through the storm. This time I didn't duck. The ring smacked into the water next the boat, but I was ready now. I scooped it up. There was a strong-looking rope securely fastened to it. Someone shouted something, but I couldn't hear it. With some difficulty, I slid the ring under the back seat and around the bench twice. Then I gave the thumbs-up. I heard more shouting. Then the rope tightened. I held on to the life-ring, just in case the bench pulled loose or something.

Carefully, they pulled my dinghy close to the lifeboat. When we were about ten feet apart, a man shouted. "We're going to grab you, OK?"

"OK," I shouted back.

The waves threw us at each other. The little dinghy slammed into the side of the freighter's life boat, and then several hands were grasping my life-vest and I was hauled like a big pike into their vessel. Someone cut the rope to the dinghy, then the outboard roared and we swept up the side of a wave toward the ship. The vessel was enormous. We motored around to the lee side. The waves were maybe a little smaller here, and the wind was broken by the vast bulk of the ship. The long, flat hull of the freighter had a superstructure – something that looked almost like a small three or four story building – at the very bow of the ship, and another, slightly smaller one at the stern. The helmsman brought us in close to the stern superstructure. Lights glowed everywhere, like some giant Christmas-decorated mansion. The waves lifted us to within five or eight feet of the railings on the ship, and then dropped us into troughs twenty feet or more below them. If my rescuers didn't know their business, we would be thrown against the steel hull, capsized and rubbed out of existence.

"I need to use a radio, right away. Lives are at stake," I shouted over the storm and the rumble of the outboard.

The helmsman never took his eyes off the ship. "Is there someone else out there?"

"They are being held hostage."

He shook his head, like he was clearing it of fog. "We'll be on board in a minute. Sit tight."

The three men in the rescue craft called out to several men who were at the rail above us. The helmsman idled the motor of the lifeboat, occasionally goosing it to keep us in position. Above us, cables were descending from large steel davits that loomed like a pair of overturned hooks. The other men in our boat stationed themselves at bow and stern. First, the bow cable was snagged and clipped into position. The men above allowed plenty of slack. The stern cable was trickier, but they managed it.

"Hold on," said the man at the outboard. "We have to do this quick."

I nodded. He gave a signal to the men above and killed the motor. Great winches took up the slack in the cables, careful to keep them evenly balanced, and then jerked us suddenly out of the water into the air, where we hung for a moment like four babies in a giant cradle. We rose higher, swaying with the motion of the ship. The rail slowly came to our eye level, and then we were above it. With a few minutes of shouting and grinding machinery, we were swung inboard. Hands reached for me, and then I was standing on the solid steel deck of the Great Lakes freighter, Superior *Rose*.

I had not often been so aware of my dependence upon the kindness and strength of others. I slumped a little against the wall of the structure beside me. I looked at the small circle of men around me. "It doesn't seem adequate, not at all. But thanks. Thank you."

"Can you walk?" asked the man who had handled the motor of the lifeboat. I could see now that he was tall and thin, with brown skin and tight curly hair cropped short. He looked about thirty, and carried his back and neck tight and straight.

"Sure," I said. "I need to get to a radio right away."

"OK, sir, I heard you," he said. "This way."

We took a few steps and then went through a rectangular door with rounded corners and a twelve-inch lip. Inside, it was bright and warm and very loud. The black man was waiting for me. I stuck out my hand. "Jonah Borden," I said. "Thank you again."

He smiled kindly and took my hand. "No problem. Greg Iverson."

Iverson led the way under an overhang that opened out into a vast, deep bay or hold. He seemed to limp a little bit. The bay was like a giant square hole in the ship that rose two stories above us, and two below. There were railings and walkways all the way around on every level, enclosing the big space. Pipes and dials and gauges seemed to sprout everywhere. From the bottom of the open hold, the engine rumbled and roared. Using my vast education, I deduced that we were in some kind of engine-room. Iverson skirted the aft edge of the hold to another doorway. We went through and shut the door behind us. The noise and temperature dropped considerably. We were in a long narrow room. Benches lined the walls on either side, with foul-weather gear hanging on pegs above them. There was a telephone on the wall just inside the door. Iverson reached for it.

"I need the Coast Guard," I said. "I came from a sailing yacht where two people are being held hostage at gunpoint. One of them has already been shot. The kidnappers are also bank robbers."

Iverson replaced the phone and swiveled around to stare at me. "Say that again," he said in a calm voice. I repeated it. "You don't look crazy," he muttered.

I pulled off my life vest, then my jacket, and showed him the bullet holes. "Bullet holes" I explained helpfully.

"Holes, anyway," he said. He muttered under his breath and picked up the phone again, punching a few buttons.

"Cap'n? Iverson here. Yes, I've got him. Yes sir, just one, but he says…" He looked at me while he spoke. "I'd like to bring him up to see you, right away." He listened a minute more. "Okay." He hung up.

The door swung open and a sailor appeared with a bundle under one arm and a thermos. "Dry clothes and blankets," he said, pushing the bundle at me. I stripped and rubbed myself with the wool blanket, not caring how it made me itch. The clothes didn't fit exactly right, but they were clean and serviceable, a pair of jeans, too big in the waist, too short in the legs, with a belt to keep them up, and a gray flannel shirt.

"Gear up," said Iverson, pointing to the foul weather gear on a nearby hook. "We're going up to the bridge. Better accommodations up there anyway." He looked at the sailor. "Hang his clothes out there," he jerked his thumb at the door. "They'll dry out pretty fast." I dug in the pocket of my jacket for the GPS, and then handed the coat to the sailor.

"What you got?" asked Iverson.

"GPS," I said.

Iverson narrowed his eyes like maybe he might think about believing me after all. "Come on," is all he said.

It was fully two hundred yards between the stern superstructure and bridge superstructure up in the bow. We walked along the rail on the starboard side, out of the worst of the wind, but it still plucked and howled at us, and I held on to the safety line that had been rigged along the endless row of giant hatches that led to the belly of the boat. Three times on our trip, waves washed up over the railing to my right, soaking my new dry jeans up to the knees. Walking behind Iverson, I could see now that he definitely had a limp.

We finally made it to the superstructure in the bow, and Iverson led me through another steel water-tight door. "Nice little blow," he commented once the door was shut behind us.

"It's OK, I guess," I said. "If you like that sort of thing." Iverson looked carefully at me and then smiled widely. "You might be all right, Mr. Borden."

"Call me Jonah," I said.

"Sure thing, Jonah," said Iverson. "Most folks around here call me 'First' to my face and 'Navy' behind my back. I like both names. I'm the first officer here."

"And you came out of the Navy?"

"Yeah. Honorable discharge, on account of my injured knee here." He pointed at his right knee. "I get around just fine, but I am no longer the perfect physical specimen required by Uncle Sam."

He led me up three flights of stairs, which he seemed to manage just fine. Better than me in fact, in my exhausted state. "Outside again, real short," he said. We stepped out and I found we were on a brief railed deck, high above the turbulent water. This high, the movement of the great ship was exaggerated. Iverson led us aft a few feet, and then we climbed a very short stair up to the bridge level. Without pause, he opened the door and led me into the enclosed bridge.

It was spacious and bright and lined with windows looking forward. Two great wheels stood in the middle of the area, about five feet apart, but no one was using them to steer. There were two people looking at banks of instruments, and then out through the windows into the black night. A third man stood with his hands behind his back, swaying with the ship, watching us expectantly.

"Here he is, Cap'n," said Iverson, speaking to the man who stood off by himself.

None of the sailors I had seen so far wore any kind of uniform. The captain's only concession to uniform was a blue peaked cap, much battered and worn, but braided with gold. It looked like maybe it was an old Navy officer's top. He was probably in his mid-fifties, with steel-gray hair under the cap, kept short and military style. His back was ramrod straight, and his eyes were almost the same color as his hair.

"Thank you, First," he said. He stretched out a solid, callused hand to me. "Captain Andrew Dillon," he said.

"Jonah Borden," I said, taking his hand. "I'm extremely grateful to you and your crew, Captain. We have an emergency situation here. I came from a sailboat where two people are being held hostage by violent criminals. We need to contact the Coast Guard immediately."

Dillon looked at Iverson, and then back at me.

"I know it sounds crazy, Captain, but you've stumbled across a one-in-a-million situation. The criminals are the bank robbers who have been operating on the North Shore for the past three months. One of the hostages is an FBI agent who was on the boat, undercover. The other is..." I faltered. "She is the love of my life."

Dillon continued to stare. "What were *you* doing on the boat?"

"We don't have time for all that," I said. "I'll fill you in afterward. You can listen when I talk to the Coast Guard. But we've got to bring them in right away."

"Is the vessel sinking?" asked the captain.

"No," I said. "But who knows what they will do when they find out I'm gone. And I have a bad feeling about their plans. One of the robbers is a killer, and she's already shot and wounded the FBI man."

"*She?*" said Iverson. The other two sailors had turned around and were looking at me too.

"Please," I said. "The Coast Guard? This is life or death."

"Okay," said Dillon. "But if you are screwing with me…"

"That's right," I said. "I jumped into a zodiac with a ten horse motor and came thirty-five miles from the nearest land in the biggest storm this year, on the off chance that you would pick me up so I could screw with you."

"He's got a point," said Iverson.

The captain grunted and turned to one of the other sailors. "Get me the Coasties."

FORTY-FOUR

It took a few minutes of patching and things I didn't really understand until we heard a female voice on the radio loudspeaker say, "This is Ensign Brock of the U.S. Coast Guard. Who am I speaking to, over?" There was a lot of static and fuzz.

"Ensign, this is Captain Dillon of the freighter *Superior Rose*. My crew and I just picked up an individual in a lifeboat who says he needs to speak to you. Over." Dillon handed me the mic.

"Hello," I said, feeling a little foolish about not knowing how to address these people. "My name is Jonah Borden. I came off the sailing yacht *Tiny Dancer*. The vessel is not sinking but there are five people on board. Three of them are criminals who are holding the other two hostage. One of the hostages is an FBI agent who has been shot."

Iverson touched my arm. "You say, 'over' so that the other side knows you are done talking, and you don't talk at the same time as each other."

"Oh," I said. I clicked the mic. "Over." The rest of the conversation was so punctuated with "overs" that fairly quickly, I stopped noticing them, even when I said it.

"Repeat please, over" said Ensign Brock in a metallic, static-filled voice. I wondered why everyone said that. I repeated.

"Hold on," she said.

I was feeling impatient and anxious. There was a long time when nothing happened. I looked at the Captain and Iverson. "Are we still connected?" They both nodded. Iverson said, "She's going up the chain of command. An ensign doesn't handle this kind of stuff by herself."

Finally a male voice crackled through the air. "This is Captain Kurt Moser, U.S. Coast Guard. Is this Agent Stone?" My heart leaped within me when he mentioned Stone's name. Stone must have had back-up. They couldn't have intended to get lost in a storm.

"Captain, my name is Jonah Borden. I was on the boat with agent Tony Stone. He is in serious jeopardy, along with another civilian. We need help immediately."

"Who is this? Where are you?"

"My name is Jonah Borden," I repeated. "I escaped from the sailboat *Tiny Dancer* and was picked up by the freighter *Superior Rose*. Stone and a civilian are still on the sailboat, and I'm afraid they are going to be killed."

"What about Agent Bianco?"

"You mean Jasmine? I'm afraid she's working with the bad guys."

There was a moment of static. "Doesn't sound right," said Moser finally. "Do you have any kind of position?"

"Better. I have last known position, course, and approximate speed."

"Well done, Borden," crackled Moser over the distance. "Give 'em to me." Iverson looked at me approvingly. I pulled the GPS unit out of my pocket, and gave him what he needed to know. I could feel the stress beginning to drain away. The cavalry had been summoned, and they seemed to know their business.

"Are you sure about these?" asked Moser. "*Superior Rose*, what is your current position?" Dillon took the mic from me and looked at one of the sailors who hovered near the instruments. The sailor gave him the position and he repeated it into the mic.

There was a pause, presumably while someone at the Coast Guard station plotted the course. "How did you get way the heck out there?" crackled Moser. "You were supposed to be in the Apostles. Were you crazy, heading out in this storm?"

"I'm sorry, sir," said Dillon into the mic. "What do you mean?"

"I was talking to Borden," said Moser. "We were tracking his sailboat until we lost the signal, right about when the storm started."

"Agent Stone lost some kind of pager overboard," I said, taking the mic. "He was very upset about it. The gang took over the boat right about then, and forced us to head out into the storm."

"That pager was our signal. Hold please." After a few minutes, Moser was back. "All right, we have course and position at 2200 hours. It is midnight now. We should be able to intercept in about seven hours, or 0700. Sit tight."

"*Seven hours!*" I didn't mean to yell, but I did. Iverson and Dillon looked startled. "That's too late! Captain, my theory is that they are planning to rendezvous with another vessel and sink the *Tiny Dancer*, with us in it. I'm guessing at present speed they'll make the rendezvous at five-thirty in the morning or so."

Captain Moser's voice, though attenuated by static and machinery, sounded calm. "I'm sure you have had a rough time of it, Borden, and that feels like an eternity to wait. But it will be fine, I assure you."

"Why so long?" I asked.

"We were shadowing you with the cutter *Alder* beyond the Bayfield peninsula. When the storm hit, we had to recall the speed runners, and then we got a distress call back near Duluth. Since we thought you had taken shelter behind one of the Islands, the cutter left the Bayfield station to handle it, and went back to cover the SOS. The *Alder* is in Duluth now."

They were about one hundred and forty miles away.

"Is there nothing closer?"

"The cutter *Alder* is our only full-size vessel on Superior. You're out in the middle of nowhere. The Marquette station is a hundred and sixty miles from you, and there's nothing there with more speed or range anyway."

"What about a helicopter or a float plane?"

"We can't risk it in this weather, and even if we could, it is night and visibility is extremely poor."

"Of course," I said. "I'm sorry."

The cavalry was coming, but they would be late. Far too late.

FORTY-FIVE

Captain Dillon got back on the radio with the Coast Guard.

"Captain," said Moser through the speakers, "I can't order you to do this, but I wondered if you could stay in the area for a few hours?"

Dillon looked out of the dark windows of the bridge for a few moments, tapping the hand-held mic on his thigh. He brought it back to his lips and pushed the send button. "I need to check with corporate on this. If I don't, it could be my job."

"Understood," said Moser through a burst of static. "Please get back to me when you have your answer."

"Will do, Captain," said Dillon. "Over and out." He reached up and hung the mic back on its bracket. "Get me corporate headquarters."

"Sir," said the sailor who operated the radio, "it's after midnight."

Dillon swore. "I forgot. I'm going to have to wake someone up."

I stepped away from the action. Iverson took my arm. "Coffee?"

I brightened. "Absolutely."

"Sorry we didn't get you something earlier, but you were pretty insistent about your call. I see why now."

Iverson led me through a small passage behind the main bridge and into a kind of sitting area. A big industrial-style coffee maker was bolted to a wall and a counter. He grabbed two mugs from a cupboard, filled them and handed one to me. The first sip was heaven. The second sip sobered me up.

"I have to get back to the *Tiny Dancer*," I said numbly. Iverson looked at me without expression.

I met his eyes. "You married?"

He shook his head.

"Ever been in love?" He nodded.

"How would you feel, if you were safe drinking coffee somewhere, while your love was tied up in a boat, prepped for execution in a few hours?"

Iverson said nothing, just regarded me thoughtfully as his sipped his coffee.

"You cut the lifeboat free – the one I was in."

"Yeah," he said. "Those conditions, I made a judgment call. The boat, or your life. I picked your life."

"Can I take one of your lifeboats?"

He put down his coffee. "What are you talking about?"

"I need to get back to the *Tiny Dancer*. Look, the bad guys don't even know I'm gone. I was steering the boat for them while they held my sweetheart – her name is Leyla – hostage. I set it on autopilot and got in the lifeboat and tried to make it to you guys when I saw your lights. As far as they know, I'm still up there at the wheel."

"How long ago was that?" he asked.

"I don't know, maybe an hour and a half. If I go quick, I could get ahead of their course and wait for them, and get back in the boat before they know I was gone."

"You are one crazy dude, you know that?"

"I've done hostage negotiation before," I said. "I'm the police chaplain in my town."

Iverson was silent.

"I can't let her die," I said. I sipped some coffee and looked away miserably. "My first wife was killed by a burglar."

Iverson began swearing. I realized maybe there was a reason for the expression "swear like a sailor." He got up.

"I'll be right back."

He was gone for fifteen minutes, which gave me time to finish my coffee, plus a second cup. I was warm and comfortable, but nothing could ease the anxiety that chewed away at me inside. I was starting to wonder if the *Superior Rose* had any of those automatically inflating life rafts that I could steal. The problem would be getting ahead of the *Tiny Dancer* with nothing but a tiny plastic paddle. The *Superior Rose* had been going roughly parallel to the *Tiny Dancer*, but downwind, and of course, much faster, so I would have to paddle against the force of the storm.

I stood up just as Iverson walked into the room. He limped directly to me and met my eyes. "Let's go."

"I can't stay," I said. "I'll take one of those inflatable rafts if I have to."

"No," he said. "I mean, 'let's go get you back to the *Tiny Dancer*.' Captain's letting us take his launch."

I was speechless, but I followed Iverson with alacrity when he turned and led the way back down to the deck level. As we made our way out into the howling wind and back toward the stern, Iverson called out over his shoulder.

"Cap'n is an ex-Coastie. We both miss the action a little sometimes, and it seems like this one was made for us and dropped in our lap."

"I am a pastor, my boss is God," I shouted back. "Maybe it *was* made for you."

He flashed me a tight grin in the dark, and we continued on.

The launch was more substantial than the lifeboat that had pulled me out of the lake. It looked like a large narrow speedboat with a covered bow and a windscreen and roof protecting most of the cockpit. The outboard motor looked huge. By the time we got back to the stern, a crew of men had already hoisted it on a pair of davits and were lowering it into a position where we could get on. Without any ceremony, Iverson and I scrambled aboard, followed by a short, broad muscled sailor and then another one, taller and slimmer.

"What're we doing now, First?" asked the short, muscular man.

"Covert insertion," said Iverson absently, checking the cockpit. He tested the radio, examined gauges and then gave the thumbs up to the davits crew.

"Huh?" asked the muscled sailor.

"Sorry Jones," said Iverson. "We are taking this man," he pointed at me, "back to his yacht, but in secret, so the folks on that boat won't ever know he was gone, or that we were there."

"Why dint ya just say so?"

"Never mind," said Iverson.

I heard Jones mutter, "Crap navy-speak."

The taller sailor was called Felix. The crew lowered us back into the waves. Iverson had the engine going as soon as we hit the water. There was a little bit of maneuvering and hassling with the davits. It seemed to take forever to me, but probably it was only a few seconds. Finally, we were under way.

The storm had abated a little. The wind still whipped spray everywhere, but the rain seemed to have quit, and the waves were averaging maybe twelve or fifteen feet now, instead of twenty or more.

"Let me see the GPS, said Iverson, gunning the engine.

I held on with one hand, and pulled out the unit with the other, and thumbed it on. Iverson glanced at it for maybe half a second, and then lifted his eyes forward and kept them there, steering the launch. He cut the engines back to idle and we drifted, just a hundred yards or so from the *Superior Rose*. Iverson started intently at the waves and the freighter. I continued to hold the GPS for him, though he didn't look at it. Finally, he glanced at me and said, "Got it, thanks. I heard you when you gave it to the Coasties. Just wanted to double-check." I guess the U.S. Navy still trained them pretty well.

"Listen up," he said to Jones, Felix and me. "We need to do this quietly, which means with the engine off, so we're only going to have one shot at this. We'll get ahead of the sailboat, and upwind a little. I'll try to time it so we can cut the engine and drift across their path. If we can get close enough, Borden will jump. If not, we throw a hook into the rigging, tie him on and it's up to him. You two need to be ready to push us off – quietly – if I miss the mark."

"He's kidding," said Felix to me. "Navy never misses."

"I heard that, Felix," said Iverson.

"Just bolstering your confidence sir," said Felix without a trace of a smile.

Iverson pushed the accelerator forward, and we roared north into the night.

"C'mere," said Jones to me. I scooted over to him. He wrapped a rope around my waist and tied a bowline.

"Gotta knife?" Somehow in all the fuss I'd lost the one Stone gave me. It was probably adrift somewhere miles from here, in the abandoned lifeboat. I shook my head.

Jones pulled a clasp knife out of his pocket. It was spring-loaded with a four-inch blade. About an inch and a half of the blade was serrated.

"The other end of this line is a fifteen-pound spider anchor." He picked it up from the bottom of the boat. It was a cylinder about eighteen inches long. The rope was attached to one end. The other end sprouted eight or ten thin steel spines that curved up and out.

"If this ends up in the water, and you are on the other end of it, you'll go down. Cut the rope."

"How about a life vest?" I asked.

"Might help," said Jones. "I'd still cut the rope." He dug around under the bow and brought back a life vest. It was stamped with the name of the freighter. I put it on.

After an extremely rough half-hour, Iverson cut the engine to idle again. He looked at me. "GPS," he said succinctly. I gave it to him. He thumbed through some screens and looked at it for a minute. He looked at the waves and then back at the GPS, and nodded in satisfaction.

"If you were right about their speed, it'll be about ten minutes."

We drifted. I looked at Iverson. "Aren't we going to get into position?"

"If you were right about their speed, we *are* in position."

Jones slapped both of my shoulders. "Don't worry," he said. "First is the best officer on the Great Lakes. He'll get you there."

"He's not lying," said Felix.

I glanced at Iverson. He was grinning. "Aw shucks, fellas," he said, wiping the corners of his eyes with the back of one hand. "You're making me tear up."

"If you tell anyone I said that, I'll deny it," said Jones grimly.

"Me too," added Felix.

Iverson's grin got wider, but he said nothing. He watched the waves and glanced back at the GPS from time to time. He nodded in apparent satisfaction, probably for my benefit.

"Sure we can't just storm the boat, take 'em by surprise?" asked Jones.

"We went over this, Jones," said Iverson, never breaking the rhythm of his eyes, which rested first on the waves and then the GPS, and then back to the waves. "They have hostages and firearms, and they've already used them." For a moment he pulled his eyes out of their rotating vigil and looked at me. "Speaking of that, do you want a gun?"

I thought for a moment. "I don't think so," I said. "I could really blow it, and if they found it on me before I was ready to use it, I don't know what they might do."

He nodded, his eyes back to their flicking rotation. "Good choice. But I thought I ought to ask."

"Thanks," I said.

Iverson glanced quickly at the watch on his wrist, and then reached forward and cut off the idling engine. "Any minute now," he said.

We drifted silent, four pairs of eyes straining through the darkness and spray. The minutes passed, and we saw nothing. Iverson glanced back at the GPS. Time slowed down. Babies grew up and had babies of their own while we waited. It seemed like nothing had ever come before or after the moment we waited in the wet, cold darkness.

Finally, faintly, I thought I heard a splashing and murmuring of water that didn't quite fit with the random sounds of the storm. Jones and Felix tensed. "There she is," said Felix in a hoarse whisper. Iverson visibly relaxed, though I wasn't aware that he had been tense. A few seconds later, I saw it too, the ghostly graceful shape of the *Tiny Dancer* plowing doggedly through the icy waves.

"A little behind schedule," muttered Iverson, calmly. "We're going to pass in front of her. Jones, get that hook ready."

Jones grabbed the hook and climbed out the cockpit, holding on to the roof with one hand, the hook in the other. Iverson was right, we drifted in front of the Tiny Dancer, about ten yards before she crossed our path. Felix swore in admiration, and Iverson gave a tight grin. As a feat of seamanship, it was like breaking a world record at the Olympic Games not by seconds, but by minutes. To navigate through the storm and dark and time it so that we drifted so close was almost miraculous. The Navy still trained them well, all right.

"Now," said Iverson in a low voice.

Jones heaved the hook, and then pulled it back quickly. The rope tightened, angling up into the darkness of the *Tiny Dancer's* rigging.

"Go!" said Jones.

There was no time to thank them, to express my swelling admiration for their skill and daring and sheer luck. Felix grabbed my life vest and rolled me out of the boat.

FORTY-SIX

I had been in the water a few hours ago, but the mind tends to blur the most unpleasant and dangerous experiences. The first shock of the cold stole my breath and never gave it back. I gasped and wheezed. My muscles locked up as they had before, and it was difficult to move. Sometimes, on a hot summer day, you can get used to cold water. But this water was far too cold to become used to. Almost immediately, my feet and hands began to ache.

Before I could gather my wits, the rope around my waist tightened and I was jerked forward, face down, and towed through the water like a buoyant sack of potatoes. I inhaled water, and panic imparted a strength to my limbs that nothing else could. I flung my arms in front of me and got hold of the rope. Twisting and flailing, I managed to get on my back, and coughed and hacked while I plowed through the water like a giant Great-Lakes Atlantic salmon on the end of a line.

I knew I wouldn't last long like this. Unless I got out of the water quickly, I would freeze to death on the end of the line. Still on my back, I reached above my head as far as I could and grabbed the rope. I twisted it around my wrist and pulled myself backwards toward the boat, against the rush of water caused by our passage through the waves.

I couldn't feel my feet anymore, and my thighs were aching with the cold. Holding the loop of rope down by my waist, I reached up and pulled myself toward the boat again. A big wave flung me upwards, and abruptly the upper half of my body was out of the water. Just as quickly I was slammed back down into the trough, and for a moment my entire body was submerged, even my face. This continued to happen periodically.

Slowly, I pulled myself toward the boat. My arms were shaking with the cold and effort. Twice, I looped the rope around my wrists and held on, unable to keep going. But both times I thought about the alternative, and once more reached above my head to pull myself along.

At last, I saw the boat out of the corner of my eye. The rope I was on went up to the hook that was caught in the rigging of the mast cross-tree. That meant that the closer I got, the further to starboard I was swinging. I wasn't going to be able to scramble up the stern – I would meet the boat on the side, where the starboard rail met the water.

There wasn't much I could do about it, so I kept hauling myself toward the boat. I couldn't feel the lower half of my body, and I shook uncontrollably. I no longer reached as far behind me as far as I could, but settled instead for smaller, easier pulls. Finally, I was up against the starboard side. The *Tiny Dancer* was receiving wind from port, so as it met the waves it dipped down to starboard. It rolled right on top of me, pushing me under water, and then releasing me as it climbed the next wave. Just as I recovered, it did the same thing again. I held the rope with my left hand and flailed desperately with my right hand for the starboard rail. I couldn't reach it. I tried again, timing it as the hull heeled over to bury me again. I vaguely felt my numb fingers contact the steel cable of the lifeline, but I couldn't clench my hand fast enough. It slipped away, and I realized that in my focus on the rail, I had let go of my rope. I began to slide quickly astern. With my left hand, I tried to grab the rope as far up as I could while I continued to try to grab something along the hull with my right.

I couldn't find the rope, and my right hand was now slipping off the corner of the stern. In a moment I would have to start the entire exhausting process again. I wasn't sure I could do it; I had almost no feeling anywhere in my body anymore. In fact, I was beginning to imagine that I was warm, which I knew was a very bad sign. In desperation, I twisted over to my stomach and flung both hands at the stern.

I missed.

Just as I slid away into despair and darkness, a hand locked onto my right wrist. For a moment I blacked out, but then I realized that I wasn't dead, and I wasn't even back to my starting point at the end of the rope. The first hand was joined by a second, further up my arm. I tried vainly to kick my legs and assist by moving myself forward through the water, but I couldn't do it. The hands pulled me closer, and then my left hand found the rail and I began to pull too. I'll never know where I found the strength for the last heave that brought me flopping into the cockpit like a confused lake trout.

I lay there gasping and shivering, black clouds pulsing like blood in front of my vision. At last, when my body calmed down to the point of merely shivering uncontrollably. I sat up.

"Hello, Jonah," said a voice. "You've been a busy boy, haven't you?"

It was Jasmine.

FORTY-SEVEN

I fumbled with the zipper of my soaked coat pocket while Jasmine watched patiently. I dug my hand in and came out with Jones' knife and flicked it open. Jasmine reached out gently and took it away from my weak and trembling hand.

"You don't need that for me anyway," she said. She folded it up and handed it back to me. My numb fingers dropped it to the floor of the cockpit. I picked it up again, looked at her, hesitated, and then put the knife back in my pocket.

"Why didn't you just cut the rope, or let me freeze?" I asked.

Jasmine regarded me for a long time. "I thought I saw a boat out there," she said.

"Superior does strange things to you in a storm," I said.

She bent closer to look at me. Suddenly she snapped on a bright flashlight, causing me to wince. She pulled me forward and looked at the back of my life jacket. She killed the light.

"Where did you get that life-jacket? It says *Superior Rose*."

"It was on board," I said. "They probably have all kinds of old life jackets from who knows where."

"That's not your coat," she observed.

"Says who?"

"What were you doing in the water?"

"I like a midnight swim. It keeps my head clear."

Jasmine glanced at the GPS next to the wheel and then sat down on one of the benches and drummed her fingers on her knee. I shivered in time with her drumming. I'm musical that way.

"I guess you have this on some kind of autopilot?"

I saw no need to answer the obvious.

"I guess I don't have a choice," she said, apparently to herself. She looked at me. "I'm working with the FBI."

"I know that," I said. "Most of me is frozen, but my brain still works."

"No," she said. "I mean I'm *still* working with the FBI. Angela thinks I've turned dirty, but I haven't. You and I are on the same side. So tell me what you were up to."

"Midnight swim," I said. "Extraordinarily refreshing."

"Jonah," said Jasmine. "I mean it."

"How happy for you," I replied.

"I saved you just now," she said. "You said it yourself – I could have just let you drown or freeze. Doesn't that show that I'm on your side?"

"If I had frozen, then you wouldn't have a chance to know what I was up to." I paused for a moment. "I may yet freeze, come to think of it."

"I gave you your knife back."

"After we found out I'm in no condition to use it anyway."

"I'm asking you to trust me."

"And giving me no plausible reason."

"Okay," said Jasmine. "I have some coffee here."

"Now that would be a start," I said eagerly.

"I'm going to give you some. Do you think you can stay warm enough while I tell you some things?"

"I'll try not to expire."

"I'll talk quickly," she said, pouring coffee from a thermos into a mug.

"In a minute, Angela is going to check on us anyway. She sent me up here to see how you were doing, and to make sure you weren't trying any funny business. When I talk to Angela, I will say that a wave washed you overboard and I found you clinging to the rail. I won't say anything about the rope. And I'll try to get it down once you go below. How's that for building trust?"

"I'll believe it when I see it."

"The problem is, this is our best time to talk. We can't communicate freely in front of Angela and Phil."

"So talk," I said.

"Okay," she said. "Angela and Phil and their gang operated in northern Washington for a few years, which you already know because your mother sent you some of your father's old case files. They had already got our attention because of the havoc they were wreaking on the small towns there, and because of the shootings. They were also operating close to the Canadian border, and finally Homeland Security stepped in, because no one else really had jurisdiction. They brought us in – sort of seconded the case to the FBI – but we're still working under their auspices. We have more expertise with bank robbers, even if they are only robbing the customers in the lobbies."

I sipped some coffee and felt the warmth begin to spread. Maybe that was why Jensen and Lund had been getting pushback when they tried to investigate the Charles Holland angle. Homeland Security was big and powerful enough to cut out other law enforcement agencies.

"Anyway," said Jasmine, "after your father killed Charles Holland, they went to ground for a while. We began doing some undercover work, and because we learned the identity of Holland after he died, we started getting leads. We began to suspect Holland's older sister. We noticed also that she was using the robberies as an excuse to shoot people – usually men in uniform, or men in some kind of obvious authority position.

"It appears that their plan in Washington was to take the money on a sailing trip up Puget Sound to some remote spot on the Canadian coast. Holland had rented a yacht just a few days before he died, and we were lucky enough to get to it shortly after he was ID'd. So, their plan for leaving the country was a bust. Border crossings into Canada aren't really a big deal, but still, it was a pretty big chance to take, just driving across. Once they started hitting banks, Homeland Security put out a border watch. The gang must have figured that would happen."

The coffee was helping, but not enough. I was still shivering.

"So the gang decided to try basically the same thing, only here on Lake Superior," continued Jasmine. "They added a nice refinement, inspired by you, I'm afraid."

"What do you mean?"

"Well they were going to rent a sailboat and go to some remote spot in Ontario. But Red Holland and Angela – the two siblings of Charles Holland – wanted revenge on your father. Only, he died inconveniently before they could do it, so they decided to take their revenge out on you. That's where they started getting elaborate, which made them a little sloppy. Still, the plan is brilliant."

"And what is it?"

"They are meeting Red Holland out here somewhere. They're going to sink the *Tiny Dancer* with you, Leyla and Tony in it. Everyone else will think that all hands perished on this trip, and so the authorities will stop looking for them. They go to Canada in a different boat, that Red has already rented or purchased, and start new lives."

This was pretty much what I had already figured out, with a few extra details thrown in about Homeland Security and the FBI. But the fact that Jasmine was telling me outright meant something. I assumed that Angela and Phil didn't want us to know the plan, because if we did, we wouldn't cooperate by sailing the boat, and we would be desperate, knowing we were doomed anyway. So if Jasmine was telling me this, it meant she didn't care if I was desperate, or if I cooperated with Angela.

"All right," I said. "You've taken the first step in earning my trust. But I've got some questions."

"Go ahead."

"You guys – the FBI – were closing in on them. Obviously, you knew who they were. Why didn't you just arrest them?"

Jasmine shook her head in the darkness. "Sadly, we didn't have any hard evidence on them until they pulled guns on us yesterday afternoon. We didn't even have enough for a search warrant. It was all circumstantial connection to Charles Holland, and no one in the gang even has the name of Holland – probably fake IDs, or in Angela's case, she's married, so her name is different."

"OK," I said, trying to make my numb brain work faster. "How did they think you were dirty, and why didn't you just stop them after they pulled guns?"

"I approached Angela directly. Our profiler thought that she had serious unresolved issues with men, so I told her I hated the male-dominated culture of the FBI, plus that I was looking for money. I don't think the greed alone would have convinced her, but she is so immersed in her view of an evil male-dominated world that she was very ready to believe I felt the same way. It's a kind of sister-hood, woman-power thing."

"OK, so you had no evidence until this trip. But why didn't you stop her as soon as she pulled a gun?"

"It wasn't so easy. Phil pretended to hold me hostage to stop you and Tony from doing anything, and I really had no choice but to play along. We feel pretty strongly about protecting civilians, so having you and Leyla here has made it tough. Also, I think Angela believes me, but I'm on probation. She made me give her my gun before we got on the boat. We had the Coast Guard hiding in the Apostle Islands, but the storm must have screwed them up, and Tony lost his pager. It was really a tracking signal. That, and the storm, was rotten luck."

I tried to react as if I was shocked and angry. Mostly I was tired and cold. I made a decision.

"I managed to contact the Coast Guard," I said.

"What?" asked Jasmine. "How?"

"Never mind how," I said. "You probably wouldn't believe it anyway. The point is, we've got help coming. They aren't going to get away with it."

I figured that if Jasmine was, in fact, a dirty cop, working with Angela, it wouldn't hurt to put the pressure on. People who are afraid and pressured make more mistakes. Now I would see if she shared this information with Angela or not.

"So..." Jasmine looked astern. "How did getting in the water help you contact the Coast Guard?"

"I got in the lifeboat," I said, truthfully enough. "There was a radio in it."

"Where is it?" asked Jasmine eagerly.

She could have wanted it to send a message to the Coast Guard to call off the rescue. But it didn't seem like it to me.

"The dinghy overturned," I said, "the tow rope broke, and all I had left was this life-line I rigged up."

Jasmine swore regretfully. "We sure could have used a covert radio. But I guess you got the main thing accomplished. Thank you." She seemed sincere. But she also seemed like there were two of her. I shook my head, but the fuzzy image remained. Definitely two, maybe three. My teeth chattered noisily.

"You don't look so good. Can you get below?"

"Wait," I said. "Here's one more test of trust. Obviously, I put the yacht on auto-pilot to get out to the dinghy. It's draining the batteries. If you leave it on, the batteries will drain all the way out. We'll lose power and lights and the onboard GPS. They'll have to bring their GPS out here to keep on course, and one of them will have to stay to make sure we follow the course. That will make them tired and cold and wet. I speak from experience. It will be dark in the cabin. They may start making mistakes."

Jasmine considered me. "You sure you're a pastor? You have a devious mind."

"Be wise as serpents but innocent as doves," I said, but it took me four tries to say it, I was shivering so badly. Jasmine helped me up, and I stumbled down the companionway to warmth and rest.

FORTY-EIGHT

"What happened to you?" asked Angela. I was still dripping water and shivering uncontrollably.

"Almost fell overboard," I said. "I was holding on to the rail trying to get back on board for five minutes."

"So, no all-nighter?"

"Sorry," I said. "I need to warm up a bit first. Maybe I can go back out in a while."

I glanced around the cabin. There was only one dim light on, but it seemed bright compared to the stormy night outside. Phil was blinking at me sleepily. Leyla was still asleep, her head on her arms which were stretched out on the table in front of her, held together by the plastic handcuffs. Stone's eyes were open and filled with pain. I wanted to reassure him somehow. But then I realized that the Coast Guard was going to get to us too late anyway. That was the whole reason I came back on board – to try and delay or stop Angela and Phil until we could be saved.

"Watch them," said Angela to Phil, and got to her feet and went up the companionway. Now was the moment of truth. Either Jasmine would tell her everything I said, or she would keep my secrets.

The storm was definitely past its peak. It wasn't calm by any means, but the front that had blasted down upon us was far to the southeast. I wondered if this was one of those Alberta Clippers that broke hard, and then kept the lake churned up for days afterwards.

I couldn't stop shivering. I wanted to get out of my wet clothes, but I couldn't think of a way to do so without revealing my secrets. I settled for stepping over to the galley for more coffee. I wanted to wrap up in a blanket and rest, but unless I somehow changed things, there were only a few hours before we all died.

"So, Phil," I said, the hearty pastor making small talk, "you know Angela had an affair right?"

Phil looked at me cautiously. "She told you that?"

"She did. I'm sorry." In the scheme of things, I wasn't as sorry as I might have been.

"She probably just said that to get us into counseling."

"So, you guys never had any trouble with your marriage then?"

Phil's face looked pinched. I wasn't playing fair. The fact is, *all* couples have various issues in their marriage sooner or later. It was normal and natural; the working through of marriage problems is part of God's plan to give people an opportunity to mature. But I was playing for our lives, so I didn't say that to Phil. I tried to make him think he was the only one.

"The guy she cheated with was a professor at UMD."

Phil looked even more sour, and also sad and strangely vulnerable. I began to dislike myself a little bit, but my only choice was to find a weak link and hammer at it until something gave.

"He was into feminism. You know how she likes that. She probably thought he understood her or respected her, but I doubt it. He was probably just after her body."

"Shut up," said Phil thickly.

I wanted to shut up, I really did. Now, I was disliking myself a good deal. But I thought of Leyla and Stone lying there helplessly, watching me, and the Coast Guard getting to the wreckage of the *Tiny Dancer* long hours after we were lost in the cold darkness of Superior's depths.

"She doesn't think a lot of you, does she, Phil?"

Phil screwed himself together with effort. "Shut up," he said again. "I know what you're doing, and it won't work. You're just trying to get us mad at each other, and then you'll jump us."

"Could be," I said. "That's a pretty good idea, now that you mention it. But even if I was doing that, what I am saying is true. You know it is."

"Stop it," said Phil. He was almost pleading. It was going to be a long time before I wanted to see my face in a mirror. But I kept my expression cold and blank toward Phil.

"How long are you going to let her do this stuff, Phil? How many more affairs will you let her have before you stand up for yourself?"

I sipped some coffee, choosing my words with as much thought as I could muster.

"Phil, you aren't a murderer, but Angela is. Even if you don't care that she looks at you like chopped liver, don't you care that she's killing people? How many more lives will you let her take? She's out of control. Be a man, Phil. Do the right thing, and stop her."

With a supreme effort, Phil got ahold of himself. "You killed my brother," he said.

As a conversation stopper, it was a pretty good one. I didn't know what to say. It was true, I guess, and there wasn't any way to change it. I stared at him and felt my shoulders slumping. He wasn't going to listen to me. I was the one who killed his twin. The silence began to lengthen.

"Angela started the shooting." It was Stone who spoke, startling Phil and me. His voice sounded like sandpaper on limestone, but we could understand him just fine. He slowly eased himself up a little on the settee until he could turn his head and see Phil. "If Angela hadn't started the firefight, Borden wouldn't have shot back. Fact is, Borden didn't even have a gun to use until Angela shot the guard." He coughed a little and grunted with pain.

"It's true," I said sadly. "I was shooting back at Angela, though I didn't know who it was, of course. I missed her and hit your brother. I didn't mean to. When someone shoots at you, you shoot back if you have the chance. It's a defensive reaction."

"The fact is," said Stone slowly and clearly, though painfully hoarse, "Angela got your brother killed. If she didn't start shooting, no one would have been hurt, and he'd be alive. If she hadn't made you guys keep on with the robberies, no one would have been hurt, and he would be alive. It wasn't the first person she got killed either, was it? She got her own brother killed first, same way, by Borden's father."

"She'll never quit, Phil," I said quietly. "Who is it going to be next time? You? There aren't many left."

"We're done with this now," Phil said in a tight voice. "We've hit our last bank."

"I bet you thought that when you left Washington, too," I said. "You really think she'll quit for good?"

At that moment, Angela blew back down the companionway. I looked at her, trying to read her face. Now was the moment of truth – did Jasmine keep my secret or not?

She saw me staring at her. "Were you hoping I got blown overboard?"

"The thought had crossed my mind," I said.

She laughed, but there was no humor in it. "No such luck, Borden."

I sipped some coffee while she took off her coat. She glanced at me, and then looked more closely.

"When did you change your clothes?"

"I didn't," I said, surprised. A half-second later I was grateful for the fact that I had completely forgotten that I had been given new, dry clothes on the *Superior Rose*. My reaction had been perfect.

"You must have," said Angela. "I don't remember those clothes. Those pants look too short for you."

"You're crazy," I said loudly enough to emphasize the point to Stone and to Leyla, who was wide awake now. "You think I keep spare clothes stashed up there in the cockpit?"

"I don't know what to think," she said, looking at me closely.

"Those are his clothes," said Leyla. "He's been wearing them all night. I've bugged him about those stupid short pants for months, but he says he loves them. I think they make him look stupid."

That's my girl! I wanted to hug her, but I was careful to not even look at her.

"Something's going on," said Angela.

"Right," I said. "I jumped off the boat, swam over to some convenient freighter that was in the neighborhood, got myself some dry clothes and a cup of coffee, and then swam back here because I missed you so much, and I wanted wet clothes anyway."

"I think those must be his own clothes Angela," said Phil.

"You're a moron, Philip," she said. "You wouldn't even recognize your own pants if I didn't pick them out for you in the morning."

I watched Phil's face get pinched again. It broke my heart, but gave me hope at the same time. Angela dropped the business with my clothes. I sipped some coffee to cover my relief. I am always discovering new uses for coffee.

I noticed that the light seemed to be dimmer. Even so, we were no nearer to being safe. I had to try again.

"So, Angela," I said, "you killed your professor-lover in Duluth, huh?"

Her eyes locked onto my face. So did Phil's.

"I heard it on the news, right before the storm. Professor of counseling and women's studies shot to death in his own home. First name Ethan. Same first name as the lover you claim you *invented*, Angela. Professor of the same things." I looked at Phil. "You see?"

Phil looked like a man struggling through a thick swamp. "We've only got your word for it, Borden," he said.

Angela lifted her chin. "I did it."

Phil stared at her. Even Stone looked surprised through his pain. I myself didn't expect her to admit it all so easily, but then I was cold and tired and wasn't really thinking straight about Angela and her twisted view of the world.

"I had the affair, Philip, because it is wrong to be confined by the artificial social construction of marriage, which is merely used as a tool to oppress women."

"Yeah," I said. "It sure looks like Phil's done a lot of oppressing in this relationship."

"Shut up, Borden."

Phil was looking like someone had just clocked him with a right hook. "Why did you kill him?" he asked. I wanted to cry. In Phil's voice there was the sound of pathetic hope, as if he thought maybe Angela had killed her lover out of true love and commitment to himself.

"I realized he was just using me, like men always do," said Angela. "Plus," she said casually, "it's not like we're going back to Minnesota. I wouldn't be seeing him again anyway."

I saw Phil's world brutally implode. He looked away from Angela and wouldn't meet her eyes. His shoulders slumped, and through the dim light, I thought I saw tears in his eyes. I didn't know what he would do, if anything, but he was facing the truth now in a way that he probably never had before. I wanted to give him time and space to make up his mind to do the right thing.

"So did killing the guy help your guilt problem?" I asked Angela.

She leaned back against the desk underneath the radios. "You know, I haven't really had time to think about it," she said. Incredibly, she seemed genuinely interested in the question. Then she shook her head. "No, guilt is an artificial construct used by the elites of society to oppress others and maintain control. I already told you that."

"So the answer is, no – you still feel guilty."

"Well, your approach isn't really an option now, is it? I think we're a little past forgiveness."

"Nobody is past forgiveness," I said. "You know the song *Amazing Grace*?"

"You think some stupid platitude from a *hymn* is going to change my mind?" She sounded incredulous. She shook her head. "I used to think you were intelligent."

"The writer of that hymn was a slave trader."

"What – what do you mean?" asked Phil. There was a catch in his voice.

"I mean the guy who wrote *Amazing Grace* was a slave trader. He captured innocent people, imprisoned them, and transported them across the ocean in unimaginably horrible conditions. A lot of them died because he didn't take care of them. He sold them like cattle, and got filthy rich. And when he finally admitted that what he did was evil, he also found out that *even he* could be forgiven. That's what inspired the song."

"Religious propaganda to further oppression," said Angela.

"How does forgiveness oppress you, Angela?" I asked.

"You want me to admit I'm wrong," she said in a voice that sounded like nails on a blackboard.

"You think killing, kidnapping and stealing are not wrong?"

"Morals are made up by societies to control the masses. But it's not just that. It's everything. You want to justify what was done to me."

"I'm not trying to justify anything, Angela. Forgiveness is exactly for things that cannot be justified."

She gave a little groan. "Shut up."

"That's always an intelligent argument," I agreed.

There was an explosion of pain on the left side of my head, a scream from Leyla, and I staggered against the galley counter. Angela had struck me with her pistol, very close to the same spot where Phil hit me earlier in the night. Now she held the weapon pointed at a spot between my eyes, her hands trembling.

"I could blow you away right now," she said. "End your little corner of oppression in this world."

I looked into her eyes of death, and knew with certainty that life waited for me on the other side. No one gets out of this world without dying anyway, and a few years more or less doesn't alter the final result. A bullet from her gun was merely a shortcut to the life I was looking forward to more than anything in this mortal frame. I took a deep breath. Death held no fear, but I had unfinished business here. It didn't seem like it was my time yet. I wondered if it ever did. I wanted to save Leyla, Tony, and maybe Jasmine; maybe even Phil and Angela. I took another breath. "How many men have you killed, Angela?" I asked. "Has it ever really helped?"

Her hands shook more. I could feel blood trickling from my temple, and my head began to throb again.

"Go up there and relieve Jasmine," said Angela at last, lowering the gun. "She shouldn't have to be cold and wet while you're warm."

I felt it was an unwarranted exaggeration to say that I was warm, but under the circumstances, it seemed better to remain quiet. I refilled my coffee mug and turned to the companionway. As I pulled the door open, I thought that when Angela freely admitted to murder in front of three witnesses, she might as well have said right out loud that we would all be dead within hours.

FORTY-NINE

"You didn't tell her," I said to Jasmine. She was sheltered under the dodger, letting the autopilot steer.

"I really am on your side."

"Angela just admitted to murdering someone," I said. "I think we don't have much more time."

What little I could see of Jasmine's face, under her dripping hood, was grave. "I wish I knew the whole plan," she said. "I know she'll sink Tiny Dancer, but she hasn't said how."

"Does it matter?" I asked. I had a pretty good idea of how, but I still wasn't completely sure I could trust Jasmine. She might be fishing for more information before she passed it all on to Angela. I said nothing. Later, I bitterly wished that I had spoken.

"Maybe not," said Jasmine, "—if you are right and the Coast Guard is on the way." I felt slightly guilty that I hadn't told her the Coast Guard would be too late. If she was really on our side, she should know that. But if she was really working with Angela, I wanted the pressure to be on.

"I thought for a minute she was going to shoot me just now," was all I said. "I better stay up here, at least until she calms down."

"What did you do?"

"I was pushing buttons, trying to get them to screw up or something. Probably stupid."

I couldn't see her eyes, but I could feel them on my face. "You sure you're just a pastor?"

For some reason, that sort of question always irritates me. "Of course I am. Pastors are just people, like everyone else. Are you sure you're just an FBI agent, or just Italian? Quit categorizing people."

"How did you know I was Italian?"

"Lucky guess."

She looked at me for a long time. "You're not telling me everything, are you?"

I returned her gaze. "No."

She was quiet for a minute. "Jonah, I'm your ace-in-the-hole. You need me."

"So you say – no offense."

"I left the autopilot on. I got your rope out of the rigging. I didn't tell Angela anything."

"Look, Jasmine," I said. "Nothing in our relationship up until this very night has been based on truth or reality. I just can't trust you yet."

She turned away abruptly. "Fine. I'm going below," she stalked to the companionway and disappeared.

I considered the dim lights glowing dully through the cabin windows. If I let the autopilot drain the battery completely, I might have a few minutes afterwards to steer us off course and delay us. I could claim it was an accident, since I wouldn't have the GPS any longer. But whenever the Coast Guard did show up, they'd be looking for us on the course I gave them.

I went back to the wheel and looked at the GPS unit. We were within about ten miles of the waypoint – maybe two, or two and half hours at our current speed. Once Angela and Phil were on the other boat, our lives would be forfeit. Under the circumstances, delay seemed like a good idea.

I waited under the dodger. The cabin lights looked washed out and old. I wondered when someone would notice, and what they would say. Leyla would probably figure it out, but she might not know it was deliberate. Jasmine, of course, would know. Maybe her response would give me the assurance I wanted in order to trust her.

I am not a swearing man, but I almost gave in to the impulse when I realized that a dead battery meant no more coffee. I cheered up again a moment later when I remembered that the stove was run on propane, and I could boil water and still make cowboy coffee, thick and full of grounds.

Suddenly, there was no more light coming from the cabin. In the same moment, I felt the *Tiny Dancer* swing to starboard, but this time she did not swing back, as she had done under the influence of the auto-pilot. I stepped quickly to the wheel and steadied her, holding her maybe ten or fifteen degrees off the original course. I punched the GPS, but to my satisfaction, it was dead.

I reached over and loosened the jib-sheet, spilling air out of the sail, and slowing us down. I tried not to do it so much that it caused a noticeable difference in the feel of the boat.

I heard muffled voices from below and some banging around. I wondered if Jasmine had taken a chance at Angela's pistol in the dark. Even as I thought it, I hoped she hadn't. Phil had a pistol too, and shots in the dark could hit Leyla or Stone. After a moment, I saw the gleam of a flashlight through the windows.

This time it was Phil who came up, five minutes after I saw the flashlight. "What did you do?" He said. He looked tired and even more pinched than before.

"What do you mean?" I asked. I was glad for the dark. It made it easier to pretend surprise.

"All the lights went off. We don't have any power."

"Did you check the fuses?" I asked.

"We just did," he said. "Everything looks OK."

"I don't know much about boats," I said.

"You must have done something. The rest of us were all just sitting there."

"The storm probably loosened something. All this pounding can't be good for the boat."

He stood there for a few minutes, flinching as the spray and rain crashed onto his back.

"What did you do?"

Brightness may not have been one of Phil's strong points. He didn't seem to know what else to say.

"I've just been out here all night, keeping us on course," I said. It was true, but of course, I was using the autopilot to do it.

He looked at me. I looked at him, and then out at the storm. The twelve foot waves were pounding the port side about halfway along, sending spray flying as high as the mast. Every third or fourth wave caught us and washed over the deck, dumping water into the cockpit at our feet, which then drained out the scuppers.

"Look at it," I said to Phil. "And this is calm compared to earlier. Something got wet, or got shifted by the movement and shorted out."

"Do you mean it?"

I looked at what I could see of his face in the dark and under his hood. "Mean what?"

"Do you mean it – what you said about forgiveness?"

I blinked spray out of my eyes and wiped my face with my right hand. "I do, Phil. There's nothing I believe more."

"Is it really true, that guy who wrote *Amazing Grace*?"

"It is," I said. "He was a slave trader named John Newton. I think they made a movie about his life or something. He was abused when he was younger and forced into a kind of slavery himself. But that didn't stop him from making slaves of others."

"And he was forgiven?"

"I believe he was. I don't know how you could write that hymn if you weren't sure you were forgiven."

Phil was quiet for a long time. Then, without a word, he turned and went below.

FIFTY

The wind was strong and steady from the northwest, and I let it push us father east. I didn't have the GPS anymore, so I wasn't sure just how far off course we were. But the waves had moved from our port bow to our port rear quarter. That meant I started getting very wet again, because they were hitting the boat right next me, and when they washed over the deck, most of it came into the cockpit. Several times water swirled up to my knees before draining out. I was cold and sore and desperately tired. But I ran Rich Mullins' *I Am Ready for the Storm* through my head, and pretended it was true.

It took them about half an hour to realize I wasn't on course anymore. Jasmine came up, dressed in raingear and holding the portable GPS.

"They noticed you are off course. Angela was all for finishing the job on Tony as an object lesson, but Leyla pointed out that you wouldn't know where to go, once the electronics went dead."

My difficulty was that I had only Jasmine's word for it. This is what I wanted to hear – that she hadn't sold me out. But I wasn't down there when it happened, so I couldn't know for sure. At least no one had been shot – surely I would have heard that over the sound of the storm.

"I was hoping Angela or Phil would come up. That would leave only one against you, Tony and Leyla."

Jasmine looked at me. "That's a bad plan Jonah. Tony's badly hurt, and couldn't help. Would you really want Leyla fighting down there?"

I felt foolish. "Sorry, of course not. I was just thinking of numbers."

"It's just too risky – guns in small spaces with several people is a bad combination. That's how Phil's brother got killed."

"Thanks for that."

"Sorry, Jonah, but that's the truth. Once it starts, it's pretty hard to control what happens. That's why Tony's down there fighting for his life."

I was torn with a desire to tell Jasmine about Tony. If she knew his wounds were not vital, maybe she would be willing to work with him to try and take out Phil or Angela while the other one was in the cockpit with the GPS. On the other hand, I would be literally killing Tony if I gave away his secret and Jasmine was really working with Angela.

"Screw it," I said. It was a phrase I had picked up at seminary. "Tony isn't going die. He wasn't hit in the lung."

Jasmine's black eyes glittered under her hood. She swore softly. "That fox. He's good; freaking good. So how bad is it?"

"He's not hit anywhere vital," I said. "But his shoulder looks like raw hamburger. I don't know how much action he's capable of. Certainly, I would guess his right arm is basically out of commission. And whatever else he does is going to hurt him like the blazes."

"What're you, from 1955? No one says 'hurt like the blazes.'"

"I just did."

Jasmine surprised me by reaching up and kissing me gently on the cheek. "You're good too, Jonah Borden. I never would have guessed."

I still wasn't sure if I had made the right decision, but at least I had got a sweet kiss on the cheek for my trouble. That was something to feel good about.

"So now what?" I said. "Do we try to get one of them up here with me, while you guys take out the other one down there?"

"I'm not sure," she replied. "If what you say is true, it doesn't change too much. Tony is still gonna have a hard time helping. I would guess he's probably only got enough energy and pain-resistance for one try, and we don't want to waste it."

"On the other hand," I said, deciding to at least proceed as if I was sure of Jasmine, "we've got two of the good guys in one place here. What can we do? Can we get Angela up here by herself while you and I are both down there? That would help our odds."

"We could try," she said. "Maybe I could send you back down. You could tell Angela that I said I didn't see the point in having one of the hostages up here when one of us has to be here anyway. Maybe eventually she'd send Phil, or come up herself to relieve me."

"A lot of 'maybe's and 'ifs' there."

"Got anything better?"

"Well, *we're* both here – the fox is watching the henhouse, so to speak. Why don't we keep veering off course? It'll buy us time and maybe options."

She thought about it. "But if we get too far off, they'll realize that I had to be letting you do it. That blows my cover, for no purpose."

"Give me ten more minutes on this course. They probably won't know exactly how far off we were or how long it will take to get back. After ten minutes, we'll start coming back to the right course, but we'll take another ten or fifteen to do it. I've already been doing this for a half hour so, that wins us almost an hour, total."

"Why are you so concerned about time?" asked Jasmine. "I thought you said the Coast Guard was on the way."

"They are, but who knows when they'll get here."

"They aren't close?"

I shrugged. "It's a big lake, bad weather – a lot of things could go wrong."

"You have the makings of a fine agent."

"I don't think so. I'm allergic to hierarchy and authority."

"Jonah, you're a clergyman, for Pete's sake!"

I laughed. It was pleasant to talk about something besides impending doom. "I'm not part of *that* kind of church. There are a lot of churches and denominations, like mine, that use minimal, streamlined leadership and bow to local congregational authority."

"You don't have bishops and such, telling you what to do?"

I shook my head. "Nope. I couldn't function like that. I truly have faith. But I recognize that over the years, a lot of nonsense has been said and done by church hierarchies. Thankfully, it's easy enough to demonstrate that they weren't following Jesus when they did those things."

"Huh."

We stopped talking for a bit while we rolled on through the unsettled darkness. After another wave had crashed over the edge of the cockpit and soaked us up to the knees, Jasmine said, "That's a lot of water."

"We'd be in trouble if the companionway was open when that came in," I agreed. "Leyla says she'd fill up and drop like a rock."

"The *Tiny Dancer*, not Leyla, right?"

"Right."

I was tired right through to my teeth. I was so used to being cold that it felt more like an aching numbness. A sudden heave of the great lake pushed me off my feet. I fell to the starboard and ended up sitting on the cockpit bench. While the wheel spun, the wind pushed our bow further to the east and we turned our stern to the waves and wind. The sail, out of sync with the new direction, flapped and shuddered.

I got up and grabbed the wheel just as Jasmine got there.

"Angela's gonna come up and check. She had to feel that," she said.

"Should we jump her?"

She grabbed my arm. "No. Phil's still down there with Leyla and Tony. The best we get is a stalemate. But one of us could end up dead."

It was Phil who burst through the companionway door. "What's going on?"

"A big waved knocked Borden off his feet and us off course," said Jasmine, tapping the GPS.

A sudden inspiration hit me. "We'll need to tack to get back on course," I said. "We need Leyla." A wall of rain and spray showered us all. Phil shivered. "OK," he said, and went below.

A few minutes later, Leyla came up. She looked at Jasmine and at me. I reached out and pulled her to me, holding her with my right arm, and the wheel with my left. After a moment we broke apart.

"What's going on?"

"We're pretending that we need to tack in order to get back on course. Maybe we can fool around and delay things a bit."

Leyla looked meaningfully at me. "*Jonah,*" she whispered, cutting her eyes at Jasmine.

"Apparently, Jasmine is with us still," I said. "She is double undercover."

"Double undercover?" Leyla's eyes were puzzled.

"Under two covers?" I suggested. "Under double-cover?"

"Never mind," said Jasmine. "Just say, I have always been on the side of truth and justice, that is, on your side."

Leyla looked at her doubtfully.

"It's a long explanation," I said.

"Okay," she said, taking a breath. I loved how quickly she was able to adapt. "What did you want to do here?"

"Instead of coming back toward the wind, let's go all the way around in a circle to get back on course. Maybe we can sort of take our time doing it."

"Can't we do anything else?"

"They've still got Tony," said Jasmine. "This is a hostage situation. As long as they have the ability to kill someone if we misbehave, we have to play along, or at least, *appear* to play along."

I wanted to hit something. Three of the four of us were at liberty. But we couldn't do anything. It struck me that often, this is how evil holds Good captive. Good refuses to sacrifice the innocent; it always tries to save those who might be saved. But in so doing, Good must often let evil run free, at least for a time. People often ask why a good God would allow evil to continue in this world. He was doing it for the same reason that we didn't stop Angela and Phil at this moment – there was still someone that might be saved. But God also promised us a day of reckoning, when evil *will* be called to account, when crimes left unchecked will be finally and irrevocably served with justice. I surrendered myself once more to trust that Good and Just God, and found in that trust, the strength to face whatever was to come.

FIFTY-ONE

We managed to waste the better part of an hour turning to starboard and coming almost in a complete circle to get back on the GPS course. Leyla estimated that in that hour we made little, if any, forward progress along the course.

The weather settled into what she called a "fresh gale." The wind ripped across the water, tearing white streaks into the dark waves, throwing rain and spray at us in sheets. The waves seemed content to heave up to twelve or fifteen feet or so, with occasional specimens both lower and higher. But at least it wasn't getting any worse.

The night was old. It was too wet for my eyes to feel gritty, but my body knew I had been awake for most of the last twenty-four hours. I could sense the change before I could actually see it. Slowly, dawn struggled into the thick atmosphere like a drunk waking up the morning after a binge. The light grew sullenly, and when it reached a dark-gray, reminiscent of a stormy late-afternoon, it seemed to give up, like that was the best it could do today. With all the low light and flying water, visibility was less than half a mile.

"Take the wheel?" I said to Jasmine.

She nodded, and I moved over to where Leyla was tightening the jib sheet after our final adjustment. Leyla straightened and turned to me.

"I don't know what's going to happen," I said to her.

She stepped over and embraced me. She held me tight. "I thought you were dead more than once during the past twenty-four hours."

"I thought I lost you once tonight too," I said. "I don't want to have that feeling again."

The storm was probably loud enough to keep Jasmine from understanding our low voices, but she politely looked away from us as we stood there, balancing together against the roll and sway of the boat.

"Ever read the *Chronicles of Narnia*?" I asked. "*The Voyage of the Dawn Treader*?"

"I think I saw the movie," she said.

"Aslan came to Lucy in her darkest hour and spoke. He said, '*courage, dear heart.*'"

We were quiet, holding each other while the boat rocked us both.

"Courage, dear heart," she said at last.

"Yes," I said.

The hug was sweet, but after all, kind of wet. We let go of each other at last, shortly before Angela came up the companionway.

"Let me see the GPS," she said to Jasmine.

Jasmine took it out of her jacket pocket.

"Not much of a morning, is it?" said Angela to no one in particular. She checked the unit as Jasmine handed it to her.

"Shouldn't we be farther along?" she asked sharply.

"I'm no GPS expert," said Jasmine. "These guys said the weather has been working against us."

Angela glared at me. I shrugged. "I want to be done with this and go home as soon as possible. Delay doesn't help me."

She held my gaze a moment longer. "Fine," she snapped. "Leyla, you get below."

Leyla gave me a soft look, and then turned and went down the companionway. After a minute of simply staring out into the gauzy gray of the storm, Angela turned back to me. "Now you," she said. "Don't be thinking of trying anything on Philip – I'll be right behind you."

I went down the companionway. It was still warmer than the cockpit, since the heat came from propane rather than electricity, but it was dark; the dim light outside barely penetrated the narrow windows.

"Nice and easy Borden," said Phil. "I'm holding Leyla, and my gun is in her side." I could dimly make out their two figures near the front of the cabin.

"Okay," I said.

Angela came down behind me, and I felt her gun grind into my right kidney. "I've got him covered Philip," she said. Phil took another pair of plastic cuffs out and secured Leyla's hands in front of her. He helped her sit on the starboard settee, and she shifted around the U.

"Now you," Angela said. She walked me forward to where the mast descended from above. She fastened my hands together around the pole. "I think we're better off without you moving around," she said, jerking on my wrists to make sure I was secure.

"Any chance I could get some coffee?" I asked hopefully.

I couldn't see Angela's eyes very well in the dimness, but she looked at me for what seemed like an unreasonably long time.

"No electricity," she said at last. "If you could fix that, maybe I could get you some."

"I don't know how to fix it," I said truthfully enough. "But you can make coffee on the stove. Boil a few cups of water, and add a tablespoon of coffee for every cup."

She shook her head, "You never quit, do you?" she asked.

"It's one of my best things," I said.

"Says who?" she muttered and turned away. "I think it's time, Philip," she said.

My heart began to pound. But Phil only went over the wall where the radio was mounted and began unscrewing the face-plate. He pulled out the non-functioning radio and stuck his hand in the hole beyond. He came out with a big orange plastic radio that looked a lot like the dead one I had found in the dinghy.

However, this one worked. He turned a knob and the sound of static flowed out of it. Angela snatched the radio from him. She turned a few knobs and then held it up to her face.

"*Tiny Dancer* to *Great Escape*, *Tiny Dancer* to *Great Escape*, come in please."

I thought that was a very nice name for the getaway boat. I said as much, but no one paid any attention.

Angela released the talk button and static hissed again. She repeated the call again. Suddenly the unit crackled to life.

"I've got you *Tiny Dancer*," said a voice, hollowed out by the radio waves. "This is *Great Escape*."

"The day our father died, over," said Angela cryptically.

"Was a happy one, over," replied the voice.

"What a sweet little password phrase," I said. No one acknowledged me. It seemed to be a trend.

"OK," said Angela, "switch to sixty-seven."

"Sixty-seven, roger," said the voice, which had to be Red Holland, Angela's brother.

Angela leaned toward the dim light of a window and changed the channel. The digital LED on the radio read "sixty-seven."

"Red?" she said, holding down the talk button.

"I'm here, over," he said.

"What's your position, over?"

Holland read out some GPS coordinates.

"We're a little behind, too" said Angela. "The storm slowed us down, the engines died, and we ran out the battery, over."

"Any trouble? Over?"

"Borden tweaked Phil a little, and the FBI pig took a shot at us, but we're in control."

"I will proceed along the course further, over," said Red Holland over the radio.

"OK," said Angela. "Expect to find us along the same line, maybe two to five miles from our original rendezvous point. What's your ETA? Over."

"It's a little rough," commented Holland. "I can't really plane in this weather. Should be maybe half an hour to forty minutes, over."

"You tired, over?"

"I expect to sleep while you get us home. You've had all that help, and I've been up all night. Over."

"We'll see," said Angela. "See you soon, over and out."

There was relative quiet in the cabin.

"Can I make Jonah some coffee?" asked Leyla suddenly.

Angela looked at her. My eyes were a little more used to the dimness, and I thought her expression was contemptuous. "He's just a man," she said. "You don't need to serve him."

Leyla tossed her hair back. "He's *my* man," she said. "I want to." I suddenly felt warmer.

"You're brainwashed. He is part of the patriarchal system that keeps women like you oppressed."

"I'm sure you wouldn't understand," said Leyla.

"You're right."

"I want coffee too," said Leyla.

"Fine. You need to do it with your hands the way they are."

Leyla scooted around the table and slipped past Angela behind the galley counter. With her wrists together, she rummaged around and found a small pot. She put it in the sink and then used both hands to turn on the faucet. Nothing happened.

"Rats," she said. "I forgot – the pump is battery operated." She looked at Angela. "You mind if I go up and dip some out of the lake?"

"You're crazy," said Angela. But she reached up and unlatched the companionway door for Leyla. Leyla went up, but she wasn't gone long. The pot was about half full. "It's about the cleanest water we'll ever drink," she said. She bustled around some more with the stove and coffee. I slid down the mast and sat on the floor, leaning back against the bulkhead next to the door to the forward sleeping quarters, my arms stretched in front of me around the mast pole. No one said anything.

After a few minutes, the most beautiful aroma in the world began to fill the cabin. I was filled with vicious longing for the dark elixir of the gods. After a few more agonizing moments, Leyla came forward and knelt in front of me.

"Can you hold and drink?" she asked. I took the cup in my hands. If I scooted in close to the mast and craned my neck to the left, I could drink awkwardly without spilling too much. As I experimented with this, Leyla leaned closer and whispered, "Channel sixty-seven is a commercial shipping frequency. If there is a ship around, they might have heard."

At first, I was filled with a rush of hope. Then I remembered that Lake Superior is bigger than a lot of East-Coast states, and the chances were good that no one was within radio range out there. The *Superior Rose* had a schedule to keep and had moved out hours ago. And even if someone else overheard, it was just two boats figuring out a rendezvous – they really hadn't said enough to make anyone suspicious. However, hope is good, and sometimes hard to come by, so I didn't say anything to Leyla.

"Thank you for the coffee," is all I said.

As I finished the hot drink, I began to finally feel warm again, and with the warmth came a powerful drowsiness. I had slept less than an hour all night. Twice, I felt my head jerk downward. I cursed myself for a fool, sleeping away my last hour on earth, but it was hard to see what else I could do.

FIFTY-TWO

I was startled awake by the popping of sound from the radio. I didn't hear what was said at first.

"Okay," said Angela. "I'll go up and watch out. Over."

I squinted my eyes as Angela walked over to the table. She faced Leyla. "How do you stop this boat when it's under sail?"

"Why should I help you?" said Leyla.

Angela took two more steps and regarded me dispassionately. She took out her pistol and held it by her leg, bending over a little to see me better.

"Wait," said Leyla.

But Angela drew back her hand and struck me with her gun exactly where she had done so before. The pain exploded above my eye. I couldn't cover my head with my hands, so I scooted up to the mast and tried to shelter my head from further blows. But Angela was finished. Leyla was standing up.

"Stop it! Stop and I'll help you."

"That's better," said Angela with satisfaction.

"I'll need my hands," said Leyla. I was waiting for the stars to stop interfering with my vision, so I didn't see for sure when Angela cut her free.

"Philip," I heard Angela say, "Why don't you secure Agent Stone, too? I'd rather not trust to his injuries at this critical moment."

I looked up to see Leyla's feet disappear up the companionway, followed by Angela. I was alone with Stone and Phil. Stone was straightening up. He glanced toward me and dropped his left eyelid smoothly and slowly. My head throbbing, and fresh blood beginning to drip over my eyebrow, I hitched myself up and gripped the metal mast pole. Phil tucked his pistol into his waistband and reached out with both hands to shift Stone. He put his hands under the armpits of the wounded man. I watched, like a cat stalking a bird. Stone reached up to grab Phil's right hand with his left. "It hurts," he rasped. Phil shifted awkwardly, his arms tangled up with Stone. I swung my body around the mast and drove both feet like a scythe into Phil's legs. Stone held him with his left hand, so that Phil's legs went out from under him, while his body fell toward me. As he hit the floor, the breath exploded out of him, and I scooted down and wrapped my knees around his neck. Stone winced, but moved quickly for all that, and pulled the gun out of Phil's waistband and held it up to his head.

"Be still, OK?" he said. Phil blinked. I released some of the pressure on his neck, and he nodded.

"Lock it in again, for a minute," said Stone to me. I put one foot behind my opposite knee and squeezed a little. "I don't want to hurt you, Phil," I said quietly. "But I will if I have to." He blinked.

Stone lurched to his feet, stumbled, and slid back to his knees. He tried and failed again, and finally stayed up on the third try. "Didn't realize how much blood I lost," he muttered. He went to the galley and got a knife, came back and cut my handcuffs. He handed me the gun. "I'm right-handed," he said, and collapsed back onto the settee. I felt dizzy, and my head was throbbing, but I held the gun in both hands and pressed onto the top of Phil's head.

"I'm going to get up, Phil," I said. "You stay right there, Okay?"

He coughed and groaned and finally rasped, "Okay."

The *Tiny Dancer* suddenly swung firmly to port and then seemed to hover, wallowing in the waves. Leyla had swung into the wind to stop our progress.

"Get him up and use him as a shield," said Stone, grunting with pain.

"Okay, Phil," I said. "Get up now." He stood, and his right knee was clearly giving him pain. I stepped behind him, wrapping my left arm firmly around his neck and keeping the gun in his back.

I felt awkward and mean. "Sorry," I mumbled.

Stone looked at me incredulously. Phil said, "That's okay. I did it to you guys."

For a minute, I thought that little exchange might finish Stone off, where bullets had failed. He looked like he was having a heart attack. "I must be delirious," he muttered. He shook his head. "Okay, get in position and wait for Angela to come down."

The companionway door thrust open, and Angela started down the steps. "What was that noise?"

"I've got Phil," I said. "Come down slowly."

Angela gave an unearthly scream, something like that of the cougars I have heard in the hills above my cabin. She bent down, and in one smooth motion drew her gun, and fired at me. This was not how it was supposed to go. My reactions slowed, and my mind churned uselessly. I ducked behind Phil. I felt terrible about it later, but there it is. Phil made a little sound in his throat, almost a squeal. I stuck my gun around his body and fired twice, quickly. The boat was heaving, so accuracy was not really an option, though with my ignorance of handguns, it probably never was. Angela screamed in rage and backed up the stairs.

"You have thirty seconds to let him go, or I'll kill Leyla. I *mean* it!"

There was a hole in the cupboard next to Phil's head, and a splinter of wood drawing blood from his cheek. "She shot at me," he said in a low moan. "She *shot* at me. She shot at *me*." He kept repeating it like a mantra, emphasizing different words, as if that would somehow help him understand what happened.

I glanced back at Stone. His eyes were wide and shocked. "I guess he isn't much of a hostage," he said. "She's willing to trade his life for Leyla's."

"I'm not," I said. I released Phil. "Get up there," I said. "You've got to control her somehow. She's going to kill us all."

He slumped limply toward the companionway, and then turned back. "She coulda killed me," he said.

"She nearly did," I said.

He hobbled up the stairs.

"Borden!" Angela's voice was shrill. "The gun – now!"

"Send Leyla down," I called. "We'll stay here, and you can leave with your brother."

I heard Jasmine murmur something, and then Phil.

"Borden," shouted Jasmine, her voice harsh and impersonal. "Give us the gun now. We aren't messing around here."

I turned quickly to Stone, who was sitting on the floor, eyes closed, leaning against the wall and breathing heavily. "Jasmine – whose side is she on, really?"

He opened his eyes and looked at me. "She's good, isn't she? She's playing dirty-cop, but she's still with us."

I breathed a deep sigh of relief.

"Come on now!" said Jasmine.

"Empty the magazine," said Stone in a low voice.

I pushed the button, pulled out the magazine, and furiously thumbed shiny brass bullets out of it.

"Quick," said Stone.

I slammed it back in, checked the safety and called, "I'm tossing it up now." Stone was crawling on the floor, scooping up the bullets. I walked to the companionway and gingerly flipped the weapon up into the cockpit.

"Did you get the one in the chamber?" Stone's voice was low and tight.

Of course I hadn't. They really hadn't trained me for this at seminary. Maybe I could go back and teach a course on pastoral weapons handling. I just shook my head.

I could hear Angela yelling from the deck above. "You are a moron, Philip. You can't do anything right. I just asked you to watch them for five minutes, and I can't even trust you to do that." She said more, and it wasn't very lady-like. It know it's stupid, but I felt sorry that we had jumped him.

"You two stay put," called Jasmine. "If you show your face, someone will shoot it."

Now I could hear the roar of a marine engine, which quickly turned to a low rumble. I couldn't really see out of the high windows. There was some shouting and more engine sounds. I assumed Red Holland was here and was maneuvering the power-boat into position. Abruptly, I felt the Tiny Dancer shift and start to bounce out of rhythm with the waves. I heard a banging and scraping from the stern. A minute later, Angela called out.

"Borden? Stone? I'm coming down. You two sit on the settee, back behind the table. If I so much as squeal, Leyla loses a knee. If I scream, she dies. You understand?"

"Got it," I said. I helped Stone get up onto the settee and scoot around. He groaned twice.

Angela came down the companionway. She glared at us, and then marched forward into her cabin. She came back with two heavy-looking bags, and dragged them up the companionway. After a moment, she returned to the forward cabin for a third. My heart began to pound. She hauled that up the companionway as well.

She didn't come back. Instead, she called, "We're leaving now, and we're taking Leyla to ensure your good behavior. Don't even think about trying anything." She pulled the companionway door shut and did something to it.

Stone began to curse, low and steady, and with surprisingly few repetitions. I felt the same way, though I refrained. I contented myself with leaping across the table, and jerking open the cupboard that held my duffel bag. I pulled it out and opened the zipper.

"Stone!" I said sharply. "Shut up and listen. They were going to blow the *Tiny Dancer* to pieces with explosives. But I switched the bags. Now, when they hit the switch, they'll blow themselves up, and Leyla and Jasmine along with them."

FIFTY-THREE

I grabbed my bag and raced up the steps. I thrust at the companionway door, but it wouldn't budge. I backed up and threw my shoulder against it, but it still didn't open. Angela must have locked it or jammed it from outside. I tried again, and pain shot from my shoulder up to my bruised head. I felt dizzy and sick, but I stepped down and threw a side kick at the seam of the doors. I have splintered two-by-fours with that kick, but at the time, I wasn't dizzy with pain and exhaustion; I wasn't standing two steps down from my target on a rocking and rolling sailboat in the middle of a gale on Lake Superior. The doors gave a little, but held.

"Here," rasped Stone. He had pulled the fire extinguisher off the wall of the galley. I held it like I've seen the police hold door-rams on TV, and slammed it into the doors. They gave a little more. I pounded it frenetically, again and again, and then I turned and put every ounce of force I had into another kick. The doors splintered and fell open.

I pushed them aside and thrust my way up into the cockpit, dragging my bag with me. I knelt down, unzipped the bag and grabbed a bundle of money – the money that I had taken from Angela's luggage and put into my own. The money I had replaced with explosives in her bags. I snapped the rubber band off the stack, and stood up and threw it in air, scattering green bills into the wind. I shouted "Angela!" as loud as I could, and then dipped down and latched on to the bag with my left hand.

I stood again, with another bundle of money in my right hand, and held the bag out over the water with my left.

"Stone," I called over my shoulder. "Get the other two bags in the starboard cupboard, quick."

The getaway boat was idling its engine and heaving with the waves, about thirty yards away. They had apparently pushed off, and were preparing to watch the explosion from a safe distance.

"Angela," I shouted again. "I've got your money. The explosives are on *your* boat." I threw the money in my right hand up into the wind. It disappeared into the rain and spray of the dull-gray morning. "Now," I yelled, "You drop your guns and the explosives over the side, and give us Leyla and Jasmine, and we'll let you have your money, and go wherever you want. If you don't, the money goes to the bottom." I shook the duffel bag over the water.

Something strange was going on. I expected every one of them to be fixated on me and the money, but they seemed to stop paying attention long before I was finished. There was a flurry of movement, and then Angela was saying something urgently to Red Holland. Jasmine thrust something into Leyla's hands and then suddenly they both jumped overboard into the waves. Phil, Red and Angela followed almost immediately. They all started swimming away from the power-boat, frantically battling the waves and kicking up spray.

"Oh no," said Stone behind me.

The swimmers had covered maybe half the distance between us when there was a massive "thump" that I felt deep in my chest. A huge fountain of spray burst into the air where the power boat had been.

I turned and hurled myself down the companionway, grabbing life vests and racing back to the cockpit. I didn't know if anyone on the other boat had had time to get them. I emerged to see a giant wave swelled up over us. It grew bigger and very steep. As the wave loomed higher, an awful realization grew within me. I threw the life vests at Stone, and turned to pull the companionway doors shut. But they wouldn't latch – I had broken them in order to get out in the first place. I tugged frantically, and then the wall of water fell on top us.

I was slammed into the side of the cockpit, and then swept down into the cabin by a raging torrent of icy water. It poured in like a river. I scrambled to my feet, the water already to my waist, and saw another life vest bobbing by the galley. With extreme effort I managed to push forward and grab it. I buckled it on securely and pulled the straps as the water reached my chest and lifted me off my feet.

A second later, the cabin was completely full. I took a deep breath, and then I was under water, but there was no longer a current against me. My life jacket floated me up toward the ceiling. I opened my eyes, and saw the dim outline of the companionway. I could feel the pressure building on my ears. Frantically, I pulled myself up the passage and then I was out. A piece of wire rigging snagged me for a moment. I struggled insanely, and then suddenly I was free, floating upwards, while the ghostly shape of the *Tiny Dancer* dropped like an iron bar into the clear timeless depths of Lake Superior, carrying with it more than half a million dollars in unmarked bills.

My lungs were bursting by the time I hit the surface. The top of the mast was just disappearing below the waves maybe eight yards away. Even in the dull light of the storm, as I looked below my feet, I could see the white sail and the dim shape of the hull slowly receding into the deep darkness far below.

I looked around me. Wreckage from Red Holland's vessel was spread out all over the surface. Bits of wood, pieces of cushions, a water bottle.

Tony Stone was ten yards away, riding up a wave to my right. I could see the dark heads of the others a little beyond him. As before, the icy water was stealing my breath and strength, but I forced myself to swim towards them. I saw Stone toss someone a life vest. As I got closer, I could see that something had reopened his wound, and blood swirled in the water next to him. At least in this vast freshwater sea we didn't have to worry about sharks.

After what felt like a long time, I reached the others. They were all there: Leyla, Jasmine, Stone, Angela, Phil and Red. By the time I reached them, everyone had a life vest. Even if Superior did have sharks, I figured the cold would kill us long before any predator would have found us. I figured we had less than half an hour.

"Huddle," I gasped. "Our body heat will help."

"I don't have any body heat left," muttered Jasmine. But we all dog paddled toward each other, grabbing on to arms and life vests. I worked my way to Leyla and put my arms around her, grabbing Stone's vest on the other side. Someone else held mine from behind.

No one said anything for a while. We bobbed high, riding a wave, and then slid back into a valley.

"Anyone know how close we are to land?" asked Leyla.

"Maybe fifteen, twenty miles from Isle Royale," said Red. A lot of teeth were chattering. Every face that I saw had blue lips. By some strange, common, unspoken consent, we avoided talking about the strife between us.

"Not likely anyone will be out and about in this weather," commented Jasmine.

I put my face close to Leyla's. "Courage, dear heart," I said. She squeezed my arm.

"I love you, Jonah."

As I hung in the bone-numbing cold of the water, feeling the heat slowly ebb out of me, certain things became very clear.

"Leyla," I said in a low murmur, close to her ear. "I would not have planned it this way. This isn't the atmosphere I would have aimed for. But I need to tell you some things. I know now that I cannot stand the thought of losing you. Ever. I can't picture a life without you in it. I have made peace with my past, and the only thing I can see in my future is you."

She turned to stare at me with wide eyes. I pulled her closer.

"Leyla Bennett," I said softly, "will you marry me?"

Her shoulders began to shake. Her face twisted strangely. Then her whole body was shaking. It took me a moment to realize that she might be laughing. I waited with difficulty.

"You –" she gasped, "you – wouldn't have *planned* it this way?" Now she was laughing in earnest. I felt Stone twist to look at us. A smile began tug at the corner of my mouth. I could see her point.

"Yeah. I meant to salvage a bottle of wine and two goblets. And we were supposed to sink in Fish Lake, not Superior."

Now we were both laughing out loud. The others were starting to stare at us. Suddenly, Leyla stopped laughing and hugged my neck with so much force that it set my head to aching again. She released me and looked at my eyes. There were tears in hers. "Yes," she said. "Yes, Jonah. Yes, here, yes in Fish Lake, yes whenever, wherever."

I wasn't sure how much the others had heard, but I didn't really care. We bobbed in silence for a while, holding each other tightly, alone with each other even the midst of that miserable huddle.

Another wave washed over us, and my head went under water. In the second before I bobbed back up, I heard a thin whine. I came up, and then dipped my head forward under water again, though the cold made it ache even more. The whine was still there. Anyone who has ever swum in a lake in the summertime knows that sound. It is the noise a motor-boat makes in the water when it is near.

"Boat," I spluttered. "I can hear it."

Several people thrust their heads under quickly. "I hear it too," said Leyla.

"Where is it?" asked Phil.

"No way to know," said Stone. He sounded very hoarse. The only one who did no talking at all was Angela.

After about two minutes, we heard a sound above water – the sound of a powerful, high speed motor.

"Here!" shouted Holland. He flung his hand over his head and shouted again. It was ridiculous, of course. They wouldn't be able to hear us over the sound of their own engines. And seeing us was only slightly more possible. However, they might slow and start to search when they encountered the wreckage of Holland's boat. All of us began to shout and fling our arms into the air, especially whenever we were at the top of a wave.

And then, incredibly, Phil shouted, "I see it! Over here!" He let go of Angela next to him, and threw both hands into the air. "Over here! Over here!" Then I saw it too – a powerboat, circling slowly, through the flotsam, about sixty yards away. We went insane, shouting and waving. I kicked my feet to try and rise up higher above the water. Miraculously, the boat circled closer, and then we could see that they spotted us. Less than a minute later, it pulled up next to us.

Iverson leaned out over the side and looked at us, Felix and Jones beside him. "You folks need a ride?" he asked.

FIFTY-FOUR

With some difficulty, they got us all on board the launch. None of us had much strength to help, so Jones and Felix had to dead-lift us out of the water like fish. Stone cried out once as they pulled him up by his arms, but after that he was quiet. When I was on board, I pointed to Angela, Phil and Red. "Those are the bad guys," I said to Iverson. He jerked his head at Felix who moved and stood over them.

"Just sit still now," he said. It was probably the easiest guard duty anyone had ever had. Not one of us had the strength in our frozen limbs to even point a gun, much less lift one.

The rest of us huddled forward, sitting up under the bow-deck, in front of Iverson's feet as he piloted the boat. Jones found two canvas tarps. He wrapped one around Angela, Phil and Red, and the other around Leyla, Jasmine, Stone and I. We all moved close together, and eventually began to feel a tiny trickle of warmth, though none of us was able to stop shivering.

Iverson gunned the engines, and the noise was too loud for conversation. I held Leyla's hand under the tarp. At least, I hoped it was Leyla's. She smiled at me, and the hand seemed too small for Stone, so I guess I was all right.

Time seemed to go on forever, but it was probably less than an hour when Iverson cut the engine back, and we slowed. From my low vantage point, I caught a glimpse of the great hull of the *Superior Rose*. While Felix stood relentless guard on Angela and her gang, we were hoisted up the side of the freighter and swung into deck. I saw that this time we were at the forward superstructure, rather than the rear one where the engine was. After we were all off the launch, Iverson led us into the ship, to a large room walled with cheap fake-wood paneling. The floor was shiny, dark-blue linoleum. There were tables and chairs and inexpensive wood-framed couches bolted to the floor of the room, and two long windows in one wall.

"This is our crew's mess," he said. "The captain will be down in a little while."

We stood on the floor, dripping. After a minute, two sailors walked in, carrying towels, blankets and dry men's clothing. One of them was Jones. Jasmine and Leyla held one of the blankets in a corner for each other while behind it, they dried and changed. Stone and I did the same. Phil held a blanket for Angela, and then he and Red held it for each other.

When we were dry, and I was beginning to feel warmer than I could recall ever feeling, we sat down, wrapped in blankets. Leyla and I cuddled on a love-seat under one of the windows. Stone and Jasmine shared a couch to our right, while Phil and Red sat at a right-angle to our left, against a wall. Angela was across from us, next to the door, in a chair by herself.

"*Superior Rose*," said Jasmine, looking at a life ring hanging on the wall, stenciled with the name of the ship. "Jonah, your life vest said *Superior Rose*."

"Oh yeah, Borden's been here already," said Iverson. "He was here last night."

Six pairs of eyes swiveled in unison to stare at me. So I told them briefly about my adventures of the night before. Then I turned to Iverson. "But what were you doing out there, still? I thought you guys would be long gone."

"Cap'n got permission from the company to remain in the area," said Iverson. "At least until the Coast Guard gets here."

"So you aren't the Coast Guard?" asked Angela, speaking for the first time since we had all gone into the water.

"No," said Iverson.

"Wait," said Leyla. "You were safe aboard here, and you came *back* to the *Tiny Dancer*?"

I nodded.

"Stupid fool," muttered Stone.

"We'd all be dead if he hadn't," said Jasmine, looking at me.

I was getting uncomfortable. "But why were you out there in the launch?" I asked Iverson.

"No way was I going to throw you in the water and sail away," he said. "We waited and made as sure as we could that you got back on board. It was hard to tell, but we came slowly up behind to pick you up, in case you hadn't."

"Thank you," I said.

"Anyway, Cap'n and I talked about it. We decided before I left that if we got permission, it would be best for me keep trailing you, but out of sight, at least until the cavalry got here. With such poor visibility and the noise of the storm, we were able to keep pretty close to you. You weren't using running lights, but you did use cabin lights, so that helped. Then, all of sudden, we lost you."

"We veered off course for a while," I said. "To try and buy time."

"Plus we ran out the battery," said Jasmine, "so you probably quit seeing our cabin lights about the time we went off course."

Angela's face darkened, and she looked at us with venom in her eyes.

"So that was it," said Jones. "Anyway, we thought it was over. We circled around for an hour or two along the course you were supposed to be on, but we couldn't pick you up. And then all of sudden, just before dawn, there you are in high-fi sound, talking on the ship-to-ship channel. That was the same channel we were using to talk to the *Superior Rose*. They heard you too, so we triangulated your position between the launch and the *Rose*. We were coming up kind of slow, trying not to let you know we were there, when all of sudden we hear an explosion. After that we raced to your last known position and starting circling. You're lucky we found you. Another fifteen minutes, you'd all be frozen to death."

"Maybe not that long," said Jones, leaning against a wall.

"What happened anyway?" I asked, looking at Phil. "Why'd you guys detonate the bomb?"

"Angela pushed the button before you got out of the *Tiny Dancer's* cabin," said Jasmine. "Luckily they had programmed a two minute delay between the activation and the detonation; I suppose to give them a little time if something went wrong. It saved our lives. When we saw you had the money, they figured it out and started jumping overboard."

There was a brief silence, and then the door squeaked open. Captain Dillon stepped into the room. This morning he was in uniform, apparently in honor of so many guests. I felt a little hurt that he hadn't dressed up for me the night before, but then, no one likes to be overdressed at midnight.

"Here they are, Cap'n," said Iverson.

"Thank you, First," he said. He found my face and nodded. "Borden."

I opened my mouth to thank him, when suddenly, Angela stood, threw off her blanket and wrapped her left arm around the captain's neck. Her right hand held a small pistol – maybe a twenty-five or thirty-two caliber. She pulled him into the center of the room, pushed the gun into Dillon's temple and looked at Iverson.

"That's my gun," said Jasmine.

"Get on that phone, and tell someone to get the launch ready," said Angela to Iverson. "We're leaving again."

He just gaped at her. We all did.

"Angela," said Red. "It's over."

"Shut up Richard," she said. "It will *never* be over. I will not let them win. I will not let him hurt me again. We are going to get away, and he is going to die. Philip, get Leyla. Richard, get Borden."

For three heartbeats, it was like we were in a wax museum. No one moved. We all stared at Angela's white face, twisted and working with fury and desperation. Red was just starting to rise when there was a tremendous echoing boom. Angela screamed and dropped her gun, clutching at her shoulder and staring at her husband.

Phil sat calmly, holding his big automatic. A wisp of smoke curled out the end of the barrel. The slide was locked in the open position, because he had fired his last round, the bullet I had inadvertently left in the chamber. Angela began to curse him, shrieking out a vicious, poisonous flow of invective in some of the most hurtful words I have ever heard. Iverson picked up her pistol, and Jones and captain wrestled her out of the room, still screeching hatred at the top of her lungs.

Phil put his weapon carefully on the floor. "I guess I finally did one thing right," he said to no one in particular. Then he put his face in his arms and sobbed like a broken-hearted child.

FIFTY-FIVE

It was a gorgeous sunny day on the North Shore, though not much above freezing. We had been back in Grand Lake for about a week. My bruises had healed, but I still felt cold all the time. That could be, however, because I lived on Minnesota's North Shore, and it was the end of October. I tried drinking a lot of coffee to keep my core body temperature up. It seemed to help, so I decided to stick with it.

Alex Chan was in his office. As it happened, Julie was not.

"She's working for you today," said Chan, morosely, ushering me in and taking my coat.

"She doesn't work for me, she works for the church," I said.

"I didn't realize your church was so disorganized and forgetful."

I sighed. "She's rubbing off on you."

"It's one of the things that draws us together – a mutual love of keeping you humble."

There didn't seem to be much for me there, so I changed the subject. "Thanks for taking care of my cat."

"Sure thing," said Chan. "We left you some cat food in your kitchen closet."

"We?"

"Julie helped me."

"I didn't realize it was so much trouble."

Chan grinned his wide, white-toothed grin. "No trouble at all. A pleasure, in fact."

"Be careful with Julie," I said. "I mean it."

"We're fine," he said, waving a hand. "We're having fun, and taking it slow."

"She doesn't even know you like her, does she?"

"I'm Asian. I am inscrutable, difficult to read."

"You're Californian, and you're an open book."

"You do realize you're paying me for this time, don't you?" said Chan, picking up a pencil and looking businesslike.

I sighed and we got down to business.

~

An hour later I got out of the car in my winter coat and knocked on Ethel Ostrand's door.

"Well, hello, Pastor," she said, smiling. "What are you wearing that great big coat for? It can't be much below freezing."

She invited me in, and I took my coat off and sat down in her big green wingback chair. The place was unchanged in the weeks since we had planned her funeral. She offered me cookies and coffee, and I felt it was only good manners to accept.

She insisted that we discuss her impending death, and so we did, and it seemed to make her happy. When there was a break in the conversation, I said, "Ethel, I almost got your money back, but I lost it again."

She looked at me through her thick glasses, a little old white-haired lady of Norwegian extraction. "Oh, it wasn't you pastor, I know that," she said in her kind, grandmotherly voice. "It was those damn criminal sons-of-bitches from Washington."

"Ethel!" I said, surprised. She started laughing, a rolling chortle that gurgled low in her throat. After a minute, I couldn't help smiling. Her mirth grew into a full-throated belly laugh, and it was impossible not to join her.

"Oh my," she said finally, wiping her eyes. "Your face was something to see. I've wanted to do that to a Lutheran pastor for fifty years."

"I *am* sorry about the money though," I said.

She waved her hand. "I may be old but I can read. I read all about it in the papers, and heard about it on the radio. There was nothing you could have done. In fact, you did a great deal more than most people would have."

I was quiet.

"Besides," she said. "I've still got the rest of the money. I'm not likely to use it all up before I die."

"The *rest* of the money?" I watched her face carefully, but she didn't seem to be joking this time.

"Oh yes," she said leaning forward seriously. "I never did trust banks, so I only gave you about half to put in the vault. The other two-hundred and fifty-thousand is under the mattress in the guest bedroom."

Some things, you just can't make up.

FIFTY-SIX

They took our depositions on a cold, gray, rainy day in Duluth. Beforehand, I went to see Phil, where they were holding him at Arrowhead Corrections Center.

When they called my name, I stepped into a little boxed-in corridor. A steel security door slid shut behind me, while the one in front stayed firmly closed. A guard watched me from a window. After the first door made a heavy snap, indicating the lock was engaged, the second door opened. Another guard led me down a hall to a bare room with little cubicles along one wall. Each cubicle looked into a Plexiglas window. There was a phone beside the window. I sat down in the end compartment and waited. After a few minutes, behind the Plexiglas I saw another guard escort Phil to my little section of window. He sat down and picked up the phone.

"Hey, Phil," I said. They teach you that in seminary.

"Thanks for coming to see me," he said.

I was quiet.

"I've been doing a lot of thinking," he said. "About what you said out there on the lake – Angie and the slave trader and everything."

"You get anywhere?"

"Not really," he said. "Only that I need what the slave-trader guy got."

"Grace."

"Yeah. I need that."

"Basically, you ask God for it."

He said, "What about Angie?"

"She's got to make her own choices," I said.

"Why doesn't she seem to want this?" He waved his hand. I presumed he meant grace.

"She was abused as a child, wasn't she?" I asked.

"Yeah, I guess so," he said.

"So, I think it is two things. First, she is so caught up in what was done to her, so angry about it, that she can hardly see that she has done so much wrong herself. She feels that the wrong done to her is greater than anything she could ever do to anyone else. In her eyes, the world owes it to her to let her do as she pleases."

"What's the second thing?"

"Well, I think she also knows deep down – probably not even consciously – that if she can be forgiven, that means that her abuser can be forgiven too. It even means that if she receives forgiveness, someday she would have to work to forgive him herself. She's just not ready to accept those things."

"Will she ever be?"

"I don't know, Phil. We can't solve her issues for her. What about you?"

He nodded as if I'd asked a yes or no question. "I want to believe it is true. I want to believe that the slate can be clean, that I can be a different person."

"You can," I said. "But I can't do the believing for you."

"I need to think on all this," he said.

"Call me anytime," I said.

~

Later on, after we had repeated our adventures in front of the authorities for what felt like the seventh time, Leyla and I paused, hand in hand by the door of the justice building, looking at the dismal day outside.

"Hey," called Jasmine, coming down a flight of stairs. "Hold up."

Stone came up after her, moving more slowly, his arm in a sling to stabilize his wounded shoulder. We waited for them to catch up.

"We're taking you out for lunch," said Stone. His face was as expressionless as ever. "You're buying."

"Tony," said Jasmine, slapping him on his shoulder. He winced and cringed, and immediately she cried out, "Oh, I'm so sorry, I keep forgetting."

"Third time today," said Stone to me.

"He's working it too," said Jasmine. "Acts like he's dying every time."

"All right," I said. "Where was I taking you to lunch?"

"Bellisio's."

Bellisio's was in the Canal Park district, the kind of place where you can drop twelve bucks on an artisan cheese plate, or eighteen on an order of Sicilian ravioli – for lunch, that is, dinner is more. It was good, but steeper than my normal dining out. With drinks and appetizers, I was easily looking at more than I would spend on groceries in about three weeks. On the other hand, Stone and Jasmine had recently been deeply involved in trying to save our lives.

"Okay," I said.

We drove down to the restaurant, which featured a glimpse of the harbor. As it turned out, the ravioli tasted pretty darn good, and so did the cheese plate, which we all shared. Stone ordered a bottle of wine for all of us, which was generous of him, considering I was paying. I smiled and thought of Jesus. *Turn the other cheek. When a man wants your ravioli, give him your wine as well.*

Actually, we had an enjoyable time together. We joked and laughed, and Stone even almost-smiled twice. Leyla and Jasmine were vivacious and beautiful, and several patrons glanced at our table in what I imagined was envy. Ah, the high life.

"Do you have any more questions about everything?" asked Jasmine after the cheese plate.

"Well, someone tried to break into my place a few weeks ago. Was that related, or do we have a crime problem in Grand Lake?"

Stone grimaced. "Those knuckleheads in Homeland Security were running the show. They were watching Lynden, and they knew your mom sent you something. At that point, we hadn't eliminated you as a suspect. They were afraid your mom sent files or something that would put you on to what was going on. They figured if they got a warrant, and you were one of the bad guys, it would tip you off. And it would have been tricky to get a warrant anyway. So those idiots decided to just break and enter."

"Is that legal?" asked Leyla.

"Of course not," said Jasmine. "Unfortunately, you never heard any of this from us."

"How could anyone think I was part of all this?" I asked. "My dad shot one of them. So did I, for that matter."

Stone shook his head in disgust. "I never suspected you. But the bright stars above argued that maybe you hated your dad. They pointed out that we didn't really know if you shot one of them – all we had was blood leaving the bank."

Jasmine looked embarrassed. "I'm sorry to say, I did wonder for a while. Until that night."

"What night?" asked Leyla.

"Never mind," Jasmine and I said in unison. Leyla looked from one to the other of us speculatively.

"Jasmine had an unorthodox approach to establishing my innocence," I said to Leyla.

"Just say, Leyla, you don't need to worry about your man. He's gold," said Jasmine.

"Okay," said Leyla slowly. She looked at me. "But I reserve the right to bring this up again later."

We ate in silence for a few more moments.

"Oh, by the way," said Jasmine. "Our boat was not actually called *Tiny Dancer*. Red – Richard – Holland didn't own it. It was just a boat they rented, called the *Zephyr*. Holland had to paint over the name because he didn't know the name of the boat when he recruited you, so he told you *Tiny Dancer*."

"Something has been bothering me," said Leyla, swallowing some wine. "If they knew you two were FBI, why didn't they search Tony for weapons right away?" Her reporter's inquisitiveness was strong as ever.

"It's kind of complicated," said Jasmine, "because of the double-triple-cross thing. But basically, if they had searched him right away, he would have known that they knew he was an agent, and that would have alerted him that I was double-crossing him. As a result, they could not have used me as a hostage."

"But Tony already knew all that," I said, feeling a little confused.

"Yes, but *they* didn't know that he knew."

"This sounds like something out of *Mission Impossible*," said Leyla.

"Why didn't you wait for Jasmine to get free, before you made your move then?" I asked Stone.

He looked at me impassively, and then shrugged. "It was a gamble either way. Once they admitted that Jasmine was on their side, they would have searched me and taken my gun. I had to make my move before that. Plus, I saw what you did to Phil when he tried to beat you. You're fast, and you have good instincts. I thought that between the two of us, we could take them. As it turns out, I was the one who failed. I'm just glad no one else got hurt because of it."

After the meal, Stone insisted upon dessert as well, and I began to think maybe the bill would equal something more like a whole month's worth of groceries. However, coffee came with dessert, so there were compensations. When we were completely stuffed and the sky was growing even darker as the sun began to give up for the day, Stone leaned back in his chair and eyed me mysteriously.

"You nailed 'em," said Stone. "A lot of law enforcement worked a long time, but you were the one who brought home the bacon. Without you, we never would have held on to the Kruger-Holland gang."

"You helped," I said.

"But we are paid to help," said Jasmine.

"And now," said Tony, with uncharacteristic expression, "So are you!"

"What do you mean?" I asked.

"Quarter-million dollar reward for the Kruger-Holland gang," said Stone. "It's all yours." He actually smiled. Then he actually chuckled. Somewhere, ice was forming in the nether reaches of hell.

"You're sitting here, trying to be all stoic about dropping two hundred bucks for a late lunch. You're treating us because you can afford it!" He laughed again.

I looked at Leyla, and then Jasmine. "Did he just laugh?"

"Yes, he did," said Jasmine smiling.

"Wonders never cease." I took a deep breath. "Well," I said, "that's a load off my conscience."

Leyla looked at me and nodded.

"What do you mean?" asked Stone.

"He's going to give it to an eighty-year-old widow," said Leyla.

Stone stared. "You're crazy."

I nodded. "Very likely."

~

After supper, I said to Leyla, "Take a walk with me?"

"Sure."

We walked two blocks through the drizzle, to where some old brick buildings had been renovated to hold offices and shops. We climbed the stairs to Tom Lund's office.

I knocked on his door. "Come in," I heard him call. We walked in through the bare reception room into Lund's sanctum sanctorum. There was a pile of files on his spare chair, and his feet were on his desk, hands behind his head.

"See?" I said, turning to Leyla. "I told you detecting is hard work."

"Borden," said Lund, not moving for a moment. Then his eyes shifted to Leyla. He took his feet off the desk and stood, moving toward the chair piled high with files.

"Don't worry," I said. "We won't stay long."

He looked relieved. "Thanks," he said. "Last time I moved that stuff, it took me a week to get organized again."

"I'm here to pay you."

"I didn't do squat," he said. "You did all the heavy lifting."

"I bet you sat there by the window with your feet up and hands behind your head and thought about my case, though."

He nodded. "It's tough, but someone's got to do it."

I took out my checkbook and started writing.

"Hey, I'm serious – I got shut out on the Charles Holland thing, and that's about as far as I got 'til you blew up their getaway boat."

"About that," I said. "Did you ever hear why you were shut out, why all the push-back?"

He shook his head.

"Homeland Security. You were going against them. They were working the case and they didn't want anyone else in it, screwing it up, as they thought. So they shut down the flow of information."

Lund swore in appreciation. "So you're saying maybe I'm still the best private detective on the North Shore?"

"*Are* there any other private detectives on the North Shore?" asked Leyla sweetly.

"You're pretty, but you've got a bite," said Lund, grinning. Leyla smiled at him.

I finished writing Lund's check. "Besides," I said. "They gave me the reward."

"They *what?*"

"They gave me the reward money. I have a little bit extra, so I thought it wouldn't hurt to pay you. I may need you again someday."

"You have a 'little extra?' What's that supposed to mean?"

"Well, two-hundred and thirty-seven thousand rightly belongs to a little old lady in Grand Lake. Turns out I only lost half of what she had, but still, right is right. It's her money."

"So you are going to make a wealthy old widow wealthier."

"Wealth has nothing to do with it. I lost her money. I owe it to her."

Lund shook his head. "I always knew you were a few sandwiches short of a picnic."

"Yeah," I said, "but I'm a heck of a lot of fun."

FIFTY-SEVEN

Leyla and I were walking by the waterfront in Grand Lake. Another weather system had moved in and we could see the waves exploding against the breakwater, sending spray forty feet into the air. The wind was cold, and it howled across the water, whipping Leyla's hair around her face.

"I'm not ready to enjoy this yet," said Leyla. "It brings back some bad memories."

"I don't think it would be enjoyable even without the memories," I said.

We drove up to my cabin on the ridge and I built a fire out of seasoned birch and oak. When it started to crackle and roar, we sat on my couch and looked at it.

"Hot cocoa?" I asked.

"Tea."

I made the drinks and brought them back to the couch. Leyla sipped her tea. I sipped my hot cocoa.

"Jonah," she said, turning to me. "I want to talk about something. I want you to just listen to me for a minute."

"I'll try," I said. "It's just that I love the sound of my own voice so much."

She patted my cheek. "I know." She sipped some more tea. "I – I don't really know how to start. I guess…I just know that when we were in the lake after the boats had gone down, we all thought we were going to die."

I opened my mouth.

"No," she said. "Let me finish. I have known for a long time that you are the man for me. But it sounded like you only realized that I was the woman for you when we were about to die. I understand that in the cold light of everyday life, things may feel differently for you. I want you to know that I will not hold you to your marriage proposal."

I met her eyes steadily and waited. She kept looking at me. The silence stretched on.

"You can talk now," she said suddenly.

"Oh," I said. "Sorry." I sipped some cocoa and then put the cup down. "Hold on a sec."

I lit several candles that I keep around for power outages and romantic evenings. I went to my stereo, where my iPod was plugged in, and started playing Marc Cohn's *True Companion*. Then I turned off the main lights. Outside, the silver light of dusk softened the lines of the gray lake and the endless horizon. I came back to the couch and knelt down in front of Leyla.

"I realize," I said, "that the first time, conditions were not ideal. I remember that I said our situation had caused me to realize how I really feel. But today, being of sound mind and body, with, as a far as I know, decades of life ahead of me, I do not want to contemplate those decades without you. So here, with candles, a fire and music and tea, I am asking you, Leyla Bennett, to become my wife. I love you. I want you. Always. Leyla, I am asking you again – will you marry me?"

She looked at me. I could have waited contented in that gaze for a very long time. "Yes," she said at last. She reached for me and we held each other tightly.

"You think this one took?" I asked, my voice muffled by her hair. She punched my shoulder in response.

~

Four days later, I drove through moody jack-pines and bare-branched birches. I was listening to a mix of Bruce Cockburn, Jackson Browne and band called East Mountain South. The sounds and the drive were peaceful, even hopeful. It was cold, but the sun was out in full force, bringing joy to the wild, empty land around me. I shared that joy, and more.

After a couple hours I pulled into a quiet street lined with leafless trees, the lawns still shedding the first melting snowfall of the season. I got out of the car and waited for a minute, and walked to the door of a neatly kept ranch house. I knocked.

A voice called, "Just a minute."

The door opened, and for a moment I was looking into the past, down a long, fondly remembered trail I could never walk again. Then I met her eyes, and I saw the future too.

"Hi Ma," I said to Robyn's mother. I shifted to give room to my companion. "This is Leyla."

THE END

ACKNOWLEDGMENTS

I want to say, first of all, thank you to the most important person in my life, Jesus Christ. I think you are crazy to let me write this stuff, and I think I'm crazy to let you sucker me into it. Even so, thank you.

Thank you also to my wife Kari. Your unfailing encouragement means more than I can express. I finish this, just days after our twentieth anniversary. I love you, and I trust the next twenty will be even better. For my fans, if you like Jonah's kind of music, you might want to check out Kari's. Just Google Kari Hilpert.

Dr. Mark Cheathem took on the gargantuan task of copy-editing, as well as giving me feedback on early chapters. I have come to believe he is the world's foremost expert on the use of commas in the English language. Any mistakes that remain are mine alone, of course. Dr. Cheathem's expertise is not limited to commas, however. If you have an interest in nineteenth century American history, you really should Google him, also.

The cover was designed by my extremely talented cousin-in-law, Lisa Anderson. If you need excellent graphic design, you need Lisa. Find her at www.opinedesign.com

Ms. Emma Watt, seasoned sailor, and who knows what else, provided extensive and helpful feedback on the technical parts of the story that involved sailing. I kept Jonah largely ignorant of the mechanics of sailing, so if he referred to a "roller thingy" instead of a "winch," that is not due to any failing on Ms. Watt's part. Any genuine mistakes, as always, are mine alone.

Ms. Lyn Rowell gave me a great deal of useful and encouraging feedback. Though I wanted to bring back Alex Chan, it was her who actually convinced me to do it. She also encouraged me to give Jonah a pet, another thing I had been unsure about.

Best-selling author (but more importantly, good friend), Eric Wilson has given me steady and constant encouragement in my writing through several years. Thanks again, Eric! Others in the encouragement arena include: Michael Kosser, Kristin Wolden Nitz, and Rob Shearer.

A JONAH BORDEN PLAYLIST

Days in Between – Kari Hilpert

Moth Around the Moon – Charlotte Ryerson

Jungle Love – Steve Miller

Nobody's Cryin' – Patty Griffin

The first Cut is the Deepest – Sheryl Crow

I am Ready for the Storm – Rich Mullins

Pacing the Cage – Bruce Cockburn

Toccata and Fugue for organ in D minor – J.S. Bach

Seventeen – Stevie Nix

All Will be Well – The Gabe Dixon Band

Made in the USA
Charleston, SC
07 November 2012